mammon inc.

by the same author

foreign bodies

hwee hwee tan

mammon inc.

MICHAEL JOSEPH
LONDON

MICHAEL JOSEPH

Published by the Penguin Group
Penguin Books Ltd, 27 Wrights Lane, London W8 5TZ, England
Penguin Putnam Inc., 375 Hudson Street, New York, New York 10014, USA
Penguin Books Australia Ltd, Ringwood, Victoria, Australia
Penguin Books Canada Ltd, 10 Alcorn Avenue, Toronto, Ontario, Canada M4V 3B2
Penguin Books India (P) Ltd, 11 Community Centre,
Panchsheel Park, New Delhi – 110 017, India
Penguin Books (NZ) Ltd, Cnr Rosedale and Airborne Roads,
Albany, Auckland, New Zealand
Penguin Books (South Africa) (Pty) Ltd, 5 Watkins Street,
Denver Ext 4, Johannesburg 2094, South Africa

Penguin Books Ltd, Registered Offices: Harmondsworth, Middlesex, England

First published 2001
1

Copyright © Hwee Hwee Tan, 2001

Set in 11.5/14.75 pt Monotype Sabon
Typeset by Rowland Phototypesetting Ltd,
Bury St Edmunds, Suffolk
Printed in Great Britain by Clays Ltd, St Ives plc

A CIP catalogue record for this book is available from the British Library

ISBN 0–718–14256–X

1

Steve got his dick caught in the window. He blames me, of course. As if anything like *that* could be my fault. But I'll tell you what happened, and you can decide.

It all began with the arrival of the Red Dragon, with Mammon Inc.'s logo – a 3D flying hydra – looking as if it had been lasered on the letterhead in holographic blood.

Steve ripped open my mail (like he always does) and did a Blur-ish 'Song 2' yell – 'Woo hoo!!! Break out the Bolly, you've hit the giant jackpot!' He twisted his fingers like the National Lottery logo. 'You're going to be rich, young and beautiful. A money honey.'

'Thanks for opening the letter,' I said slightly sarcastically. 'Every day I praise Jesus that our friendship has evolved to such an intense intimacy that you feel totally comfortable reading my private correspondence without asking for my permission.'

'No problem. Permit me to announce these glad tidings to thee,' he said. Then he read the letter out loud:

Dear Ms Chiah Deng Gan,
   Mammon CorpS is a subsidiary company of Mammon Inc., the largest corporate entity in the world, serving more

1

*than seven billion consumers in over 170 countries. The
Mammon Company (mc) is the world's leading brand
name, and last year net sales for mcProducts exceeded $66
billion.*

*Mammon CorpS provides Adaption services for the
modern international professional élite: those executives
who grew up in one country, were educated in another, and
are now working in a third.*

*These are the bankers, diplomats, lawyers and consultants
we call the Global Nomads. When they relocate to a new
country, they need help learning how to gain social
acceptance, and Mammon CorpS helps them adapt.*

*We are looking for a new Adapter to liaise between our
Oxford and Singapore offices.*

*A highly selective agency, Mammon CorpS recruits only
one Adapter a year.*

*We do not advertise openings, and we never solicit
applications. Our private investigative firm screened all this
year's Oxbridge graduates, and came up with a shortlist.*

You were the only person on the list.

*We would like you to undergo some of our special Tests
to determine your ability to adapt people. If you succeed,
you will automatically be put on our mcManager fast-track
promotion program, which guarantees a highly competitive
pay package which includes mc stock options, and a lifetime
of free global travel on our mcTransport Network (mcAir,
mcRail, mcAuto).*

Can you accept our challenge?

*If so, we would like to invite you to an interview at
the Company's world headquarters in New York.*

*We hope that you will consider this opportunity to join
the world's premier Company.*

Sincerely,

Dr Draco Sidious

CEO, Mammon CorpS

'What do you think?' Steve said.

'It sounds like an invitation to Corporate Hell.' I didn't want to be a cog in some capitalist machine, and spend the rest of my life stressed about faxes, meetings, reports, mergers and the worrying question of why I hadn't been cc:-ed to receive that memo that even went to the biscuit lady. The only fun I would get would be from photocopying Dilbert cartoons to pass round the office during my fifteen-minute coffee-break.

I crushed the letter into a ball. 'This is just another one of those dial-a-suit deals and I have no interest in signing up.'

There's a small metal bin attached to the wall in our flat, eight feet above the ground. The words 'Recycle Me' are Tippexed on it. I Michael Jordaned the ball, and it arced gracefully into the basket.

'Yes!' I said, pumping my arm. 'An amazing three-pointer.'

'Don't just dunk that,' Steve said.

'That wasn't a dunk. That was an eighteen-foot jumper from the left baseline with six seconds remaining.'

Time for brekkie. I went to the sink and extracted my Tasmanian Devil mug from the dirty pile. We never wash up, because we believe in the theory that if you let the germs develop on the dishes, sooner or later they'll start a war and wipe each other out.

I opened the cupboard. 'Where the hell is the tea?'

Steve peered at the empty shelf. 'Oh, bollocks. Was it my turn to shop at the Co-op this week?'

I glared at him. 'Uh-huh.'

Steve opened the fridge and took out a bottle of mcCola. 'Here, have some coke instead,' he said.

'How on earth can coke be a substitute for tea?' I said.

'They both have caffeine in,' Steve said. 'And mcCola is a lot easier to prepare. You don't even have to boil water. Just unscrew and enjoy.'

Steve glugged down half a litre. 'Here – you can have the rest.' He burped. 'If you work for Mammon, you might get a discount on mcCola. You really should go for that interview. Mammon Inc. owns everything. Everyone reads, eats, wears mcstuff all the time. Imagine the freebies you'd get if you worked for them.'

But that was what scared me about Mammon Inc. There seemed to be nothing that they didn't own or couldn't buy. Whether you were in London, Singapore or New York, you would find people in mcJeans drinking mcLite beer while talking about the latest mcMovie. I looked at the headlines of the *mcTimes*, which announced that Mammon Inc. was taking over Apple Computers to form a new company – mcMac.

'Mammon Inc. might be able to buy everything,' I said, 'but they can't buy me. It's a matter of principle.'

'Principle!' Steve snorted. 'You can't afford the luxury of having principles. Now, I say this as your best friend who loves you with unconditional positive acceptance – you're an idiot. This is the fifth interview you've turned down. You've only got two weeks left before the Nazis from the Home Office kick you out of the country. Or do you really want to go back to Singapore and live with your parents?'

'No,' I said.

'So why don't you get a job here?' Steve said. 'I don't know why you're being so stubborn about this.'

'I don't know if I want to stay here permanently. I miss my sister.'

'Miss what?'

'You won't get it,' I said. I missed her *kia-su*ness. Steve never understood that Singaporean 'afraid of losing out' mentality, which is why he freaked out when I came back from Asia last summer with a portable table fan and five thousand straws.

Last year, when I was in Singapore, I went with my sister

to the grand opening of the Golden Bamboo Emporium. While we were pondering the difficult question of what flavour Pot Noodles we should get, a voice boomed out from the PA system, 'DEAR CUSTOMERS, BECAUSE TODAY IS OUR GRAND OPENING, THE FIRST TWENTY CUSTOMERS TO SPEND OVER FIFTY DOLLARS WILL GET A FREE MYSTERY GIFT – COLLECT AT THE LOBBY.' 'Free' is one of the key words in the Ten Commandments of *kia-su*ism, namely, 'Anything that's free, you must get.' We looked around for the nearest and quickest thing we could buy. The Emporium was doing a 'Golden Bamboo Special – 100 plastic straws for only $1'. We quickly bundled a lifetime's worth of straws into our trolley and drove it with Schumacheresque speed towards the cashier. After paying up, we grabbed the receipt from the cashier and rushed down the escalator towards the Mystery Gift collection booth, shoring two eight-year-olds and a pregnant woman with pram out of the way. I would have been ashamed of my behaviour, but I was too stressed trying to outrun the granny who was hot on my heels, who also pushed the kids and mother in an attempt to overtake me. We finally reached the free-gift counter. There were at least ten people ahead of us, but my sister kept shouting, 'I spent $50! I spent $50! Free gift! Free gift!' Finally, with a combination of sharp elbows and ever sharper voices, we penetrated the crowd, handed in our receipt, and collected our mystery prize – the portable table fan.

'Why the hell did you bring that back?' Steve stared at my prize. 'You're always in Singapore in the summer and it's not as if it ever gets hot enough here to use a fan.'

'It was a gift,' I said. 'It would have been rude not to accept. I don't know, maybe we could use it to dry the dishes.'

Steve nearly choked himself laughing. 'Yeah, like you ever even *wash* any of your dishes.'

5

'I can use it to dry my clothes, then. I wash those,' I retorted.

'And what the hell are we going to do with all these straws?' Steve said.

Steve was right. We never used straws. We hardly ever even used mugs. We usually drank everything – milk, beer, mcCola – straight from the container. I didn't tell Steve why I got the straws 'cos he probably wouldn't understand the concept of getting something out of sheer *kia-su*ism, which is basically the acquisition of an object that is free. It doesn't matter if it's something that you don't need and could afford to pay for anyway – the important thing is that you didn't lose out. I knew Steve wouldn't understand this, because the whole *kia-su* approach – rushing and pushing and yelling – definitely lacked the British reserve he so prided himself in possessing. But my sister understood, which is why I always went back to her.

Yet there would be too many things I would miss if I left England.

Steve was so different from all the boys I was used to in Singapore. They had no fashion sense, they all wore jeans, trainers, and faded school T-shirts with exciting slogans like 'Raffles Institution Debate Team'. I mean, like good grief, these men were at university, they could wear what they liked, and they went and chose an outfit that used to be their school uniform. If you walk around Oxford and see a Chinese man with a rice-bowl haircut, glasses and an old school T-shirt, you can be sure he's from Singapore.

When I first met Steve, he was lying on the grass in the front quad of St L'leh College, reading Byron. His hair was dyed Manic Panic yellow, and he wore a 70s retro Gucci shirt and plain-front cargo khakis from French Connection. After enduring years of Singapore swots, it was nice to finally have a male friend who didn't feel a need to dress as if he still lived with his parents.

6

In the past three years, I'd developed the perfect slacker lifestyle with Steve. If I left England, there would be no more sleeping in on Bank Holidays, waking up just in time for the mandatory mid-afternoon Bond movie on telly. No more Saturday afternoons at the launderette, listening to the cricket on Radio 4 on our portable radio and fighting over who gets to read the TV Guide in the *Guardian* first. No more eating strawberries at Wimbledon, swept up in Henmania; no more intellectual slumming, nursing pints of Boddingtons while deconstructing Indiana Jones with reference to James Frazer's *Golden Bough*. And nobody in Singapore understands the benefits of tea as a cure-all – there would be no more tea before dinner, tea after dinner, tea watching telly after dinner, tea when visitors come, tea after a fight, tea in the living-room, tea in the garden. If I went back to Singapore, there would be too little tea in my life.

Chiah Chen was my only sibling, but Steve had become the white brother I never had.

I looked at our Darth Vader clock. Steve was right. Time was running out, and I had to choose. 'I don't know what I'm going to do,' I said. 'If I get a job here, I'll never get to see my sister. But if I go back to Singapore, we won't be able to hang out any more.'

'Maybe Mammon can solve your problem,' Steve said.

'How?'

'If you paid more attention to the letter, you'd remember that they're looking for someone to run both their Oxford and Singapore offices. If you work for them, maybe you'll be able to live in both places.'

I frowned. Steve had a point. Yet I still really didn't want to go for the interview, but I didn't know why. 'I think I'll go for a walk,' I said, 'to sort out my head.'

I stepped out of our linoleum living-room on to the ancient road that would lead to the city of golden castles.

Don't get me wrong, I didn't always hate Oxford. I fell in love with the city the first time I saw it. On that afternoon during Michaelmas, the clustering spires swarmed the air with bells, their peal soaring over the domes, cupolas and minaret-crowned churches.

Spires and turrets, bowers and gables – before I arrived in Oxford, I had no idea what these words meant, and couldn't even *imagine* what they might look like. But arriving at the bus stop opposite All Souls, I saw the words that I'd never understood before: the sylvan suburbs and weathered cloisters, the green-gloomed waters and elm-discovering skies, the dry-stone walls and ashlar houses. I wound round medieval lanes, fascinated by the way the stones scattered their flakes on the cobbled streets. I'd read that the black walls were made from an especially crumbly stone. When beaten by the weather, it starts to decay superficially and becomes flour-like, so a fifty-year-old wall looks as if it's been there for centuries. I picked a branch off a chestnut tree, struck the wall, and watched it come powdering down, the black giving way to the grey underneath. Rot never looked so picturesque.

As the day passed, the city metamorphosed from hour to hour, quietly offering a kaleidoscope of spectacular sight after spectacular sight. The sunset turned the ivory towers, white in the daylight, dark red, bloodying the battlements and cathedral spires; but as night fell and the Thames mist dissolved on the cow-spotted meadows, the city turned a strange blue, like an ancient and immortal Atlantis.

This was a fantastical world populated by commoners and fellows, guarded by black-bowlered bulldogs, run by dons and serviced by scouts. During formal Hall, I stared up at the High Table, envious of the professors who sipped wine from the college's private vineyard in Tuscany while discussing the contents of dusty folios and quartos. They seemed like sentinels who guarded secrets from an enchanted age. I wanted to be one of them, to rise from Junior to Senior Common Room, to become one of the wise guardians in this mysterious, magical wonderland.

But they excluded me. They did it not with a slur but with a compliment. Everyone I met, from the Dean to the porter, smiled and said, 'You speak very good English.' Only when that praise passed their lips did I realize that I was different – I was the only non-white person at my college. No one at my college had ever met a Singaporean before, and their knowledge of my country was restricted to three facts, namely: a) it's in China, b) it's very clean, and c) they cane people there. (And by the way, fact a) is completely wrong.) So there's no way they would know that it's not surprising my English is good, since English is the main administrative language in Singapore. We used to be a British colony, so all the signs are in English, and all our school lessons are also taught in English. But here in Oxford, whenever I spoke English, people would react like I was a chimpanzee who could recite lines from the University Statutes in Latin.

I'm always conscious that I clash with the Oxbridge décor. Whenever I enter those pale English monuments, I radiate a bright yellow Chinkness. I stand out in rooms filled with a blizzard of white people, and when I go out into the winter air, the snowstorm continues to surround me.

'So are you going for the interview?' Steve asked me when I returned home.

I stared at our dirty 'Welcome' mat. It looked like some grey alien substance, like Jabba the Hutt had finished moulting and left his skin behind. 'No,' I said.

'Why not?' Steve looked at the mat. 'You need to make more money so we can buy a mat that doesn't look like a natural habitat for slugs.'

'I'm never going to be able to pass the Tests,' I said. 'They want someone who knows how to make people fit in, and

9

you know how useless I am at that.' I'd spent the last three years in Oxford feeling like I had an extra hand growing out of the top of my head. You know, possessing an unusual physical feature that makes it difficult for one to blend in, and is fairly useless, apart from giving one the ability to scratch one's forehead when one is puzzled. 'Why fly all the way to New York to embarrass myself in front of a bunch of white men in Armani suits?'

'God, you really need to work on your self-esteem,' Steve said. 'Develop a more positive self-image. Awaken the giant within. Harness the love from Mars and Venus. Or something like that.'

'You're not very good at giving pep talks, are you?' I said.

Steve shrugged. 'Do you know where my BlasTech DL-44 pistol is?'

'Under those magazines,' I said, pointing at the pile that had avalanched from the table to the floor. 'Why do you need your Star Wars gun?'

'I saw a rat in the kitchen,' Steve said. 'I'm going to try and drown it.'

I saw the red light blinking on the answering machine. 'Did I get a message?'

'Oh yeah, you did,' Steve said. 'It was from your Jedi Master.'

I rolled my eyes. 'Thanks for remembering to tell me.'

Steve was busy tossing magazines over his head. 'No problem. You know, it would be nice if one of us started making more money soon, so we can move. This place has more pest problems than the back alley of a Chinese restaurant.'

I pressed the 'Play' button.

'This is Professor Ad-oy.' His grandpa voice, a mongrel mix of accents and idioms, gripped my attention with Zenist ease. Nobody was sure where he came from. Athens, Jerusalem, Constantinople and Samarkand – these were the miracle-filled cities where he was said to have sojourned. Nobody knew how long he had been at Oxford. Rumour had it that he was the founder of Dagobah Hall, the HQ for the Order of St Cassiodorus. But still, nobody could be *that* old, though his wizened figure did glide through the bowers and cloisters of Oxford with an eternal calm. 'I'm looking for a research assistant. If you're available, please call me at your earliest convenience.'

I rang the Porter's Lodge at Dagobah, and they put me through to Ad-oy. 'I'm definitely interested in the research position,' I said, 'though I'm also considering an opening at Mammon CorpS.'

'Will you accept it?' Professor Ad-oy asked.

'I don't know. Maybe.'

'We should talk about this. I've seen some disturbing things about Mammon Inc. Can you come round later today?'

'Of course,' I said.

'Holy Teletubbies,' I said, putting down the phone. 'This is so cool. Professor Ad-oy wants me to be his assistant.'

'Why is that better than working for Mammon?' Steve said.

'Don't you get it? If I become a professor, then I can still swing between here and Singapore. Spend the academic year here and the summer in Singapore.'

'So why didn't you apply for graduate studies in the first place?'

'Graduate work is only for students with rich parents. My parents are so poor they want me to get married so they can get rice at the wedding,' I said. 'But if a big cheese like Professor Ad-oy wants me as his assistant, he'll probably get Dagobah Hall to give me a full graduate scholarship.'

'Yeah, but why would you rather hang out in the library with a bunch of spectacle-faced swots, instead of jetting round the world with the beautiful bonus babes? It's much

11

cooler working for Mammon than being a professor's assistant.'

'How do you know it's much cooler?'

'I know because it's my job to know what's hot and what's not.' Steve was a researcher at Zog! Entertainment, a TV production company. He took out a magazine from his Diesel slingbag. 'Guess what I saw in this month's *Generation Vexed*?' *Generation Vexed* (or *Gen Vex*) was our pop culture *Encyclopedia Britannica*, a thermometer for the heat-seeking crowd. At first it was dismissed as nothing more than 666 pages of designer eye candy. Then the French semiologist Jean Baudrillard delivered a lecture at the Sheldonian, where he proclaimed that it was 'the arbiter of taste in contemporary discourse'. This made all the dons with long ear hairs realize that *Gen Vex* was more than just glossy coffee-table fodder. It was the I-Ching for our wired, e-everything age.

'It's cool to be a CorpS,' Steve said.

'A what?' I said, confused. 'I guess if you're dead, you would be pretty cold.'

'Not corpse, stupid. A CorpS. That's what they call the members of Mammon CorpS.' Steve flipped to the middle of *Gen Vex* and pointed out the article – 'It's Cool to be a CorpS.'

'See that guy in the black Prada sitting with Cardiac Stompers?' Steve's finger was pointing at the executive in the centrefold with the magazine's staple through his chest. The man with the MBA sat sandwiched between the international grunge rock superstars, the votive candles on the spider-shaped table lighting his sunglassed face. 'He's one of the CorpS.'

I read the caption beneath the photo:

Most corporate managers are all bar graphs and pie charts. Dead boring. But regular appearances in 'Out on the Town' gossip sheets with Vogue *models and Hollywood starlets make the Mammon CorpS the Brahmins of corporate cool.* Gen Vex *asked this pretty Prada-clad boy what he does when he's not downing Martinis at* Wax, *but he was quieter than East Midtown on the weekends. Such a secretive lot, these CorpS. But who cares? They're rich, hip, good-looking frequent fliers, and that's all that matters to us media mavens.*

'Face it, any corporate job would probably Hoover your soul,' Steve said. 'And for 90 per cent of the people in the world, all they get in exchange is discounted cafeteria food, unlimited paper clips and free photocopying. Mammon CorpS is offering you glitter and glitz galore. Hey, maybe you'll get to be like Lara!'

Steve pointed at our TV. The screen was beaming out *Lara*, Mammon Inc.'s international monster hit dramedy about beautiful New Yorkers who managed to afford penthouses despite spending most of their nine to five office hours drinking cappuccinos and analysing their fear of intimacy. The only reason why we weren't (like 35 million other UK viewers) glued to the idiot box was because this was a repeat of yesterday's show. *Lara* was more addictive than *Neighbours* and *EastEnders* combined, thus it was on twice a day, with an omnibus edition over the weekend.

'Yeah, but that life is so shallow. Lara's greatest moral dilemma is usually what shade of highlights she should use for her hair,' I said. 'I want something more than that.'

'What?'

'Nothing,' I said. 'I'm not telling you.'

'Why not?'

'You'll only take the piss out of me.' I hesitated for a moment. 'I feel like I don't fit in anywhere, like I can't connect. Like I'm a three-pin plug living in a two-pin world. I want to feel loved by something bigger than myself, to not always feel so alone and abandoned.'

'I feel like that too,' Steve said. 'But that's just life. And life, as Bertrand Russell once said, "is a long march through the night, surrounded by invisible foes, tortured by weariness and pain, towards a goal that few can hope to reach".'

I shook my head. 'No, I think there's a way out of the Dark Side. And I think Professor Ad-oy can show it to me.'

I was drawn to Professor Ad-oy because his books set down everything I wanted to believe in, ideals that floated in my mind like angels' wings. His words gave flesh to those shapeless flames, made earthly those heavenly thoughts.

I remembered the first time I saw his work. I was sixteen, and felt like there was no cure for my curse. I had grown up in Singapore, in a land of pagodas and dragon boats, where men with purple faces sang operas for hungry ghosts. But I also grew up loving Plato's shadows, Edward Hopper's staring windows and Donne's bracelets of bright hair about the bone. Most people in Singapore thought those things were dead boring, so I couldn't share my passions with anyone. So that was my plight – to love the culture of a society that would never accept me. I longed to find some special place, a world where I would no longer feel alone and abandoned.

One evening when I was sixteen, to prepare for my O-levels, I went to the Popular Bookshop, a bargain-basement joint selling second-rate stationery and third-rate books. I went there to pick up some assessment books, filled with exercises, sample essay questions and mock tests in academic subjects. My favourite assessment books are the Ten Years Series, which reprint exam questions (and model answers) set by the Cambridge Examination Board. Apart from assessment books, Popular usually only stocked Chinese comics, and remaindered books with titles like *Practical Knowledge in Shares*

14

Investment: Answers to Your Needs, *The Asian Microwave Cookbook* and *Sword of Vengeance*.

But this black hardback with the gold words *Fire of Love: The Mystics* by Professor Ad-oy suddenly caught my eye. I opened it and immediately became enraptured by his descriptions of the great Christian mystics. I wanted to be like those mystics, to experience that love spectacular. I wanted to be like St Teresa, feeling the love that shot through her like an arrow, burying its sweet poisonous point deep in her entrails; or like St Francis, who was so overwhelmed by the loving face of the crucified Christ that his hands started bleeding; or like St Paul, who was snatched to the third heaven and told unutterable things, things not lawful for man to know. I was particularly struck by Professor Ad-oy's description of the mystics' heaven:

The very fervour of their sweet love ravishes them with the sight of their Beloved. Their mind is changed and passes into lasting melody. From now on their meditations become song. Melancholy has been driven out of the mansion of their spirit, and it now resounds with wondrous melody.

The evil mind destroys itself with attractive poison as it searches for happiness in created things. But the lover of God rejoices in the fire that consumes everything that is dark. He inhales joyful heat into his soul, and breathes his soul out in a honeyed flame, and is swept up to the stars, to be held in thrall with those who sing their Maker's praise.

The mystics show that man can be one with God. We can feel the eternal joy of the soul's marriage to the Divine. The Sufi mystic of Islam Rumi sighs in the same words as the Christian mystic Angela de Foligno: 'I am you and you are me.'

'Maybe if I work for Professor Ad-oy, he'll show me how to be a mystic,' I said. 'Maybe he'll show me how to feel that fiery ardour that will consume my dark aloneness. I want him to teach me how to be a skywalker, to feel the flight of my spirit, and join the Council of saints and angels who sing around God's throne.'

'I know you always believed that,' Steve said, 'but it still amazes me.'

'What amazes you?'

'Your ability to sustain weird beliefs over prolonged periods of time. You're the only person I know who has a Jedi fixation on your college advisor. He's just a professor, you know, not a guardian of the mysteries of the Force.'

'Well, I'm not saying that I'm definitely going to take the job,' I said. 'But I do want to see what he has to offer.'

I went to the bathroom to shower in prep for my meeting with Professor Ad-oy.

As soon as I shut the door, Steve slammed his fists against it. 'What?'

'I need to piss,' he said.

'Get lost,' I said. 'It's your own bloody fault for drinking so much mcCola.'

Steve pounded on the door. 'Hurry up! I really need to piss. It's like I'm holding in a tidal wave. I can see the opening scenes from *Hawaii Five-O* playing in my head, ninety-foot waves and all.'

'Yeah, yeah, I'll be out in five minutes!' I said.

I turned on the shower and closed my eyes. I remembered my first walk around the city, and began to feel more and more oppressed. Why? Maybe it was because of the way the shadows of the giant walls eclipsed me. Oxford was built like a fortress, her buildings defended by military fortifications like battlements and ramparts, balustrades and parapets, spiked fences and iron doors – Lady Margaret Hall even had a moat! All these were designed to keep someone out, and the question was, who? When I first arrived, I thought – surely not me. After all, I had the same great A-level results as every other student there, but the smiles they received were different from the ones I got. I tried everything to be accepted: I wrote my tute partner's essays, joined the Union, the Boat Club, but everyone still talked around me at cocktail parties, like I was a fart they were trying not to smell.

The city was a medieval stronghold, so every architectural detail felt like a snub, every stone and spike seemed planted there to keep out foreign invaders like myself. I pictured the cold citadels built by the rich for the rich, and sighed. If I couldn't adapt myself to fit into Oxford, how was I going to adapt anyone else? There was no way I could pass Mammon's Test.

The door shuddered violently.

'You're taking fucking forever! I can't wait any longer!' Steve shouted. 'My bladder is going to burst. Any minute it's going to explode and the carpet is going to be drowning in my piss. Let me in, damn it!'

'Why don't you just pee out of your bedroom window like you always do?' I said, irritated.

Now, according to Steve, this is the part where everything becomes my fault. Like it was *my* fault that his bedroom window had a dodgy latch. And of course I was also to blame for that unfortunate convergence of hot and cold fronts that caused a hurricane-like gust of wind to pass by our house at the precise moment when he was watering the bushes with his stick.

I don't know what actually happened, but this is how he tells the story to others:

'You know how badly I needed to piss? I'll tell you how badly I needed to piss. When I hung my dick out of the window, it was like, whoosh – tidal wave – I could have flooded the Thames. Jesus, you have no idea how good it felt. It was like a religious experience, purging myself of all that pent-up piss. So, you know, I stood there, shaking loose the last droplets on to the flowers

17

beneath my window. I just stood there, letting the moment sink in. The peace, the relief, the total bliss. You know those statues of the Buddha? That's what my face looked like, you know, fucking beatific. I should have been canonized on the spot. Then I felt this wind, heard this rattle, looked at the latch trembling, shaking. I think my last words were – "Oh shit".'

But anyway, in conclusion, this was why it was *my* fault that while Steve was spraying the roses with his hose, the wind blew and the window slammed down on his wee wee.

2

Undoubtedly, Dagobah Hall gave Oxford much of its esoteric local colour. Her monks went around the city in swamp-green bathrobes, lifting them as they skipped over puddled streets. Their tonsures made them look like walking thumbs. Coaches downloaded American tourists, eager to snap shots of these mysterious creatures – these Merlin look-alikes who smoked pipes beneath the glare of fierce gargoyles.

Since the Middle Ages, the Order of St Cassiodorus (the patron saint of libraries) had drawn scholarly fanatics. These were men who happily took vows forsaking wealth and bonking, so that they could live in cell-like scriptoriums, hand-copying manuscripts. Academics revered them as saints. Dagobah Hall, the order's HQ, had the most coveted private library in the solar system. The monks, like fearless knights, had roamed battlefields, braving pestilence and pillagers to rescue artifacts from ruined libraries. The St Cassiodorus Collection contained treasures like no other. All her books sat chained to the shelves, and when you glanced through the catalogue you understood why. There were scrolls from the Library of Alexandria, papyrus from the volcanic edge of Mount Vesuvius, and the first copy of the Septuagint, taken from the island of Pharos, where

Ptolemy II shut seventy Jewish scholars in cells until they produced the first Greek translation of the Old Testament.

Even the route to Dagobah Hall sounded surreal: in order to reach the college from my house, I walked up Jackdaw Lane, passed by the Radcliffe Camera (which is a library and not an instrument of photography), crossed the Bridge of Sighs before I arrived at Logic Lane.

There, at the entrance of Dagobah, I was greeted by the bulldogs, the bowler-hatted men who guard Dagobah's iron doors. I smiled. You know you're at Oxford when cyclists pedal around the city in black gowns, and even the security guards look like prime ministers.

I entered the Porter's Lodge and looked up at the notice-board to see if anyone had left any messages for me. The board was filled with announcements like: 'Master's Handshaking will take place in the St Frideswide Room by the Great Hall. Please wait in the passage outside', 'The Condensation of Determinants – Monday 2 p.m.' and 'WRC 1st and 2nd XV practice Wed 8 p.m.' – announcements that must seem as cryptic to the uninitiated as the Celtic script that decorates the door-frames. But that was a feeling that Oxford sought to cultivate among its members, the feeling that they were the possessors of some sort of esoteric knowledge available only to the élite.

Across the moat, Dagobah Hall stood before me like a castle from another universe. Frozen in fantasy, her fog-wreathed spires breathed promises of myth and mystery. That had always been the lure of Oxford for me, and for everyone who was sick of our modern, factory-strewn, dotcom i-universe. With her creeper-hung walls and cobbled courts, her shining domes and trim-arcaded bowers, Dagobah Hall seemed to be a magical time-capsule. She was a link to an age when sorcerers brewed potions in cauldrons and knights battled winged snakes. As you walked across the drawbridge into her courtyard, you could easily imagine

20

unicorns flying through those stone portals. Once inside, you were immediately surrounded by weird and wonderful creatures: mermaids and saints in armour; bronze eagles perched on fruit baskets; a Madonna that filled the fountain with her green tears; stone lion heads sprouting from the centre of lush acanthus bushes. When you're at Oxford, you see what inspired a young mathematician, the author of *An Elementary Treatise on Determinants with their Application to Simultaneous Linear Equations and Algebraic Geometry*, to devise stories about mad hatters for his young friend Alice. Not far from here, at the Eagle and Child pub, two medieval literature professors used to swap notes about hobbits and lions that lived in wardrobes. At its worst, Oxford seems like a heritage theme park, with arcane traditions, bad food and even worse weather. But at its best, Oxford becomes the land of Matthew Arnold's 'dreaming spires', a place that 'whispers from her towers the last enchantments of the Middle Ages'.

Faces of stone frowned down as the pitter-patter of my footsteps broke the cloistral hush. The setting sun touched the tip of Coruscant Tower, where Professor Ad-oy lived. I climbed the winding steps, spinning up the turret towards the celestial lights.

I knocked on the oak door.

'You may enter.'

I followed the voice into the dark cave of a room, into the luminous fog that swirled from the wax-lit flames. The room was filled with arcane treasures: there was an ivory holy-water bucket, medallions, a lid from a sarcophagus, and in the corner knelt an angel, gentle in white alabaster.

Professor Ad-oy sat beneath an African crucifix. Made in the seventeenth century by the Balongo people of Zaire, it showed Christ hanging on a bronze cross, with monkeys perched on each outstretched arm, clasping their tiny simian hands in prayer.

When Professor Ad-oy saw me, a smile lit up his face, making his head look even more like a light bulb. He had a tiny chin and an oversized forehead, which God must have given him to store a freakishly large brain. With his pointy ears, chubby dwarf cheeks and sagacious air, he looked like a cross between Spock and Doc from Snow White.

'I'm sorry I'm late. My flat-mate had a medical emergency,' I said. 'I had to take him to Casualty.'

'What happened?' Professor Ad-oy said.

'He got his –' I pointed at my crotch, 'caught in the window.'

Professor Ad-oy smiled slightly, looking bemused. 'Very odd. How did he get himself into such a compromising position?'

'In the morning, Steve can never wait for me to get out of the bathroom, so he pees out of his window.'

'Steve. This wouldn't be Mr Stephen Boulter, would it?'

I nodded.

'Yes, I remember Mr Boulter well,' Professor Ad-oy said. 'He always fell asleep during our tutorials, which was no mean feat considering that I was the only other person in the room. I would always have to tap him with this to wake him.' He pointed to an oak stick with an eagle's claw. 'Yet he still managed to graduate with a First.'

'Well, that's Steve. He has a Mensa-certified IQ of 236, and the emotional maturity of an infantile gerbil,' I said. 'In his defence, his liquid fertilizer has been really good for our rose bushes. It's like Valentine's Day under his bedroom window.'

'What a peculiar life you students live,' he said. He tapped his Victorian Mr Punch teapot and asked me if I would like some tea. 'It's my own special blend of Polynesian Kava Kava, Rooibos, Dong Quai and Black Cohosh from the Native Americans.'

'Sure,' I said, looking at the rococo cover of the sugar

bowl, an eighteenth-century masterpiece of flower garlands, shells and scrolls, elaborately carved in silver. Having tea with Professor Ad-oy always made me feel like I was irreverently playing with exhibits from the V & A.

Professor Ad-oy poured the steaming liquid into a five-hundred-quid cup. 'I called you in today to talk about your thesis on the Christian mystics. It was some of the best work I've ever seen from an undergraduate.'

'Wow, thanks. You really think so?' I said. Everything outside suddenly looked brighter: the domes and turrets stretched out before me, shining like eternal sandcastles against the sky.

'I remember how different you were from my other students,' he said. 'And I wonder if that difference is still there.'

'What difference?'

'All of my other students dismissed the mystical visions as fantasies, as vapours that arose from primitive, superstitious minds. But you believed the mystics, you believed in the reality of those pierced bowels and inflamed souls.'

'I still believe that, I guess.'

'Good. I'm working on a new revised edition of Richard Rolle's *Incendium Amoris*. I'm looking for someone to aid me in the preparation of the manuscript.'

'I would love to be able to work with you.' Rolle's *The Fire of Love* was my favourite mystic manuscript. I could see it now, my fantasy: I would be like an academic Indiana Jones. Professor Ad-oy would guide me through the labyrinthine holdings of the Bodleian. I would camp out there, dig through the quartos and folios, until I found It – the book that showed me how to be ravished by the love of God. Exploring the dim aisles and echoing stairs, surely someday, if I looked hard enough and long enough, I would find that Sacred Book on some dusty, shadowed shelf.

'Very well,' Professor Ad-oy said, 'I will hire you as my assistant and you can enrol to complete your DPhil with me here at Dagobah Hall. Aren't you happy to hear that, Aloysius?'

Professor Ad-oy picked up Aloysius, a human skull, and put it on his lap. Carved on the skull's forehead was the motto '*Et in Arcadia ego*'. I guess Professor Ad-oy was a big fan of *Brideshead Revisited*.

'What sort of funding will I get?' I asked.

'You will probably qualify as a St Cassiodorus Senior Scholar, which would cover your tuition and provide you with a room in College. As my assistant you'll get a small stipend that will cover your minimal living expenses. However, there are various part-time jobs that you can take on in College. They always need help in the library and the garden.'

I frowned. Stone bats with baby faces glared down at me. 'There's just one problem.'

'What may that be?'

'My parents expect me to support them now I've graduated. I think they might freak if they found out that I've taken a low-paying job in Oxford.' My family looked forward to my return with an Oxford degree with the same fanatical anticipation that crazies in Jerusalem reserve for the second coming of Christ. They had fantasies of me descending through the clouds on a silver jet, with a pocket full of platinum cards that they could charge to their hearts' content. 'I'll have to talk to my parents about this before I can give you my decision. I suspect they'd be much happier if I worked for Mammon CorpS.'

Professor Ad-oy stirred his tea, the bronze spoon spinning like a magic wand in the thick golden brew. He sighed. 'I was hoping that you might have changed. You wanted to know how to be a mystic, but the same thing that hindered you two years ago still hinders you now.'

Two years ago, when Professor Ad-oy first introduced me to the mystics, I nearly became a Christian. I wanted to be like those souls consumed with the fire of love, shot through with that flame which gladdens and glitters with heavenly light. All my life, my parents had taught me to light joss sticks and ghost money, but whenever I knelt to my ancestors' idols, I felt nothing but emptiness and boredom. I was tired of praying to silent glass. I wanted to experience the Christian God, to know the One who could melt the earth with His breath. Like the mystics, I wanted my soul to fly through the air, powdered with the pollen of the frosty night, dusting the stars with the clouds from my feet.

But if I became a Christian, my soul would have to fly without my family. I would be a bright star, but in a cold, dark, lonely heaven. So I decided to stay on earth, and be among my family, worshippers of porcelain statues, gold chains and jade Mercedes.

Back then, Professor Ad-oy had looked at me and said these same words with that same sad face: 'Remember the words of the Lord – "If any man come to me, and hate not his father, and mother, and wife, and children, and brethren, and sisters, yea, and his own life also, he cannot be my disciple. And whosoever doth not bear his cross, and come after me, cannot be my disciple."'

'But if I hate my parents, I'll go to Hell,' I said. That doctrine was something my parents had scared into me from childhood. When I was seven, I was sent to the principal's office for peeking at my partner's answers during our maths test. To teach me a lesson I wouldn't forget, my parents brought me to Hell. Located in Haw Par Villa, an amusement park created by the two eccentric brothers who invented the Tiger Balm muscle rub, the 'Ten Courts of Hell' exhibit re-created the punishments for the perfidious. Its gross luridness presented an oddly R-rated form of entertainment in a strictly PG kind of country. Hell was

25

located within the dragon's head, and my parents dragged me past the jagged teeth into the belly of the beast. They brought me to the Eighth Court of Hell, where a demon pulled out a naked woman's intestines. The woman stared at her bloody pink tubes as they snaked their way into the rice bowl at her feet. My parents, Virgil-like, pointed at a sign that said 'Eighth Court. Causing trouble for parents. Cheating at exams.' After that scare, I became such an unfailingly honest person that even now I was probably the only student in the deprived Oxford neighbourhood of Cowley who actually paid the extortionate fee for a TV licence from the BBC.

But what struck me most about this educational excursion to Hell was that Chinese values were different from mine. In Hell, prostitutes were drowned in a sea of blood, food wasters who didn't finish their meals were sawn in half, and marijuana addicts were tied to a fiery pillar, where they were BBQed. Rapists, robbers and murderers simply had their hands cut off. It seemed odd, and unfair, that some Son of Sam/Fred West sicko would have a less painful time in Hell than a pot-smoking hippy who had never finished eating his tofu.

'You know, after reading Foucault, I tried to dismiss the Ten Courts of Hell as a superstitious discourse invented to keep the dominant patriarchy in power,' I told Professor Ad-oy. 'But it's difficult to de-programme myself from the code that my parents have pounded into my system since infancy.' I told him how, whenever I even thought of disobeying my parents, I got nightmares about going to Hell. I have visions of myself, breasts exposed, being dragged around by a soldier with an ox's head and a steel spear. The lizard guards would yank out my tongue in the Third Court, then lead me to the next level, where their claws would pierce through my nipples and claw out my heart. Finally, without a heart to pound in fear, I would stare at the looming shadow of a boulder about to crush my bones to dust.

I looked out of the window. Monstrous heads jutted from the window's edge. The stone beakheads, with their staring eyes and sword-like mouths, leered towards the moon like grotesque angels.

'If I become a Christian and work for you,' I said, 'my family will disown me. They'll curse me. Then I'll have to go through the Third, Fourth and Seventh Courts of Hell before I can be purified and rise to Heaven.'

'Rejection by the world is the cross that Christians have to bear,' Professor Ad-oy said. 'But you will see that it is a small price to pay for Heaven's treasure.'

I looked at the porcelain statue of St Catherine. She held a spiked wheel (decorated with pearls), the wheel she was tortured on before they chopped off her head. During Bloody Mary's reign, they burnt three bishops outside Balliol College. Monks from the Order of St Cassiodorus were also tortured during the Inquisition – some were hoisted on the strappado, others had their limbs stretched on the rack, while some had their thumbs screwed in with a metal-studded vice. All of them died believing that their agony was a bargain compared to the riches of Heaven. I wasn't so sure.

'I don't know,' I said. 'It seems that Mammon Inc. offers a better deal.'

'May I look at your letter from Mammon?' he said.

I handed him the letter.

He studied the letter while I stared at the floor.

Professor Ad-oy had a really weird carpet. Woven in fine Persian fibres were the great mythical monsters: the manticore, who had a lion's body, man's face, scorpion's tail and an appetite for human flesh; the harpy, half-bird, half-woman; and the basilisk, a dragon that could kill you with its stare.

27

'Do you remember Moff Tarkin?' Professor Ad-oy said. I nodded.

'I met him at a University charity do recently,' he said, 'and he told me he was working as a mcManager for Mammon Inc. He was the best medievalist in his year and I wanted to offer him a junior research fellowship at Dagobah. But he seemed only to be interested in using his immense literary talent to come up with slogans like "Do more" to tempt consumers to get into bigger credit-card debt.'

That was an eyebrow-raiser. 'Moff Tarkin? The same bloke who wore Oxfam sweaters and served soup at the Gatehouse? The last time I talked to him, he was going to be a pilot for the Peace Corps in Uganda. Everyone who met him would swear that he was predestined to end up in a dog collar.'

Professor Ad-oy rubbed his Rudolph nose. It was perennially red, sensitive to the ancient flecks from the dusty books he was always hunched over. 'I've been disturbed by the fate of my students who have gone on to work for Mammon Inc. Do you remember Lorth Needa?'

'The Guitar Guy? Sure.' College gave him that nickname because he was in charge of leading the happy-clappy songs during Christian Union meetings. He was a leaf-chomping sandal wearer, and managed to get a First despite spending most of his Oxford years standing behind the baby-milk table outside the Virgin Megastore, trying to get people to sign petitions against Nestlé. 'The last I heard he was living in a tree to stop it from being chopped down to make way for a five-lane motorway.'

'Not any more,' Professor Ad-oy said. 'At the charity do he was arguing with Moff Tarkin about the best way to balance his stock portfolio. I'm worried that you might end up like them. I've seen them take these bright, idealistic children of mine and turn them into soulless automatons. Aren't you afraid of being brainwashed?'

I shook my head. 'I won't fall that easily. For the last couple of years I've been running a medical experiment on myself, to see how long a human body can subsist on Pot Noodles and baked beans before contracting scurvy. It'll take more than a great profit-share programme to seduce me to the Dark Side.'

I turned my eyes away from Professor Ad-oy and looked out of the window. You could see all of Oxford from the top of Coruscant Tower. Leaves tore from their branches, ripped off by the wind, which swirled the brown flakes up and round the smokeless chimneys and gardens, slamming them into brick walls and iron gates. They collapsed in dank piles against the slumbering houses.

'Do you believe in the Devil?' Professor Ad-oy said.

'I don't know. I grew up being taught that there were spirits everywhere.'

Murdered lovers dwelt in banana trees, *pontaniaks* the Malay called them, bloodsucking women who raged in the bulging fruit, bursting out of the yellow skins at night. As a precaution, my parents placed eight-sided mirrors outside our door to deflect these tormented souls. Once, on the island of Sentosa, my class-mate woke up with bruises around her neck. Nobody was that surprised, as demonic assaults were a phenomenon common to camping trips, almost like mosquito bites. We knew we were sleeping on a sandy graveyard, for before it became a tourist resort, Sentosa was called *Pulau Mati* – Island of Death – because this was where the Japanese soldiers had shot thousands of Chinese rebels and buried them in the shore where we slept. In August, during the Festival of the Hungry Ghosts, Singapore would be hidden in a grey fog, the ash from burnt money, food, and ghost BMWs swirling in the air, presents combusted to appease the wandering souls. We were taught not to walk in underground car parks or go to public toilets alone during that month.

'I guess I believe in Asian demons, but it's more difficult to believe in the Western Devil. Over here, the Devil is either a cartoon or a character from some bad B-movie. Like he's either some cutesy red thing that appears on Donald Duck's shoulder whenever he's going to do something naughty, or some weird monster that makes the heads of teenage girls spin 360 degrees while vomiting green slime.'

Professor Ad-oy nodded. 'This is the result of the Enlightenment, as after the Age of Reason, Satan ceased to exist in the Western mindset. He is seen as a mythological fantasy of the Middle Ages, a product of the age of superstition. But demythologization might simply be the Devil's camouflage.'

'You mean the greatest trick the Devil ever pulled was convincing the world he didn't exist?' I said.

'Yes,' Professor Ad-oy said. 'C. S. Lewis has written about that. I suppose you've read *The Screwtape Letters*?'

'Um, yes.' Actually I got that line from *The Usual Suspects*. Like most secular non-Christians, I get most of my theology lessons accidentally through pop culture. 'So you think Satan has been totally secularized?'

'Yes. He would not perform any terrifying supernatural acts, as that would destroy his camouflage.'

'So you think he kills with ennui rather than by sinking his fangs into your neck?'

'Yes, and I doubt that you would find him sleeping in coffins or sacrificing virgins under a full moon. It is much easier to corrupt a soul if your victim does not suspect that it is being seduced. But the wise can spot the signs.' He returned the letter to me. 'Notice the sign of Satan.'

'Where?' I said.

'The red dragon,' he said, looking at the Mammon Inc. logo.

'Why is that satanic?' I asked. I grew up surrounded by dragons. These sacred gods were engraved on the doors of our restaurants; they crouched on our roofs, guarded our temples and wrapped themselves around the pillars in our gardens. Their fiery glow scared away evil spirits, and their crimson wings carried blessings from Heaven. A jade dragon gold-chained itself around my neck, a talismanic gift from my sister.

'Don't you know the vision that appeared to St John the Apostle on the desert island of Patmos?' Professor Ad-oy shut his eyes as he recited the passage from the Book of Revelations. '*And there appeared another wonder in heaven. Behold the great Red Dragon, having seven heads and seven crowns upon his heads.*' Professor Ad-oy opened his eyes. 'Satan fought Michael and his angels but lost, and fell from heaven like a burning star.' He closed his eyes again, as if channelling St John. '*The dragon was cast out into the earth, that old serpent, called Satan, who deceiveth the whole world. Woe to the inhabitors of the earth and of the sea! For the devil is come down unto you.*' Professor Ad-oy placed his finger on the logo. 'Look at this winged hydra. Look at its seven heads, those cockatrices. Legend has it that these Egyptian cobras could kill just by looking at you.'

'But maybe the dragon isn't necessarily a demonic sign,' I said. 'My best memory from childhood was the dragon boat races.' I loved those leviathans, could hear their hearts pound in the furious drumming of the cox. Their beating hearts made me mad with pubescent excitement as I watched the magical beasts cut through the soft glass of the water. 'This is all just speculation. I have to go to New York to see what they're like for myself. If they really are some corporate cult, then I'll look for another job.'

Professor Ad-oy put Aloysius the skull back into a bowl of roses. 'I fear that just as the serpent beguiled Eve through his cunning, you too might be deceived. Let me give you something to read to arm you against the Devil's wiles.'

Professor Ad-oy got up and unchained a book from the

shelf. 'This is the Catechism of St Cassiodorus,' he said, giving the book to me.

I couldn't believe what I held in my hands. This book was over five hundred years old, a work that had survived the Black Death, the Civil War, two World Wars and the Thatcher years. The cover was damp, cracked and mushroom-brown, with knotted worm-like thingies embedded in it, making it look and feel like wet tree bark. The pages crackled as I turned them, revealing stunning figures in black ink pirouetting across the moth-brown pages. This wasn't just a book, it was a work of art, a literary jewel. But it was always the smell that did it for me. Every flip of the page lifts a whiff of musty perfume, like no other smell in the world – warm and tangy, so thick you could chew it, leaving a sour taste on your tongue.

This was the only thing I loved about Oxford. I loved the time-worn books locked in cloistered castles; their crackling pages and floating odours always sent me into a heady daze. Only at Oxford could you truly feel like the scholar explorer, digging through the relics of distant civilizations to find answers to our deepest questions in some mysterious, melodious language.

'In this book you'll find excerpts from the Book of Genesis, which recounts the fall of man in the garden of Eden. Study it well to guard yourself against the serpent's tricks.' Professor Ad-oy sighed. 'Tarkin and Needa entered the serpent's pit, and were poisoned. And you know how strong they were. What makes you think you can resist where others have failed?'

I looked for a place to lay my doubts. An angel's head lay on the table, quills and tulip stems piercing through its eyes and mouth.

'That's a risk I'll have to take,' I said, sounding cockier than I felt.

Professor Ad-oy unchained something from his neck and

dangled it before me: a bronze asp curled around a wooden stake.

'This is the Amulet of St Cassiodorus,' he said. 'It has been passed down through the centuries from one abbot to another. Moses used it to defeat the fiery serpents in the wilderness, and I pray that it will protect you also from the venom of the enemy.'

'Is this the original bronze snake? Did this belong to Moses?' I clasped my fingers around the shining serpent. I saw the Israelites, sprawled in the desert, writhing from the bites of the bright snakes. But those who lifted their eyes – beholding the bronze snake high above Moses's head – rose and were healed.

'No, this is simply a replica,' Professor Ad-oy said. 'Before he founded our Order, St Cassiodorus saw a vision of the risen snake. Then he heard a voice from the Gospels – "*Ergo prudentes sicut serpentes et simplices sicut columbae*," and so it became our Rule.'

'As shrewd as serpents, and as pure as doves.' I hung the amulet around my neck. 'And that's the Rule that will guide me when I face Mammon Inc.'

But could the amulet really protect me? As I walked away from Coruscant Tower, passing through the mouldering arches and worn courts, I looked at the scarred statues that surrounded me. Around me drooped decapitated angels and headless saints, victims of the Puritan iconoclasts who rampaged through the monastery during the Reformation and defaced any sculpture that might become an idol. I reached the gates and stared up at the Madonna with the broken nose. If the amulet couldn't protect the monastery from violent peasants, how could it defend me against the giant dragon that was Mammon Inc.?

3

'What's that noise?' I said. 'You moving house or something?'

'Oh, I'm making black pepper crab tonight,' my sister said. 'The crab go and run away, don't know where already. *Ai-yah*. Got to go look for him.'

My sister put down the phone. Furniture moaned and scraped as she moved it around in search of the AWOL crustacean.

All of my sister's best dishes flashed through my head – roasted Peking duck, steamed prawn dumplings, quail eggs in bird's nest soup, Buddhist monk's soup. If there's one thing that would make anyone go to Singapore, it would be the food. Even William Gibson, who dismissed Singapore as 'Disneyland with the Death Penalty', conceded that 'the endless variety of street snacks in the hawker centres is something to write home about. If you hit the right three stalls in a row, you might decide these places are a wonder of the modern world.' And you know, he never ate any of my sister's fried crispy oyster omelette. Never smelt the stinging pungent aroma of chilli frying, before sinking his teeth into the plump oysters surrounded by crisp egg crusts.

My sister picked up the phone. '*Ai-yah*, he crawl until where already? So annoying. Still cannot find him.'

'Hey, Ah Girl, phone call from England very expensive one,' I said. 'Talk to me more, don't waste time looking for crab.'

'Don't be so cheapo. Now you got Oxford degree, sure got many companies want to give you big money. Can afford long phone call. Any company offer you job yet?'

I told her about the letter from Mammon CorpS.

'Wah, Mammon Inc. very good. Last year, Aunty Lin's son Loong became a mcManager. You should see the things he bought for them. Gold teeth for his father, jade bracelet for Aunty Lin. They threw out all their old furniture from Yaohan and filled the whole house with rosewood antiques. But the most beautiful thing – *ai-yah*! so jealous – was their new Mercedes. Licence plate SZ 88. Everybody want the 88 licence plate, the number so lucky, you guess how much it cost?'

'I'm sure the figure was profane,' I said. 'I'm sure the licence plate probably cost more than the car.'

'Oh! Oh! I see running him behind the – got it!' my sister shouted. 'You wait a while, I got to kill him.'

She put down the phone.

I heard three loud cracks.

'OK, he's dead,' my sister said, and I strained to hear her voice amidst the crackle and splutter of crabs in boiling oil. 'See, I was right! At first Mummy and Daddy didn't want to get the DVD player, but I told them, "Chiah Deng just graduated, sure can get job with a lot of money, we can afford it."'

'What are you talking about?' I said.

My sister told me how my family had just spent ten thousand dollars on a DVD player and a new speaker system.

'Oh my God, I can't believe you spent half a year's salary on hi-fi equipment! You *xiao* or what?' Her insane spending baffled me. 'Why it cost so much?'

'The DVD player very good. THX-certified. So the movie sound just like in the cinema. And also can play CDs. So now I can sing karaoke at home! No need to go to bar any more, there so much smoke, I sing there too long, can get cancer.'

'Yah, it was a health issue for you,' I said sarcastically.

'Also, the sound very good. Not one, not two, but *six* speakers. I go and get the description for you.' After a few minutes, my sister came back and started reading from the stereo manufacturer's catalogue. '"The Bose System 8,000 is a 5.1 channel speaker system with two front left/right satellites, a centre speaker with a copolymer midrange driver and a wide-dispersion dome tweeter, a subwoofer, and two surround speakers. These speakers have a six-driver D'Appolito bipolar array that radiate sound front and rear in an omnidirectional pattern exactly the way sound is produced naturally."'

Suddenly, my sister stopped speaking and I heard Liang Wenfu moaning a syrupy *xinyao* ballad. I had heard that Chinese song a hundred times before, but I must admit that this was the first time that I noticed a subtle wave of strings cascading in the background during the chorus. Whatever the D'Appolito bipolar array was, it did a pretty good job.

'Where did you all get the money from?' I asked. Not only was my family poor, they were so stingy, they were the types who would spend half an hour bargaining with the market lady so she would sell them spinach twenty cents cheaper. I couldn't understand why they would suddenly splurge on something as frivolous as a home-entertainment system.

'Ming's Electric Emporium got special sale,' my sister said. 'All items, only 5 per cent interest. No payments for the first six months. We knew you were going to be rich once you graduate and get a job. So we buy now – you pay later. Hee hee.'

'Very funny. This is ridiculous. Even if I had extra money

to spend – which I don't – I wouldn't spend it on some home-entertainment system. I could do a million more philanthropic things if I was comfortably well off. You know, feed starving children, discover a cure for Aids, or fund research to find a way to prevent Celine Dion from ever releasing a record again.' I sipped my PG Tips. 'And I haven't got the job with Mammon Inc. yet. I'm not sure I want to work for them.'

'Why not?'

'I'm really not interested in going down the yellow brick road to Corporama,' I told my sister. 'The problem is that I suffer from a strange affliction, whereby I am seized by a narcoleptic fit whenever I hear words like "fourth-quarter profits" and "initial public offering".'

'You don't want a big-money job, then you want to do what?' my sister said.

I told her about Professor Ad-oy's offer to make me his assistant.

'You be his assistant, can make a lot of money or not?' she said.

'No,' I said. 'I might even have to take another part-time job to cover all my living expenses.'

'So you won't be able to buy the DVD player?'

'No.'

'You can't be his assistant.'

'Why not?'

'You need to make a lot of money to give us, so Buddha will see that you're very filial. When you die, you don't need to go to Hell, but can just walk across the gold bridge to Heaven.'

'I hate being Chinese,' I said. 'I want my own life. Why do I have to sacrifice everything for the older generation?' I remembered a statue at Haw Par Villa of a woman extolled as a paragon of virtue, because she suckled her toothless mother-in-law, leaving her own baby to starve.

'That's the problem when you stay too long in England. You become like them – all the children so selfish and ungrateful. You better come back to Singapore before they corrupt you some more.' My sister squealed. 'Ah, I call you later can or not? I got to get the baby eels out of the tank now. Got to use both hands, they're very slippery.'

'Why tonight eat so many special things?' I said.

'We know you're going to be rich now, so this week, we every night also eat special things. Tonight, pepper crab and eel deep-fried in KFC flour. Tomorrow, maybe I make shark-fin soup. I'm so excited! I go tell Ma Ma and Pa Pa you work for Mammon Inc., they'll be so proud! You got to send me the letter so we can frame it.'

My parents framed everything: my ten A1 exam results, my Grade 8 piano certificate, my BookWorm Club 'Merit' citation (from nursery school), even the 1981 letter from Sony telling me that I had won a free T-shirt in their 'Scratch and Win' draw. You could hardly see the living-room wall. 'Don't choke on your saliva,' I said. 'I still have to go for an interview. I might not get the job.'

'Of course you'll get the job. You're the only person in Singapore to win the St L'leh scholarship. We got frame the newspaper article, it's on the wall, so all our visitors can look and see we're not bluffing them. In the history of Singapore, you're the smartest girl!'

That night, I dreamt that I returned to Singapore as a member of Mammon CorpS. I had a briefcase with the logo of the flying snake. I opened it, and there was a nest of live eels, hundreds of sea serpents wriggling in my Gucci bag.

My family beamed.

'So good,' my father, mother and sister chimed together like an eerie Sophoclean chorus. 'Because of you we can eat special food forever.'

4

Kermit the Frog woke me, the alarm in his mouth switching on the radio at seven a.m. sharp, blasting out some early Britpop tune played by DJ Jazz Linton on mcRock 103.6 FM.

'Flipping heck. Why the hell are you getting up so early? It's Saturday. Only six-year-olds get up this early to watch *Teletubbies*.' Steve lay in the inflatable dinghy that acted as the other couch in our living-room. He moaned, grabbed the pizza box off his tummy and placed it over his face to block out the light.

'Got to catch the New York plane today,' I said as I stumbled towards the wardrobe in a sleepy blur. 'How do you feel?'

It was Steve's first day back from the hospital.

'I don't feel anything,' Steve said. 'I'm up to my eyeballs in painkillers. I can't feel my hands, my legs, my dick. I'm so numb, if I weren't actually talking to you, I'd think I was dead.'

I opened the wardrobe and checked out my fashion options, which were: a) Marks and Spencer, b) Bobby Chng, or c) Versace. The navy M & S suit would be safe and sensible and sound and all those boring bourgeois words. Bobby Chng is a Singaporean designer, so that suit tries to do this Chinese thing with the cheong-sam collar and skirt with a slit that goes up rather daringly to my right hip. Then of course there is the Versace, which I bought during one of my regular summer trips back to Singapore, when, in a moment of weakness, I caved in to the Asian gene that is programmed with a hereditary obsession with designer labels. As a general rule, the more difficult the designer name to pronounce, the more popular the brand with Singaporeans. The hip knew that 'Versace' was pronounced as 'Ver-sar-chi', and not 'Versace', and complicated European names separated the sheep from the goats. This explains the general awe with which we regard French and Italian labels like Dolce & Gabbana (often mispronounced by the uninitiated as 'Dol cher and Gab-bah-nah') and Chanel (often mispronounced as 'Channel'). Anyway, the Versace, which cost more than all the other clothes in my wardrobe, was bought in the hope that one day it would pay back its cost by providing me with the exact look I needed for that Special Occasion. And maybe this interview would be the Occasion where a riot of purple, green and tangerine zig-zags would be exactly what the fashion doctor would prescribe. Or not. Dilemma, dilemma.

'Jesus, that looks like something that dropped out of a sphinx's nose,' Steve said, when he saw my Versace suit. 'It looks like something that you would get off the Vivienne Westwood clearance rack at Harvey Nicks.' He scrutinized my blue suit and said, 'Marks and Sparks' stuff is always safe, though it sends signals that you have zero originality or flair.' Finally, he pointed at my Bobby Chng. 'I like the Asian twist on this, though I'm not too thrilled about it being in olive. Olive is such a Spring 1998 colour. Far too pre-millennium.'

I decided to go for the pre-millennium look.

'You're so gay when you're like this,' I said.

'I'm not gay,' Steve said. 'I just like reading *The Face*.'

'Same thing,' I said. But I just said that because he spends endless evenings in his dinghy with a tissue box, replaying over and over the scene from *Titanic* where Leonardo draws Kate's boobs. That was his favourite Blockbuster rewinder, even more gawked at than the bathtub scene with Kristin Scott Thomas in *The English Patient*.

I went to check my email on my mcCorp Thinkpad. 'You've got to be kidding. It's impossible,' I said.

Steve came over to stare at my TFT screen. 'What?' he said.

'It's an e-card from Tock Seng Edwards,' I said.

'Who's Tock Seng?' Steve said.

'He's my ex. I haven't heard from him since I started at Oxford.'

'What kind of weird name is Tock Seng Edwards?'

'He was originally called Ethan. I met him in my first year of secondary school. He would sit all by himself, at the tuck shop. Once in a while, some Chinese kids would run up and smack him on the head, and say to him in Singlish, "You Ethan or not? You eaten or not?"'

Singlish is Singapore slang. It's like pidgin English but not really. It uses English but mixed with Chinese, Malay and Indian slang. Often, English words follow the Chinese word order. I explained to Steve that in Tock Seng's case, if you translate the Chinese 'Ne Chi Le Ma?', which means 'Have you had your meal yet?' literally, word for word into the English, it becomes 'You eaten or not?'

'So the kids were, like, saying "Are you Ethan?" and "Have you had your meal?" but they both sound the same in Singlish. "You Ethan or not? You eaten or not?"'

Steve laughed. 'It's pretty creative actually. Who would think that kids could be so imaginative with wordplay at that age?'

'Cruelty is the fount of literary inspiration, I guess. So his parents decided to change his name to a Chinese one, to help him fit in. Tock Seng was the name of one of the national heroes of Singapore. A real rags-to-riches story,

41

from fruit-seller to multi-millionaire. He donated money to build a free hospital for the poor, which today is still a major medical centre.'

'Did it help?' Steve said. 'The name change, I mean. Did it help him fit in?'

'No. The kids made fun of his Chinese name even more. That's because Tock Seng looked really white. When your gene pool is as WASPy as his, having a Chinese name makes you stand out even more.'

Tock Seng's father was American-German and his mother was French-Irish. They were socialist vegetarian idealists who came to Singapore to run a non-profit-making organization called Third World First.

I became friends with Tock Seng because he was the only one in my school who had read Dante and Derrida. For our class project, we used Chinese opera conventions to perform scenes from the Greek tragedy *Oedipus Rex*. Our class-mates' response was 'Wah, very *cheem*' – which was a compliment you gave something that you thought was so profound that you couldn't possibly understand it. But that was the problem, we were the only two people who got each other. We would greet each other with – 'You! *hypocrite lecteur! – mon semblable – mon frère!*', knowing that we might possibly be the only couple in Singapore who knew that this was an allusion to Baudelaire's *Les Fleurs du Mal* via T. S. Eliot's *The Waste Land*.

'So you became friends because you were both freaks, huh?' Steve said. 'Kind of like us?'

'I suppose so,' I said. Steve and I first got together at a party because nobody else in the room would talk to either of us, but that's a story for some other time.

I clicked the mouse to open Tock Seng's greeting card.

A wooden tumbler filled with fortune sticks appeared, rocking back and forth until one of the thin bamboo sticks tumbled out.

The fortune stick popped up from the ground and filled the screen. Then these words appeared in a Tempus Sans IPC font:

The fairy crane escapes from its cage;
So you can fly wherever you will,

Tock Seng's voice came booming out of our Soundblaster speakers – 'DO YOU STILL WANT TO FLY?'

I wondered what Tock Seng looked like after all these years. When we first met, I thought he was the most beautiful creature I had ever seen. His curly hair wisped around his porcelain face like flames, making him look like the cherubs in paintings stored in museums far away in the West. All the other Singaporean boys looked like brown, skinny monkeys in comparison, screeching racial abuse at him while his pearl-grey eyes welled with tears. He looked like an angel with broken wings, trapped on this old earth, needing my help to mend his baby feathers so that he could return on dazzling wings to his Father's throne.

I clicked 'Reply' and wrote:

I'm going to New York for an interview today. Will write more when I return. CD.

I looked at Kermit the Frog and swore. 'I'm late.' I grabbed my suit and ran into the bathroom.

Steve knocked on the bathroom door.

'Not again!' I said.

'No, I don't need to piss. You've got another message from Tock Seng, he just *binged* you,' Steve said. 'He says he's in New York. He wants to meet you. What are you going to do?'

I guess I still felt guilty about the way I left Tock Seng, so I went to the computer and typed in my answer:

43

OK. I'll be staying at the Olympus. Give me a call if you're around. CD.

Mind the Gap.

Droning over and over. The doors opened, inviting me to step into the Piccadilly line, to enter those dark blue veins that would bring me to Heathrow.

Mind the Gap.

The sound of a lost soul, a disembodied voice floating above the commuters waiting to be tubed through the innards of London.

The City suits surrounded me. These were the billion-dollar men, super-humans, bionic in their wealth. They could leap over buildings in a single bound with just one swipe of their Amex. Soulless automatons.

I stared at the line across the platform, and stepped back.

Mind the Gap.

The sound of a spirit split from flesh. A ghostly voice, drifting, a bodyless being, floating, lost. The voice of a metallic siren, a woman warning of what would happen if you crossed the line. You would become like her, no will of her own, a pre-recorded noise. A cold and robotic voice, a mechanical chant.

Mind the Gap.

The train left and I stared at the dark gap above the tracks.

Sometimes it feels like the East is one mountain, and the West another, and I'm falling into the valley between both, spiralling in the gap between both bodies. I'm trapped in limbo, in the black hole between Heaven and Hell.

Mind the Gap.

Another train pulled in. Who was I kidding? If I crossed the line, it wouldn't make that much difference. I was born in the gap and would always stay there. I had always felt as lost and disconnected as the voice that floated above me. In a way, drifting between here and there, I *was* the gap.

I sighed. Maybe I just think too much. Why turn a train ride into a major metaphysical crisis? The problem was still the same. I wanted to live in England and Singapore, and Mammon Inc. was the only firm that would enable me to do that. Until someone came up with a better deal, it was an offer I couldn't refuse.

I stepped across the line.

5

A sluggish river choking with violent fish.

Windowless walls rising in the Moroccan desert.

The sheen of a fly's wing on cow-chewed bark.

I flipped through the travel photos in the in-flight magazine. *A hammock swinging over the void.* I wondered if Tock Seng went to any of these places. We were both looking for a somewhere to belong, and three years ago, Tock Seng said he knew how to find that somewhere. I wondered if he had succeeded. Should I have followed him?

We broke up on the day we went to Chinatown to celebrate Tock Seng's eighteenth birthday.

Chinatown was one of the few places in Singapore still lined with nineteenth-century shop-houses, their dusty ochres, cobalt blues, lime greens and sunset reds providing a rare burst of colour against the orderly rows of grey, skyscraping banks and concrete blocks of white, matchbox-like housing flats. With its winding alleys and illogical one-way streets, it was a rare oasis of colour and chaos in a city centre dominated by spotless hotels and shiny, identical shopping malls, all equipped with a Seven-Eleven, mcBurgers and a Visa ATM on every ground floor. Walking around the shop-houses always felt like walking into a rainbow, into a magical, arcane past, where every shade reflected one of the Five Elements, and all things maintained the tranquillity of a Yin–Yang in balance.

Chinatown had numerous shops that catered to the Asian's consumer hit-list, namely electronics (Walkmans and IBMs galore), imitation designer goods (e.g. fake Rolexes) and genuine gold chains. But we didn't go there for those products, we went there because we loved browsing through stuff that you couldn't get in the shopping malls: painted masks, waxed-paper umbrellas, kites, ivory seals for stamping documents. We walked through medicine halls that filled the air with the pungent smell of potions created by mixing snake skin with herbs and the body parts of probably at least one species on the endangered list, but then extinction is a small price to pay for any medication that claims to increase your height, extend your penis and cure cancer.

Suddenly, a smell hooked us, the aroma of the durians piled along the market stalls that lined the street.

Tock Seng walked up to a vendor who was doing a 'four for $10' offer on these Thai imports. The durian seller, dressed in the market 'uniform' of an imitation Yves St Laurent polo shirt, tennis shorts and flip-flops, grabbed a large durian by its branch, and lifted the green, spiky fruit near his face. 'Durian, mister. Very nice. You see outside –' he pointed at the spikes on the fruit. 'Sharp.' He touched one of the spikes with his forefinger. 'Ouch.' He snickered. 'You buy one, you got enemy, take durian, hit him on the head.' He pretended to brain his assistant with the durian. 'He sure die, ha, ha.' He put the durian down on the table and took out a cleaver. 'So you see, mister, durian, outside very dangerous, but inside . . . ahhhhh.' He slammed down the cleaver and split the durian in half. He dug out the yellow, fleshy fruit from the shell. 'Like gold nut. Soft gold.'

All this time, when the durian seller was doing his demonstration, Tock Seng pressed his lips together harder and harder. I couldn't understand why, because Tock Seng loved durians with a passion that most men reserve for beer and sports teams.

I squeezed his hand. 'So do you want any?'

'You tell your friend to try the durian,' the durian seller said to me in Chinese. 'I know most white people cannot stand the smell – make them want to vomit – but sometimes they like it. No try, no gain. Like last time, my brother brought back some cheese from Switzerland. So smelly, make me want to vomit. But I hold my nose and eat the cheese. And I quite enjoy it. You ask your friend to try durian. Don't like the smell, never mind one.'

Tock Seng told the durian seller that he liked the smell of durians, and that he'd eaten durians ever since he was three years old. And he said all that in Chinese.

The durian seller stared at Tock Seng for a few moments. '*Wah*, your Chinese very good. Where did you learn how to speak such good Chinese?'

'*Xin Jia Po*,' Tock Seng told him.

'You learn Chinese in Singapore? But where are you from?' he said.

'*Xin Jia Po*,' Tock Seng said.

'Where are your parents from?' he said.

'*Mei Guo*,' Tock Seng said. Then he added that he arrived in Singapore when he was one, and that he grew up in Singapore.

'Oh, you're from America. I like America. Sylvester Stallone.' He pointed at a giant movie poster that was attached to the side of the bus stop. 'You like America?'

Tock Seng told him that he'd never been back to America and didn't know anybody there.

The vendor just smiled at him and said, 'So when are you going back to America? Maybe take back a few durians?'

48

Tock Seng turned around and stomped away.

I ran after him. 'What's wrong?'

'Why did he speak to you in Chinese, but me in English? Why didn't he praise you for speaking such good Chinese? Nobody ever asks you where you came from originally. And no one ever asks you when you're going back to China. Why am I the only one who gets asked these questions?'

It was because he looked like an *ang mo*, but I couldn't tell him that. 'That guy was obviously an insensitive moron. Most people say stupid things when they're trying to sell you something. It's nothing personal. Don't let it get to you.'

'But it's not fair. I live in a white concrete housing block, like any typical Singaporean.' Tock Seng pointed out that he wasn't like those white expats, holed up in their condos, who shuttled between their office and air-con restaurants in their Mercedes. Unlike the expats, he didn't just hang out with his tennis partners at clubs like the Tanglin that only accepted American citizens. Tock Seng ate at the hawker centres and *kopi tiams*, bought his food from the wet markets, played *sepak tawak* and practised judo at the community centre, rode the bus and the MRT, just like everyone else. 'But I know that no matter how Singaporean I might be in my soul, because of the way I look, I will always be treated like an *ang mo gwei*.'

Tock Seng told me how he always felt part of this most Asian of places. He'd visited Chinatown ever since he was a baby, and his infant eyes drank in all the sights, his heart and mind too young and undeveloped to be able to grasp the concepts of ethnic identity and national background. When he heard housewives haggling in Hokkein, or smelt the red barbecue pork roasting on the hot charcoal, all through his childhood, his eyes and ears and nose didn't sense those things as Chinese or Singaporean. They were just things, things felt by his body, *his* kind of things. So if you asked him, 'Who are you?', he would say, *I am the trishaw rider,*

twiddling the knobs on the radio beneath my leather seat
while I wait for my next customer; I am the toothless
grandfather, moving my Elephant to crush my opponent's
Cannon during a game of Chinese chess; I am the plastic
canopies that protect the market stalls, striped red-and-
white like candy canes; I am the red lanterns hanging from
every shop-house like a string of giant, red garlic bulbs. All
this is me.

But as he grew older, he would always meet someone like the durian seller, who would remind him that the world saw him differently from how he saw himself. He was like every other white person they had ever seen, and they only saw white people through the glass walls of their TVs, a race from a distant, almost fantastically fictional land.

'What should I do?' Tock Seng asked me.

I looked at the crowd cramming its way into the Guan Yin Temple. 'Why don't you ask Guan Yin?' My sister always went there to *qiu qian*, to ask the Goddess of Mercy about her fortune.

'Good idea,' Tock Seng said. 'This temple's *qian* is famous for being very *ling*. The answers from the fortune sticks are supposedly really dead on.'

I liked this temple because it had no historical significance. It was first built in 1884, but was then torn down and replaced with a renovated, faux-Chinese version which erased anything that might be of interest to National Heritage seekers. This made it purely functional, which meant that it was strictly a place of worship (with – hurrah! – no gift shop attached) and consequently a tourist-free zone. Unlike the Thian Hock Seng Temple, which has always been littered with sightseers due to its status as one of the pioneer temples in Singapore, there were no hundred-seater coaches idling outside the entrance, generating a murky fog of exhaust fumes. Neither were there middle-aged men in shorts, exposing their hairy, pasty legs and pointing their Nikon cameras at worshippers while they tried to pray.

No, the crowd that crammed through the Guan Yin Temple were strictly locals, where going to *qiu qian* was a regular and important part of daily living, like going to the market or the coffee-shop. You had the grandmothers and the aunties, the Ah Mas and Ah Sohs, bearing bunches of lilies and baskets of oranges on behalf of their sons and daughters. There were the working girls, praying for the arrival of Mr Right, and the teenage bookies, hoping that the Goddess would reveal the next champion horse at the Turf Club. Students asked for good O- and A-level exam results and elderly *Ah Peis* begged Guan Yin to relieve them of their rheumatism.

Before I entered the temple, I bought a wrist-band of beads from a saffron-robed monk, putting in a five-dollar donation for the upkeep of the temple. The monk was the only legit operator outside the temple, as it was lined with tables of hucksters ready to prey on the superstitious – astrologers, fortune-tellers, and mediums who were supposedly possessed by the local temple ghost. The temple gates were plastered with many signs threatening these charlatans with legal prosecution.

We went to the side alcove and picked up a wooden tumbler filled with hundreds of fortune sticks. I picked up one of these wafer-thin strips of bamboo, about the length of chopsticks, and tried to decipher the Chinese words engraved at the end of the stick. I couldn't. Mandarin had never been one of my strongest subjects, and now, post-A-levels, I didn't have to go for Chinese lessons any more, so I was moving slowly towards being illiterate in my 'mother' tongue.

We looked for empty spots on the red carpet in front of the glass cabinet beneath the lanterned ceiling. It wasn't easy. Nearly every inch was filled, and a temple attendant

51

barked at the crowd with a bull-horn, issuing orders so that everyone could squeeze on to the mat. But we finally found a space, and I pressed my knees against the hard floor and faced the glass cabinet that housed the statue of Guan Yin.

I shook the tumbler, sloping it towards the altar so that one stick would gradually work its way out of the bunch and fall on to the floor. Guan Yin, with her long, ebony hair, porcelain skin and rosy cheeks, always looked beautiful, but distant. She seemed like an idol crafted in a shop somewhere, but I always hoped that she was somewhere in the Heavens, and that one day I might meet her somehow. So far, our relationship had been formal and impersonal. I would ask her something, and she would answer me via her fortune sticks. She was the goddess of compassion, but I never felt that love when I was praying to her. She only made me feel more lonely as I looked at her, a mute statue glued to a cold pedestal.

I closed my eyes to block out any distractions, but the lantern-shaped lamps must have had 5,000-watt bulbs. Even with my eyes clamped shut, I could still see the yellow glow. Millions of fortune sticks clattered in hundreds of tumblers, mixing chaotically with the buzz of prayers from frantic lips.

Finally, I heard a plonk. A stick fell out. I picked it up and returned to the side alcove. Tock Seng joined me, and we exchanged our sticks for a pink slip of paper.

'Which Lot did you get?' Tock Seng said.

'Lot Fourteen,' I said.

Tock Seng showed me his pink slip. 'Lot Fourteen. Isn't it amazing?'

'What?'

'Isn't it obvious? We're soul-mates. I asked Guan Yin what I was supposed to do with my life. What my destiny was. And we got the same answer. We're supposed to follow the same path.'

52

'And what path is that supposed to be?'
Tock Seng read the Lot:

> The fairy crane escapes from its cage;
> So you can fly wherever you will,
> No corner of heaven is barred on your flight,
> Even to Paradise, or as far as you please.

Tock Seng picked up a book by the alcove, the *Guan Yin Qian* by Master Han Muna, which helped explain the riddle. 'Your home is insecure, so it is hard to settle down. Migration is highly recommended.' He shut the book.

We walked to the edge of the Singapore river. The wooden bum-boats sailed out of the harbour.

'Maybe we should just hop on some boat and take a trip past the great beyond.'

'Where would we go?'

'It's obvious we'll never fit into Singaporean society, or any society, for that matter. We're freaks, mutant hybrids of East and West – like trans-cultural X-men. So forget fitting in. Why don't we get out of this place and look for other freaks like us?'

'But do you think there are any people like us?' I used to think there was a Generation X, other X-men like ourselves, a tribe that existed on the fringes of society – an indefinable group that couldn't be recruited by corporations or targeted by advertisers. But ever since the Spice Girls used that term to sing the praises of Pepsi, those words had lost all their meaning, and it seemed like a whole generation had got swallowed up by the Mammon Inc. mentality.

'We'll never know until we go and look for them,' Tock Seng said. 'If we stay here, we'll just feel like misfits all our lives. But if we travel, even if we don't find our tribe, at least we'll get to have some cool adventures. Think of all the places we could visit.' Tock Seng told me of all the places we could go, fantastical escapes far away from Singapore's concrete blocks: swamps where statues wept blood, and high mountains full of smoky huts and blinking mongols; desolate mausoleums, where vampire bats dangled from domes and red ants tunnelled through crevices, exploring the cracks in the white sepulchres. We would sit by mud wells, miles from the nearest diesel engine, listening to sounds we'd never heard before – gypsy xylophones, Arab bagpipes, pigs drowning. We would walk up gentle, dusty stairways, and smell air we'd never smelt before, the scent of a desert city, thick with cloves and incense and wood smoke.

'Will you come with me?' Tock Seng said.

Why did I say what I did? Maybe because I was afraid that if I stayed in Singapore, I would become a typical Singaporean. I would end up in a marriage arranged by the government's Social Development Unit, double-clicking my life away for some dotcom company and spending Sundays with my kids at mcBurgers. My greatest excitement would come from deciding which colour cover (opal, peppermint or tangerine) to snap on to my Nokia. No, I wanted the life that Tock Seng described: I wanted to laze on hot banks, where the ice and the dice clicked, and crocodiles yawned, startling butterflies with their jaws.

'Yeah, sure,' I said. 'Let's hit the road, Jack.'

A week later, I got a letter from St L'leh.

Tock Seng stood in line at the duck rice stall, pointing at the crispy bird that hung behind the glass cage.

I ran up to him and flapped the paper in his face. 'I did it! I got a full scholarship to Oxford!'

He did not look at me but stared at the hook that pierced the duck's jaw. 'You going to take it?'

'Of course.'

'But we were going to go to Egypt, to see the pyramids.'

The hawker slammed the cleaver down on the duck's

neck. I made some hee-hem noises, then said, 'Uh, I'm not sure about that. I've been reading up on our trip and our itinerary sounds really dangerous. I mean, like Egypt. Dangers include land mines and terrorists who bomb tour buses.'

'What about going on safari in Africa?'

'Africa. Dangers include diarrhoea. Malaria. Aids. Bilharzia. Meningitis. Rabies. Tetanus. Polio. Yellow fever. Cholera. TB. And blackwater fever – when you literally piss blood.'

'What about Tibet? You wanted to look for enlightenment there. What about our plans to trek to the cave hermitage of Drak Yerpa?'

'Mountains equal hypothermia,' I said. I stared at my feet and shifted my flip-flops, making black marks on the wet tiles. 'Your trip sounds exciting, but I have to get real. I'm not the New Age hippy traveller type. I need regular showers, and shops where I can get herbal exfoliating face washes with alpha and beta hydroxy acids. I don't want to end up on some mountain in Lower Mongolia, squatting on a toilet with no toilet paper, and worse still, no toilet door. And, you know, what if J. D. Salinger decides to publish a novel after thirty years of silence? I don't want to be in Eritrea when that happens, or anywhere else that's a breeding ground for malaria, ebola or other viruses that liquefy your intestines.'

'You're such a material girl,' Tock Seng said. 'Yeah, if you go to Oxford, it'll be cushy. All cloistered libraries and genteel gardens, and a job-guaranteed degree at the end. But you'll find that it's no substitute for love.' He played with the string of the plastic bag, winding and unwinding it open and shut. The soy sauce churned as the bag tossed and turned in his hands.

'My parents would kill me if I turned down a full scholarship to Oxford,' I said.

55

'What about us? What about the Lot?' Tock Seng asked.

'We could still be friends,' I said. 'We could still write.'

'Yeah, sure.' Tock Seng spun the pink cord around the neck of the bag, strangling it shut. He stomped away.

I ran after him, trailing his shadow as he marched past the palm trees and violet orchid beds.

'As long as we stay in touch, everything will be all right,' I said. 'You can travel and I can finish my degree at Oxford, and then after all that is done, we can settle down somewhere together. We should make it a discipline to write to each other at least every week. It doesn't have to be long, even a postcard would do. As long as we still have that commitment, you know, a card a week.'

We reached the bus stop and Tock Seng just stood there, staring at the sign silently, feigning an unusual interest in the bus schedule.

The 174 arrived. I stepped up the stairs, but Tock Seng didn't join me.

'Bye,' he said.

'Aren't you going home?' I said. We usually took this bus back to our housing estate.

'No. I'm going somewhere else,' Tock Seng said. 'I need to do some stuff. You're going some place I'm not. I need to take a different bus.'

And after that, he disappeared from my life.

As they chauffeured me across the bridge, I realized, for the first time, that Manhattan was an island. How odd. When you think 'island' you usually think of coconut trees and sun-kissed beaches, but here before me lay an island with steel banks, bordered by rusty fences and EZPass booths. They say Hades is an island, cold and dark, surrounded by the Acheron, a river of woe that flows through black gorges and goes underground. As I watched the Hudson slime itself against the lifeless piers, seeping into the sewers beneath, I worried that Tock Seng might be right. Was I a material girl, seduced by the jewelled obelisks of the West, zooming towards Hades in a champagne limo? The Greeks who worshipped the King of the Underworld called him Pluto – the Giver of Wealth. If Hades was a gloomy subterranean isle, then perhaps Professor Ad-oy was right. Maybe I was entering the kingdom of the dead, for the home of Mammon Inc. looked like the Underworld, a smog-miasmic island forested by black lamp-posts and empty of birdsong.

6

The Mammon Inc. HQ stood out from the other needles on Times Square. The other corporate HQs were stuck around 42nd Street like stiff pins, but Mammon Inc., with its curved, claw-like silhouette, arched its silver nail sensuously upwards. It pricked a dirty cloud, drawing a blood ray of sun. So this was the den of the CorpS, this sharp skyscraper, looking like a dragon's finger bursting from beneath a smoking manhole.

I stepped out of the red glow of Broadway into the cool fluorescence of Mammon Inc. A solitary guard stood by the elevator, encased in his uniform of Imperial Stormtrooper white. I showed him my letter.

He unlocked the elevator and said, 'Press P.'

I lifted a quizzical eyebrow.

'P for Pinnacle,' he said. 'Top floor.'

The elevator door opened to reveal a smiling youth. With his Euro coiffure and black-and-white suit, he looked like a Zen version of a Gucci ad. Or like a waiter who had been tipped really, really well.

'I am Sith, Dr Draco Sidious's secretary. He will be with you shortly,' he said. 'The other Adapters will be joining you via satellite.' He pointed at the six blank TV screens on the wall, blue as empty aquariums.

The geisha boy disappeared into the elevator, the doors closing with a sci-fi-movie *schwig*.

I turned around and the painting caught my eye immediately. The cold sun lit the surreal landscape, heatless flames that froze the desert in a dream. The dunes were the colour of flesh, spread like breasts and buttocks undulating across the canvas. Dali's decapitated head lay between one of those creamy bosoms, an army of ants crawling into his eye. The inhabitants looked like refugees of war. The Winged Victory of Samothrace was made out of bandages, while Venus, with drawers bursting from chest, supported herself on crutches. The crutches were shaped like rhino horns, making the goddess look like she was resting on erect penises. The frame was filled with images of decay and destruction, torture and cannibalism, but painted with such a soft fluidity that these grotesque objects, floating in the dreamy delirium of the canvas, became sweeter and more beautiful than anything I had seen in real life. Upon closer examination, I saw that the dunes formed the shape of a couple, entwined in an embrace. The woman's torso melted into a saucer like soft cheese. Her lover, with the gaze of a tender cannibal, scooped her breast with a spoon and ate the fine Camembert flesh.

'It's an original oil on canvas. Perhaps one of the best examples of Dali's paranoid critical method,' a voice behind me said. I could not place that accent, but it was familiar, like the mechanical voice you hear on PA systems in airports and shopping malls. Though the accent was hint-free with regards to locale, it exuded professionalism, as it was full of the tones and rhythms that made you feel like it would be worth your time listening to whatever deal it had to offer. It was a voice that would be accepted by business vendors around the world – sort of like Visa.

59

I turned around to put a body to the floating voice. I found myself struck by his snake eyes, that intense, unblinking gaze.

He was the epitome of corporate chic, reminding me of what Shakespeare said about the prince of darkness being a gentleman. He was tieless, with a collarless jacket that wrapped itself to his body with a wide empire sash rather than with the traditional buttons. The silk coat touched the ground, its luxurious length and rounded collar making him look like he had draped himself in Chinese Imperial robes. Yet he didn't look like a statue out of a Silk Road documentary, since his suit still had a modern Western cut to it. I had even seen a few executives on my flight donning this style into JFK. Maybe this was the latest New York look, kind of Calvin Klein meets Mulan.

'Dr Sidious?' I said.

He nodded. 'Do you like Dali?'

'Yes, he's one of my favourite artists.' I looked at the edible couple on the wall. 'I've never seen a real Dali. I could never afford to go to any of those places that had galleries with real Dalis.' Much of my youth was spent in the National Library, marvelling at reproductions of burning giraffes, blue pianos, stone heads riding bicycles, and elephants with spiders' legs. One of the things that tempted me to New York was the chance to see the famous watch melting on an olive branch at the Museum of Modern Art.

'He's one of my favourites as well,' Dr Sidious said. 'Dali was born in the Year of the Dragon, like myself. Thus I feel a personal affinity towards his psyche. The grotesque shows us a shadow world where we can marvel at the beauty of what we fear might destroy us.' He pointed at a red pond. 'Pools of blood draped on the ground like the soft cloak of a dying bullfighter.'

I was surprised. Dr Sidious poetically described what I liked about Dali. I had expected him to be some number cruncher enchanted by .xls spreadsheets and oblivious to the delights of Donatello. Yet he showed himself to be a sensitive patron of the arts, a magnate more like the Renaissance-inspiring Lorenzo de' Medici than the casino-building Donald Trump.

'Take a seat,' he said, pointing at a futon bench while he walked over to a Karuselli chair. He slid into the black leather seat encased in a white fibreglass shell. A Sixties classic, designed by the Finnish Yrjo Kukkapuro, the Karuselli chair looked like the kind of command console seat that Blofeld would swivel in as he surveyed his world-domination monitors.

'You like the Dali very much, don't you?' Draco Sidious said. 'You can have it, if you like.'

'Really?' I asked, startled.

'Our screening process is long, vigorous, even painful. Thus we reward all successful applicants with a signing-on bonus.'

'A Dali is a pretty amazing bonus,' I said.

'And our Tests are just as amazingly difficult.'

'What do you want me to do?' I stared at the painting that Dr Sidious was using to seduce me. Money did not tempt me, but Dali did. His face hovered in my mind – those devilish eyes and that stiff moustache that shot across his lip like a startled snake.

'We'll get to that in a moment.' Dr Sidious clicked on the remote. 'But first, you should meet the other Adapters.'

Six faces filled the TVs. The dragon kings, the gods of the Chinese Emperors, lived in the four oceans, and it seemed that these six majestic faces had emerged from the deep to appear on these widescreen aquariums, their faces suspended against the blue background like heads floating in glass tanks.

'Meet Mohammad Eblis, the head of our African office.' Dr Sidious pointed at the top left screen. 'Next to him is

Count Jormungand, who runs Europe. Our Finnish Ms
Louhi is to his right, and she's in charge of Antarctica and
Australia. Mr Oni and Mrs Kali are on the screens below
her, and they run Asia together. General Yama leads South
America, and finally, there is myself. I am the CEO of
Mammon CorpS and the Vice Chairman of Mammon Inc.,
and I control North America.' He pointed at the Mammon
CorpS logo, the seven-headed dragon. 'We are the heads of
Mammon CorpS.'

They looked really familiar. They reminded me of
someone – myself. Actually, I lie. I had a 25 per cent
student-discount perm from Hair in a Hurry, and a
bargain-basement suit from Isetan. The Adapters looked
like me if I'd received a million-dollar salary upgrade. They
looked like an advanced-featured version of me, like a
Microsoft 8.1b version of myself.

'What do you know about Mammon CorpS?' Draco
Sidious said.

'You adapt people who move to a different culture?' I
asked.

Dr Sidious nodded. 'Abraham Maslow, the father of
humanistic psychology, noted that we all have needs that
are built into us genetically, like instincts. He called these
instinct-like needs "instinctoids".'

'What are they?' I said.

'They are the need for what the psychologist Carl Rogers
called "positive regard" – the need for approval, acceptance
and attention. These instinctoids are essential for human
survival, and when a person is deprived of them, his mental
health deteriorates and he experiences deep anxiety that can
lead to chronic depression. This truth, of course, was not
something that was discovered by modern psychologists, but
has been stated since the beginning of time. Are you familiar
with the Book of Genesis?'

I nodded. To prepare for this interview, I had followed

Professor Ad-oy's advice and carefully studied the Temptation scene in Genesis.

'Yes, I thought you might have. I was in the same tutorials with your advisor, Professor Ad-oy, when I was an undergraduate at Dagobah Hall, and I remember that Genesis, chapter two was always his favourite passage from the Bible. I always thought the most striking part of that myth was when God looked at Adam and said, 'It is not good for Man to be alone.' That sums up our human condition. Man was created as a social organism, and without the acceptance of his community, his spirit will die.'

'That's why people need to be adapted? If they don't adapt to their society, they self-destruct?'

Dr Sidious nodded. 'Exactly. That's why Mammon CorpS has been so successful. We help our clients attain their life-dependent needs for approval and acceptance.'

'However, we are not interested in adapting the rabble,' Count Jormungand said. 'Our clients are foreigners who want access to positions of power in the fields of politics, finance, fashion and entertainment. We are an élite firm that teaches our clients how to enter the élite.'

'For example, the son of a rich businessman from India goes to Oxford,' Mrs Kali, the Indian woman, said. 'He has excellent academic abilities, but knows little about the ways of the aristocracy. Mammon CorpS, for a generous fee, teaches him how to be like the British Brahmins.'

'Our success is based on the fact that everybody wants to be in the top one per cent. People will give their souls to be in the Pantheon. Mammon CorpS sells the key to that temple for an exorbitant price. Our clients include colonels and princes, CEOs and presidents, Hollywood stars and Grammy winners. Our clients depend on us to keep them on Mount Olympus, and this has made us one of the richest and most powerful firms on earth. In order to join us you have to prove that you are the best. You have to pass our Tests.'

'What Tests?' I said.

Draco Sidious handed me a white cube.

I touched the black button on the cube and out popped three pins, like a UK/Singapore plug. I pressed the button again, and the three pins retracted and slid out to two prongs, like a US plug. Another tap of the button slid the prongs sideways, making it ready to use in Australia.

'The Tests will examine your abilities in different international arenas,' Dr Sidious said. 'We like to think of ourselves as being like a universal travel adapter. We enable our clients to go anywhere in the world, and plug into the power supply there.'

'So you want me to become like a plug-and-play peripheral,' I said, 'like one of those PCMCIA cards that you can just take out of the box and slot into any computer, anywhere?'

The CorpS nodded.

I did not want to be like them. Sure, they were billion-dollar men, but their superhuman bionic powers turned them into machines. They were androids without consciences or any other touchy-feely emotions that made humans so inefficient.

'So you are the creators of the *Übermensch*, the men of steel who rule this metropolis?' I said, half-sarcastically.

Dr Sidious laughed. 'Yes, the CorpS are the *Über*-Managers, asserting a superior Nietzschean will to profit. We are the fathers of the master race.'

Though his light tone suggested that he was only joking about being a Hitler wannabe, this place was beginning to feel more and more like the Führer's *Reichstag*. The only way out was through the red elevator doors, round in the shape of Mammon CorpS' logo.

Dr Sidious saw me looking at the firm's swastika, and

asked, 'Do you know why we chose the emblem of the Red Dragon?'

'I'm not sure,' I said. 'All I know about the Red Dragon was that it fought the angels in Heaven, lost and was cast on earth to wreak havoc.'

'That must be a different dragon from ours,' Mr Oni said. 'Our dragon has five claws. It is the sacred emblem of the Chinese Emperors. The dragon kings are benevolent deities. Living in the four oceans, they are the guardians of seafarers. Like us, they protect travellers.'

'The dragon was also the emblem for Uther Pendragon, and the coat of arms for the Prince of Wales,' Ms Louhi, the blonde CorpS, added.

I remembered what Professor Ad-oy had said about the cockatrice. 'It has the head of a basilisk, though. That's a pretty dangerous snake. Couldn't it kill with just one stare?'

'Yes, it's an asp,' Dr Sidious said. 'We chose it because it was the symbol of royalty in Egypt. We wanted an emblem that would show how our power transcends all the nations.'

Was Professor Ad-oy wrong? Maybe Mammon CorpS wasn't God's enemy, the ancient serpent. Maybe they were just believers in Neo-Confucianism, fusing Eastern traditions with Western commercialism. This 'Chopsticks and Credit Cards' philosophy has made Asia an economic boom minefield, so maybe Mammon CorpS was being more New Singapore than Neo-Nazi.

Dr Sidious gave me a file. 'This outlines our pay package.'

I jolted on the futon. I couldn't believe the digits. It was the kind of figure you usually associated with phone numbers.

Dr Sidious smiled. 'I'm glad you approve.'

'If we assigned you to turn one of our English clients into a Singaporean, what would you teach him to do?' Count Jormungand said.

'I'd teach him how to be *kia-su*,' I said. 'I'd drum that

Singaporean philosophy into him that says, If less is more, imagine how much more is more! I'd tell him to cut queues, overload his plate at the buffet table and pursue bargain hunting with the same tenacity that the Arthurian knights reserved for the Holy Grail.'

The CorpS smiled. It was the right answer. I had scored. In my head, I could hear John Motson screaming 'Goaaaalllll!' like he always does during the FA Cup Final. What can I say? It's Chiah Deng 1, Mammon 0.

'What about the reverse?' Count Jormungand said. 'If you had to turn a client into an Englishman, what would you do?'

'I would teach him to become obsessed with three things – politeness, the class system and the weather,' I said. 'In that order of importance.'

Everyone chuckled simultaneously. I was like – yes! Two–nil to Chiah Deng, she scores with a cheeky bicycle kick from the edge of the six-yard box! I resisted the temptation to do a Mexican wave. Their questions were pretty easy. I was sure to land this job.

'On paper, you seem perfect for us,' Dr Sidious said. 'Your academic record is outstanding, and you come from the right cultural-economic background. However, we'd like to test your abilities in the real world. Your first Test involves *Generation Vexed*. Are you familiar with the magazine?'

'Of course,' I said.

'*Gen Vex* will be holding its anniversary party next month. It will be at Utopia, one of the most exclusive clubs in New York. We want you to find a way to get past the bouncers by convincing them that you are one of the rulers of New York nightlife.'

'What sort of people usually get past the bouncers?' I said.

'The people who appear on Neal Adam's page-six column,' Dr Sidious said, handing me a copy of the *mcTimes*.

'You mean the stars of New York's hipster-rati?' I asked. 'Models, film directors, 26-year-old dotcom moguls?'

'Yes,' Dr Sidious replied.

I took the newspaper and stooped down to put it in my bag. While my head was out of view, I took a few panic-reducing breaths to fend off the imminent heart attack. I'd always seen myself as the binary opposite of trendiness, like the Other of Glamour, the Geek Template. There was no way I could ever look like the celebrities in Neal Adam's gossip column. They always looked inhumanly sexy, like stylish sticks with sunglasses. They almost seemed to be a species from another planet. I was sure that if I stepped into the *Gen Vex* party, the atmosphere in that world would be so deadly to nerds like myself that my face would melt, like those people who got liquefied on Mars in *Total Recall*.

This was a disaster. I had no idea how to pass this Test. I felt like Mammon Inc. had seen my keeper wandering off the goal line and had hoofed the ball from the halfway line, looping it over his head into the net, *à la* Nayim *vs.* Arsenal.

Dr Sidious handed me a green card. 'We realize that adjusting yourself to become a *Gen Vex* icon will require a budget far above your student income. Feel free to charge any Test-related expenses you may incur to this Visa.'

'Sounds great,' I said. 'Is that my only Test?'

'There are two more,' Dr Sidious said. 'Who is the most Singaporean person that you know?'

'Probably my sister,' I said.

'Why would you say that?' he asked.

'Whenever I miss being Singaporean, I ring my sister. She understands all the things my English friends just don't get. Like jokes in Singlish about *Ah Bengs*, the joys of eating shark's fin, guilt techniques for extracting the most *ang pow* money from relatives during Chinese New Year.'

'Who's the most British person you know?' Dr Sidious asked.

'Steve, my flat-mate,' I said.

'What makes him so British?' Mrs Kali asked.

'He's like your typical English lad. All his fantasies revolve around sex, football and pop music.' I tried to think of other reasons why I saw Steve as ultra-British. 'Oh yes, and the weather. We often have these hour-long conversations about the weather.'

'What do you talk about?' Mrs Kali said.

'Oh, it's a well-honed technique, almost ritualistic,' I said. 'You warm up by making moaning noises about how crap the weather is. Then you make a whining transition to how depressed you are because of it, before roaring ahead – swapping all these arcane, obscure historical details. Like how it's the heaviest precipitation since 1857, and how England hasn't had such nasty rain since the lunar eclipse that caused the Black Pox that nearly ruined South Yorkshire.'

'What's the nature of your relationship with Steve?' Ms Louhi asked.

'He's my best friend,' I said. 'I guess he's like the white brother my parents could never give me.'

Dr Sidious nodded. 'These are your final two Tests, if you choose to accept them. You'll have to take Steve to a Singapore dinner, and adapt him to fit in with the guests. Also, you'll have to take your sister to an Oxford gathering, and make her acceptable to the intellectual élite.'

I sat there, stunned. It was like I had helped Mammon CorpS equalize with a stupid own goal, and they had won the match when it went to penalties after extra-time. I felt like every footballer that ever faffed a penalty kick, like Chris Waddle, Stuart Pearce, Gareth Southgate and David Batty all rolled into one.

'But why Steve? Why my sister?' I said. 'Don't you have some other person – maybe one of your clients, whom I can adapt? I mean, someone who's actually signed up for your services. Why do you need to use my friends and family as part of the screening process? It's a really unusual corporate procedure.'

'Mammon CorpS is part of Mammon Inc. Since Mammon Inc. owns most of the world, we can have nearly anything we want. As CorpS, we get books from mcBorders, decorate our home with antiques from mcSothebys and surf the net with mc.com – all for free. Since Mammon Inc. offers us everything, Mammon Inc. also expects everything from us in return. The Tests will determine if you'll be able pay the price for being a CorpS.'

'You want me to pay for the world with my life?' I said.

Suddenly, Professor Ad-oy's warning didn't sound so crazy. All through the interview, the CorpS had stared at me, unblinking with lidless eyes. At first I thought those snake eyes were due to weird satellite reception, but now I wondered if there was something darker involved. Those predatory pupils looked hungry, hunting for a soul to feast on.

I got off the futon. 'I can't do your Tests. I can't sacrifice that much for a job.'

'What are you worried about?' Dr Sidious said.

'Steve and my sister are too important to me,' I said. 'I don't want to have to force them to do the Tests, just to get a job. Even if they did want to do the Tests, I don't know how it might affect our relationship once we went through with it. I don't want to do anything to hurt what we have.'

'That's a completely natural reaction,' Dr Sidious said. 'Most of our recruits balk when they hear about the Tests. But then we show them this.' He clicked at the screens and the CorpS disappeared, their faces replaced by six global hotspots. But the Adapters were still there, for as my eyes moved from one screen to the next, their disembodied voices wrapped themselves around the flickering images, providing a travelogue soundtrack to the Technicolour pictures.

On the first screen, Euro totty, well-heeled in Prada leather, sat at the Piazza della Signoria sipping cappuccinos. A Tuscan youth emerged from the Medici palace, looking like Michelangelo's David walking out of the Gothic shadows of the Palazzo Vecchio.

'Florence is a city where every rose roof and amber wall seems shaped by the genius of a Da Vinci or a Donatello,' Count Jormungand said.

I nodded. The video made this Italian city look like a Renaissance museum filled with lounging *Vogue* models.

The next television screen showed faces painted in red and gold, dancers with sail-sized sleeves flapping around giant cigar sticks of incense. It was opening night at a Beijing opera house, and the gongs clanged furiously as acrobats somersaulted over falsetto singers.

A Mexican marvel filled another screen. 'This is an intimate shot of Xochimilco,' General Yama said, 'where fiestas take place in barges floating on misty avenues of water that once carried vegetables and fragrant camomile from farms to Aztec royalty.'

'Who is that?' I pointed at the man on the fourth TV screen. He stood in a canoe, beneath a ray of light that arched like a bridge built of moonglow and water spray. Tiger fish jumped free from the pulsing river, while on the banks baboons huddled on the limbs of tamarind trees and black elephants dipped their bright tusks waterwards.

'He's a Zambian chief,' Eblis said.

The camera on monitor number five showed caffeine connoisseurs at the Place Sant Josep Oriol watching stilt-walkers, fire-eaters and witches caked with charcoal dust. One could imagine an art student named Dali sitting in the Catalan café, inspired by Barcelona's searing Mediterranean light and shadowy street life.

Finally, the last screen swooped over Manhattan, a giant asparagus bed of alabaster and rose-and-green blocks. Pigeons dipped and pivoted, shedding grey feathers of tumult over the million-windowed buildings. The city of mirrors reflected the light of the freshly risen moon, shimmering the violet light back out on to the surrounding black waters. I wanted to gaze on this urban Eden forever, mesmerized by the twilight falling on the garden of glass.

'These are all the places you may work in if you join Mammon CorpS,' Dr Sidious said.

How could I resist? Suddenly, I had a vision of what I could be if I joined Mammon Inc.: a cosmopolitan jet-setter, equally at home with chiefs in mud huts or tycoons in the Four Seasons. I would be like the *National Geographic* poster girl – waking every morning to learn something most people will never know. Inside every Oxford scholar is a spirit that craves a lifetime of learning – an Inner Nerd. Money is nice and glamour is fun, but there is nothing as seductive as fruit from the tree of knowledge.

'I'll talk to them about the Tests,' I said.

7

'Can you believe it?' I said to my sister. 'They have a phone in the bathroom. I'm peeing and calling you long distance for free, all at the same time.'

'Wah, so *shiok*,' my sister said. 'Don't forget to take their soap. Remember to ask the maid to give you extra to bring back home.' My sister had never bought any soap in her life, as her stinginess made her stock our bathroom with soaps that she stole from hotels, restaurants and public toilets.

'Trust me, if I get this job with Mammon Inc., we'll be able to afford to buy a truckload of toiletries. You won't have to be a bathroom burglar any more.' I stared at the green globe of soap. 'Besides, I don't like the soap here. It looks creepy, like a dragon's eyeball.'

'*Ai-yah*, I know you're going to be rich soon. But the thing is, if you don't have to spend money, then don't spend. If you can get the soap for free, why pay?'

'God, you're so *kia-su*,' I said.

'Don't forget to take their toothbrush and comb if they give you that for free as well,' my sister said. 'So when are you going to get your first paycheque? Asia Holidays got do a packaged tour to the Great Wall, but I have to put down a deposit by next week to book it.'

'*Ai-yoh*, please don't spend any more money!' I said. 'I

still don't have a job and I don't know if I'll get this one. I'll have to pass a difficult Test, but I'll need your help.'

'What Test?'

'They want me to turn you into an *ang mo*.'

'Is this yogurt fat-free or just low fat?' my sister said in a nasal twang.

'What?'

'A lot of *ang mo* come to my supermarket. That's what they always ask me: "Are these eggs organic? . . . Do you have any Equal? . . . Where can I recycle my bottles and cans?" See, I know how to talk like *ang mo*. I can help you pass the Test, easy.'

My sister worked as a supermarket cashier at Cold Storage near Holland Village, so I suspected that she was mimicking the American expatriates who lived in that area.

'I every day also meet *ang mo*s. They all ask the same questions, I know how to copy them!' She went back into that twang which I presume was her imitation of a Californian accent. 'Do you have home delivery? . . . Where's the nearest 24-hour drug store? . . . Where's the gas station? . . . Do you have this in King Size? . . . Where's the microwave popcorn? . . . Do you have any Starbucks' Arabian Mocha Java?' She went back to her Singlish accent and asked me, 'What do you think? I copy the *ang mo*, good or not?'

'It's quite good,' I said, 'only I think you're copying Americans. I have to teach you how to be like a British *ang mo*.'

'I know how to be British *ang mo* too! I always hear them talking to their maids.' Her voice went up a pitch as she put on a posh accent. 'Marissa, remember to tape Wimbledon on Channel 12 for Ma'am at eight p.m. tonight. Remember, it's Channel 12 and not Prime 12. Ma'am wants to watch Wimbledon, and not that Tamil drama *Paramapadam*.'

'We'll have to work on that accent,' I said, 'but you're on the right track, sort of. Are you sure you're OK doing the Test?'

'I OK, karaoke!' my sister said. 'Why would I not be OK?'

'I don't know. I was worried that you might be unhappy, because the Test is forcing you to be someone that you're not.'

'Yah, but being a British *ang mo* is so *shiok*, so comfortable. If you're an *ang mo* lady, all you have to do is sit by the swimming pool and tan tan. And if the weather too hot, you go to the hairdresser, sit in air con and say, "Blow my hair, massage my face, paint my nails." You got maid to do everything for you, so you can sit at home all day and shake leg. Even taking care of your children is easy – all you have to do is say to your maid, "Marissa, remember to pick up the children at one-thirty." I think I'll like being *ang mo*. Then I can finally try the expensive coffee. I always go Starbucks, but their coffee so expensive. One grande nearly seven dollars. If I become *ang mo*, will they give me money to buy coffee?'

'I think so,' I said. 'Mammon Inc. will pay for all your training.'

'Oh, goody. I always wanted to try the Colombia Nariño Supremo.'

'They'll fly you to England to do the Test,' I said. 'The *ang mo*s in England live differently from the *ang mo*s here. Most of them don't have maids.'

'I have to go to England? But isn't the weather very cold now?'

'That's something you'll have to adapt to, I guess. It's part of the Test.'

'I cannot *tahan* cold weather. What if I go there, every day ah-choo, ah-choo sneezing? What if I get pneumatic or hypothermometer?'

'You won't get pneumonia or hypothermia. Mammon CorpS will pay for you to get some proper winter gear.'

'Will I get to see snow? That is my dream! I want to build a snowman and see the Abombibable Snowman!'

'You're going to Oxford, not the Himalayas,' I said. 'The Abominable Snowman and other Yeti-type creatures only live in the mountains.'

'But Oxford got winter or not? Got polar bear, sea lion?'

'Oxford just has snow. England is in Europe. Polar bears live in the Arctic regions.' Sometimes it amazes me what I have to explain to my sister.

'Oh.' My sister sounded slightly disappointed. 'But I'll get to build a snowman? I'll get to stick a carrot under his tummy and pretend that it's his penis?'

'Um, yes. I'm sure that'll be charming.' I tried to think of a fun thing for her to do in winter that didn't involve carrot dicks. 'Maybe if it really freezes up we can go ice-skating on the Thames.'

My sister shrieked. '*Ai-yah*, skating so dangerous! Didn't you hear about the girl, go ice-skating rink in Kallang. She fell down, someone skate over her fingers, and chop off her thumb! The Test going to be make me ice-skate or not? I cannot ice-skate, I cannot.'

'Don't worry, I don't think they'll make you ice-skate during the Test.'

I looked at the Mammon CorpS logo monogrammed on the towel. I touched the 'S' of the logo, my finger tracing its red body as it snaked along the fluffy cotton. The tail of the 'S' slithered beneath the other letters like the Nike swoosh. Call it feminine instinct, primitive superstition or bad digestion – but that serpentine swish made my stomach churn. For some irrational reason, that 'S' reminded me of the cunning viper in the garden, who tempted Eve with a prize that killed her soul. So my auto reaction was – just *don't* do it.

'Maybe I shouldn't do the Tests,' I said.

'Why not?' my sister said.

'It's like the firm has no respect for personal boundaries. I don't like the way they want to get you and Steve involved. They might be able to take over any company they like, but I don't want them to take over my life.'

'*Ai-yah*, but we got no choice. You need to make big money, especially now Daddy's eyes so bad.'

'What happened?' I said.

'Nothing new, same old story. He's driving the taxi every night for twelve hours – forty years now. His night blindness getting worse and worse. He drove into a tree last week, but lucky no one got hurt.' She sighed. 'All of us very excited that you graduated and can finally get a job. So Daddy can retire. But if you don't get big job, then who going to feed us? Mummy only know how to be housewife, and I only work at the supermarket. If you become a Professor assistant, make so little money, and Daddy can't work any more, how are we going to eat?'

'But what if I hate the big money job? What if my job makes my life a living hell?' I said.

'*Ai-yah*, you don't remember the mosquito story?'

'I do.' It was the typical kind of Confucian-values, Chinese-propaganda story that my parents made up for my bedtime entertainment. It's about a boy with two elderly parents who suffered from insomnia because they kept being bitten by mosquitoes. The boy stripped naked and lay on the bed beside them, so that the mosquitoes would feed on his blood rather than theirs. I think my parents told me the story so often because they expected me to do the same for them.

'You work so you can make money to take care of your family,' my sister said. 'You like the job – good. You don't like the job – too bad. You spend so much time in England, now you think like an *ang mo*. So selfish. *Ang mo*s only

76

think of themselves. I saw this Oprah show long long time ago. Couldn't stand it. This woman leave her family because she got no . . . what did she say? . . . personal fulfilment. But you're Chinese. You cannot be like that.'

'So I have to get a high-paying job even if they suck the blood out of me?' I asked.

'Yes,' my sister said simply.

I put down the phone. One of the techno treats of the Fabulosi Suite was its turbo tub, which filled up in under thirty seconds. I turned it on.

Water shot out of the steaming tap, hissing like thousands of excited serpents.

8

'Ms Gan, this is the concierge. There is a gentleman by the name of Tock Seng Edwards here to see you.'

'Send him up,' I said.

The last time I saw Tock Seng was at a bus stop shaded by the sad arch of a palm tree. Three years later, I waited for him in the Fabulosi Suite of the Olympus, allegedly the hippest boutique hotel in Manhattan. With its 10014 zip code and Bond girl chambermaids, the Olympus had everything one needed for a stylish sleepover. It had walls in Sonic the Hedgehog blue, curtains in Marilyn Monroe blonde, and a fleet of black-clad BMWs (Bosses/Models/Waitresses) parked in its underground bistro.

Space is the greatest luxury in any city, and the Fabulosi Suite was so huge it was almost cavern-like. The chandeliers hung from the ceiling like crystal bats, while the Philippe Starck tables looked like they were about to scuttle away on their sexy, spider legs. The suite was perfect for playing out all your MTV pop star fantasies: walls that glowed like a violet Atomic Lokade cocktail and puke-green cushions – the kind of vomit colour one imagines rock stars spewing during a drugs-and-booze binge.

However, the *pièce de résistance* of the suite stood in the middle of the room: a ten-foot-long giant aquarium, the type that appeared in every *Miami Vice* episode.

I sat on the bed, watching the glittering piranhas slice through the soft water.

The elevator doors opened and Tock Seng stepped in. 'Woah . . . a lift that opens straight into your room. This is so Top 20 countdown video.'

His angelic face shone like on the first day I saw him at kindergarten, skin so pale and magical, as translucent as lunar light. The stubble that sand-speckled his jaw made my knees quiver like the reflections of our bodies in the sea on the day when we first touched each other furtively. On that day, when we were twelve, we sat by the edge of the beach, the eyes of our parents searing into our backs like the rays from the tropical sun. He slid his hand – hidden from parental eyes – between my thighs. I pumped my knees, squeezing then releasing, and even the cold water that doused our limbs could not chill his boiling palm.

He kissed me.

An olive wave surged through my breast the way it did that day when we sat by the shore, ash-white with sand dust, listening to the radio song float from the shimmering dune behind us.

'You look great. And you seem to be doing well.' He looked around the room. 'This place is humungous. It's like Batman's garage. How did you manage to land this place? Did you just sign a deal with mcRecords or something? Are you going to be the new Madonna?'

I shook my head. 'I'm interviewing with Mammon Inc.' I walked over to the couch and sat down. 'Take a seat. How have you been? What have you been doing all these years?'

Tock Seng stared at the two giant cushions that bulged on the couch. 'God, those look like Demi Moore's breasts in a

Wonderbra. I don't know if I'm supposed to sit on it or have sex with it.' He joined me within the bosom of the loveseat. 'I've been travelling.'

'Where?' I said, putting my arm around him. I thought it would be awkward, not having seen him for all these years, but I felt unexpectedly comfortable and it felt like he had never left me.

'Everywhere. You name it, I've been there. Asia, Europe, Africa – everywhere. I just came from Kenya, where I helped a friend hunt down a rogue buffalo.'

'Wow. What happened?'

'The buffalo had already been wounded by the hunters a few hours before, but had escaped. So they sent me to finish the job. I knew it would be in a pissy mood.' Tock Seng told me how he crept through the thorny bush and the dry leleshwa in total silence, breathing the air hot with the smell of sage and dung, looking for a drop of blood on a thread of grass. 'I kicked the dust to check the wind.' A crash broke the silence, the leleshwa parted, and the buffalo thundered through the thorny curtain. 'I squeezed my .458 and the air exploded, dazzling the flies and lizards.'

'But who's your Queen, Sir Walter?' I said. 'Who pays for all your global expeditions?'

'My clients have a lot of things they need to send that they can't through Fed Ex, if you know what I mean.'

'You're a smuggler?'

Tock Seng nodded. 'I've sneaked things through every border in the world. I'm always seeing new things, always expanding my horizons. Every day I wake up and I learn something I never knew I never knew.'

'Isn't that a line from Disney's *Pocahontas*?' I said.

'Yeah, scoff if you like, but you should have been with me when I went to the Feathered Pipe Ranch in Montana. That was deep.'

'What did you do there?' I said.

'Rhythm exploration, ceremonial dance and drum building.'

I choked down my laughter. 'What?'

'A Native American chief taught me how to build my own drum so that I could use it to discover my inner rhythm and connect with the circle of life and the Great Spirit.'

'Yeah, whatever.' I smiled sceptically. 'What did you do after that? Gaze into the mirror of nature, crying for a vision?'

'I went back to Asia. You won't believe the things I've seen and done. The pink dust of the Indian desert. Cow horns lye-shaped and painted blue. Sitting next to a beggar – I remember him, he wore a white dhoti and whitened his body with ash. An Arabian scale hanging in the air, wafting from the mouth of the dacoit's flute. Then a flutter behind me. I turn around, and there she is – a peacock settling in a dusty tree.'

'Well, I'm glad you've had an exciting life,' I said angrily as I stood up. 'I think you should leave. Best wishes for your future.'

'What's wrong?'

'When you left, your mother kept all your stuff in your room, just the way you left it. 'Cos she couldn't believe that you wouldn't come back for them. I mean, your clothes, your books, your CDs – they were a part of your life for eighteen years, they must have meant *something* to you, you couldn't have left them behind like shit in a toilet bowl. But you did. So now your room is like that room in Miss Havisham's mansion.'

'You're kidding,' he said.

'No.' Before he left, I thought there would surely be some way I could persuade him to go to Oxford with me. I couldn't imagine that he could leave me like that. 'I believed you would return too. But the hours turned into days, then into weeks, months, years. Then I felt like all the stuff in your room. Something you could easily leave behind, to collect dust and to grow mouldy, like some rotting wedding cake.'

Tock Seng shook his head in disbelief. 'But *you* rejected *me*! You wanted to go to Oxford.'

'So you abandoned me like that? I came up with all sorts of wild schemes to get in touch with you, maybe hire a PI, or post ads on the Internet, or put little messages in green bottles to float across the ocean. I wanted to talk to you, but you just ditched me like that. You know what I've been doing for the past three years? Making excuses for you. I kept thinking, maybe you were dead, or got into some horrible accident which paralysed your body, or at least some accident that paralysed both your hands and your mouth so you couldn't phone home to tell people how you were. You couldn't just have disappeared without a trace, leaving me with nothing but memories of you, wild and worried. Now I find out that, no, you've been fine all along. You just never bothered to write.'

'Is that the only thing that's really bothering you, that I didn't write? You know why?'

'Yes. Because you're a fucking callous bastard.'

'No. It was because you chose a different path. You wanted to get a Ph.D., a managerial position, a three-room executive condo and drive a BMW, like everyone else in Singapore. And I knew that while we were on these different paths, we could never truly be friends. We'd just be acquaintances who'd put up with each other, fondly considering each other eccentric, 'cos we'd no longer be on the same wavelength.'

'Yeah, but even acquaintances send each other Chinese New Year cards. You didn't even do that.'

'But I didn't want to be just an acquaintance. I thought it would be better just to completely break off. It would have been too painful to slowly drift apart, to see what we had

82

dissolve to nothing. Better to break up immediately, and still have the memories of all the good times.'

'So why did you come back?'

'I've been having this dream about you. It's the same dream for the past couple of months, every week.'

'What dream?'

'You're sitting in a room in some library, reading a book.'

'Well, that's no surprise. That's what I do at Oxford, read books.'

'No, but this was different. There were flames all around you.'

'What? I was being burnt to death?'

'No. It was good fire, warm and sweet. It was like you were on fire, but the fire didn't hurt you. You know, you were sort of like the burning bush that Moses saw.'

'You mean I looked like some sort of combustible shrub?' I said this as sarcastically as I could, to hide the fact that his dream really spooked me.

There was no way he could know that I'd spent the last three years thinking about the *Incendium Amoris*, the fire which consumes everything that is dark. I wanted to study under Professor Ad-oy, so that I could devote more time to studying Richard Rolle, to learn how to experience the ecstasy he felt when he wrote, 'My soul melted when my Beloved spoke.'

'No. Your face looked heavenly, like you had finally found what you were looking for,' Tock Seng said. 'Then I realized how stupid I was.'

'Why?' I said.

'Once in your life, if you're lucky, you'll find someone who can be your everything. Friend, lover, soul-mate. I've travelled all around, and I've never met anyone who could take your place. Someone who would know jokes about *Star Wars* and Shaolin Temple. We were made for each other.

Our destiny is each other. It doesn't matter where we are or what we do, as long as we're together. That's what the *qian* tried to tell us.'

He gave me a pink slip. It was the Lot that explained the *qian*.

' "The fairy crane escapes from its cage," ' I read aloud. ' "Your home is insecure, so it is hard to settle down. Migration is highly recommended." '

'You have to come and travel with me. You can't run away from your destiny.'

'So that's why you've come back after all these years? Because of a dream? Well, let's say you already have enough weird ideas in your conscious mind.' I shuddered. 'I'd hate to think of what might go on in your unconscious. You know, there's a big sign next to the place called Tock Seng's Psyche, and it says, "Don't go there." ' I laughed. 'I still remember the dream you had . . . when was that? . . . it was during the Ethiopian famine crisis. I think you had it after we watched Live Aid.'

'Which one was that?' he said.

'The one where the angel told you how to feed the world's starving children.'

'Oh, that one.' Tock Seng looked slightly flushed. 'It seemed like a good idea at the time.'

'Yeah, the angel appeared, all glowing and ethereal, and said, "Xerox Food." '

'Can you believe that Bob Geldof never wrote back to me after I sent him the suggestion? And I thought British people were supposed to be polite.' Tock Seng stubbed out his cigarette. 'Maybe you haven't experienced what I saw in the dream, but it's like Someone is telling me that you're my light. I've had all these great experiences travelling, but I always feel kind of lost. And that's because I don't have my lamp. You. After all, your name is Chiah Deng.'

My name meant 'Lamp of the family'.

'I think you're just reading into the dream what you want to believe,' I said.

'No, it makes perfect sense,' he said. 'You've finished college. You're free to do what you want. Come travelling with me.'

'I can't. Your life sounds totally photogenic, like it's just one Kodak moment after another. But I can't abandon my parents like you did. I can't just leave them to starve while I go off and play Marco Polo.'

Tock Seng jumped off the couch. 'Bullshit. Don't pretend to be Joan of Arc. It's obvious you don't want to come with me because all I own is in this backpack.' He patted his non-designer-label bag. 'You don't want to be with me because you can't live without voicemail, Pay Per View and all the other mod cons of a five-star hotel. You love being able to pick up that hell horn –' Tock Seng pointed at the curved telephone receiver, 'to get the bell boy to room-service you a plate of Lobster à la King. I thought you might have changed after all these years, but you haven't. You're still a material girl, and now you actually live in a MTV suite.'

I didn't say anything. The TV filled the silence, mcNews on 62 reporting that:

Net income and diluted earnings per share for Mammon Inc. were $15 billion and $6.66, an 83 per cent increase over the diluted earnings per share reported for the corresponding quarter last year. During the last year its stock delivered a total return of 503 per cent, contributing to a five-year compound annual total return rate of 350 per cent.

'But what else can I do?' I asked.

'Let me show you something,' Tock Seng said. 'It'll just take one afternoon. Let me show you why it's worth chucking it all – friends and family – to go and look for what I'm looking for.'

What would it be like to drop out of the system? I knew quite a lot of friends my age who had decided to do it, to reject the nine-to-five routine to go and do the whole *Zen and the Art of Motorcycle Maintenance* thing. I wondered what it would be like to get into the whole ashrams, pot-smoking, Army and Navy gear, body-piercing, tofu-eating, hitchhiking, sex-in-tents kind of life. Did this wanderlust lead to true fulfilment or were the New Age travellers just as empty as the mouse-clicker in the cubicle?

'Just come with me for a couple of hours,' Tock Seng said. 'That's all I'm asking for.'

Maybe Tock Seng could help me answer my question. So I nodded and said, 'OK, show me the grail, Mr Galahad.'

9

The number-nine train grated and howled downtown through the intestinal tunnel, finally screeching to a stop at South Ferry, where, with a groan, it disgorged us on to a balmy bed of grass. After being digested in the belly of the beast, dazed and groggy, my eyes scoured for Lady Liberty, the statue that Tock Seng promised would make it all worthwhile. Blushing leaves and whispering grass, Battery Park looked positively Edenic, a dew-fresh forest compared to the grimy innards of Manhattan. But any hopes of an Arcadian calm were quickly dispelled by the pirates who flogged their imitation CK T-shirts and ten-dollar watches by the bay. A bus-load of Japanese visitors Nikon-clicked their way towards a statue, climbing and crushing some defenceless pioneer while their guide froze this image in a Kodak moment. Still, there were signs that this place might not be just another tourist trap.

Nevertheless, I said to Tock Seng, 'I'm surprised you brought me to such a touristy place.' I had expected a dangerous, sultry itinerary, more *Naked Lunch* than this Thomas Cook package-holiday scene. I had expected hotels with cigarette butts cascading out of ashtrays, hipsters lounging against the door frames, twirling pistols and shooting junk. I thought he would bring me to rivers floating with mosaics of newspapers, a deathly ooze swallowing the gangsters in concrete.

'Trust me, I'm going to show you something that will blow your mind,' Tock Seng said.

I gasped, just a slight one, when I first saw the Lady. I'd seen Liberty's image so many times before, on the big screen and TV, on mugs and postcards, caps and cereal boxes, on giant billboards and palm-sized cigarette packs. The first time I saw her – despite usually reacting to everything with cool irony – involuntarily, I felt a shock, a tiny static jolt – crikey! – this is the real thing; this icon, though minuscule across the watery haze, was right before me, her hollow breasts open to my touch.

We squirmed on board the Circle Line ferry that would slosh us to Liberty Island. Though the passengers were from different corners of the world, they wore the same uniform. Many wore loose, comfortable clothing with sports shoes, and occasionally someone sported the memorabilia cap/ T-shirt that you knew (or hoped) they wouldn't be seen dead in if they were in a normal setting. Nearly everyone humped a bulky bag around, and I hadn't seen this much photographic equipment since I went to Ming's Electric Emporium.

Everything was priced 40 per cent above its market value. The burger, served by a sullen boy who looked as if he had just missed a visit from his probation officer, tasted like a bat that had decided to die in a soggy bun. My fears that Liberty Island might be classic tourist hell resurfaced. Tourist hell: a place designed, usually via an unholy alliance between government mandarins and corporate sponsors, to simulate a cheerful version of what the natives think foreigners want to see in their culture, rather than what the country is really like. A fake, bland, closely supervised educational experience, extorting money through entry fees, and swindling ignorant, defenceless aliens with the inflated prices in the theme restaurants and gift shops that invariably litter these national monuments.

Everybody looked at the ocean with the same blank sheep eyes.

When the ship bumped against the dock, kids with Mickey Mouse ears laughed their way towards the Lady, glowing emerald in the soft autumnal light. The childish excitement was infectious, spurring me to merge with the flock that trotted on to the tree-lined, pastured walkways. Couples linked arms and began their slow, entwined walk to join the line that slid into the dark opening between the Dame's limbs.

'The queue looks bloody long,' I said. 'I thought lines like these only existed in the former Soviet Union. How long is it going to take us to get to the top?'

'Two to three hours.'

My mouth dropped. I turned around and said, 'We're heading back.'

'The wait is worth it,' Tock Seng said. 'Believe me.'

So we planted our feet on the first of the three hundred and fifty-four steps. My face cringed inches away from a Texan buttock, its blubber fluorescent in pink polyester. This is what I had to look forward to for the next twenty-two storeys – the shadow from a crack half-eclipsing my head, and the threat that the burrito-fed belly might belch a stink bomb through that cavernous hole.

Tock Seng tugged the back of my blouse, flapping a gust of breeze to cool me. 'You should have come travelling with me. You have no idea what you've missed.'

Tock Seng went on to tell me about everywhere he had laid his hat. Mud houses, stone houses, brick houses, tree houses, houses that floated on lazy waters startled by fanged fish, cardboard houses, bamboo houses, tent houses, concrete houses, hammocks swaying beneath mosquito nets, houses in jungles and swamps and deserts, the back of a

Chevy. He'd slept in mosques and caves and sewers and churches, in safari parks and car parks, on fire escapes, in desert cities where the houses stretched starwards with their flesh-toned walls. He'd walked through alleys and catacombs and fields with sweet, chewable stalks, fields panicked with crickets, their frantic chorus strangely soothing on that wide, boundless, infinity sheet of blue grass.

'Sounds beautiful,' I said. But it was hard to pay attention, since I felt like I was listening to him from within the bowels of an iron furnace. I wiped my neck. 'How long is it going to take to get to the top?'

'Soon,' Tock Seng said. 'Any time now.'

'You said that half an hour ago.' We had jerked our way towards the crown at a speed of three-quarters of a step per minute. Much of the time was spent standing still, choking on the miasma that had vaporized from the damp armpits surrounding us.

'Anyway, it's too late to turn back now,' Tock Seng said.

I looked at the black void that spiralled beneath us. This was not my idea of a good time, stuck like a foreign body in the heart of a tin lady, surrounded by weary bones and wet flesh, trapped in this hard bosom, in these cold breasts that had never cradled a man nor fed a child.

I sat down on the steps, but then blubber butt pounded up four steps, so I had to get up and follow her to avoid being lynched by the mob below me. I felt like a lamb ascending into Hell, the oven heat boiling my blood and melting my bones, exhausting me. My watch told me we'd been imprisoned within *Liberty* (hah!) for over two hours. Stench from millions of moist hair fogging me, Liberty's stainless-steel ribs caging my body within her body, I climbed three steps, and then stopped – those idiots! – again. Standing still in her womb, like a lifeless foetus that will never see the light. Maybe I could leap off the stairs like Lara Croft, and escape down her veins of wire.

'This place smells like a hot ass on a cold day,' I complained. Tock Seng spoke of the places he would bring me, places fragrant with the smell of cinnamon, incense and smoking branches. He spoke of ruins. Shattered trees and weed-covered mansions, desecrated temples where bats hung beneath the minarets like rotting papayas and a woman stroked his face with fingers stained yellow with turmeric. He spoke of bars. Shots of clear liquor made bloody by the light from the red neon ads, while in the corner a jazz magician blew into his golden wand, changing his breath into a smoky tune that rose onwards and upwards, floating in the air like an eternal cloud, drowsy like an unwakeable dream. He spoke of storms. The wind screaming and the waves vaulting to smash white and green against a scratched window. After Ra emerged to spread his divine solar light, Tock Seng opened the streaming window and came upon a land of giant trees with beast-chewed bark, where monkeys unsettled the languid vines.

'I lay in the hammock watching this one blue bird all day,' Tock Seng said, when we finally moved on. 'How it glided through the trees! It blazed, one with the sunlight between the leaves, one with the torch flame that glittered off the night water. And then I knew it was you. You were my blue bird, the one who would lead me home.'

I would have been touched by his words, but instead felt an oil–water mix of relief and excitement: we had reached the crown!

I couldn't believe it. The place was so small that if I'd dropped a Kleenex it would have had wall-to-wall carpeting. It was empty, apart from windows that were tinier than the screen of my Palmpilot.

'Is this it? Can we go up to the torch?' I turned to Tock Seng. 'What are we supposed to do?'

'The torch is closed to the public,' Tock Seng said. 'This is it.'

I squinted at the windows. The glass was so scarred and lacerated that you could hardly see anything outside, especially since the famous Manhattan skyline was wallowing in the smoggy gloom.

'What I wanted to tell you is that in every good thing I've felt in these past years, you were there. You were in the yellow fingers, the sweet grass, the salty surf, the proud bird, that jazz lick. And I realized that those things weren't It for me. I loved those things, not because they were wild and dangerous and exotic, but somehow because those things felt like you. Whenever I went to some amazing place, and then remembered that you weren't with me, a shadow would fall into my flame. Because you're the one who makes me feel It.' Tock Seng fell to his knees. 'Will you marry me?'

What I did next was pretty brutal, but I couldn't help it. Tock Seng had promised me visions of celestial skies over a coral city, but instead he'd brought me to this vacuous skull, this bimbo head. I was flesh, blood and bone. My head held memories of fire, sand and secret salty kisses swapped within the fluttering groves of the sea bed. There was nothing between Liberty's ears but a black hole that never loved or dreamed, a brainless cranium that never wrenched wisdom from a lighted page, that never echoed with the mattress moan from a lustrous horn. I looked round the room, surrounded by visitors from around the world, all looking cheated, a rainbow of unsmiling faces. We had slapped down mucho-money to fly mega-miles, and our only pay-off was the view of a ship coughing smoke on the grey, petrified waves.

'Don't be ridiculous.' I left the room and stomped down the stairs.

'What's wrong?' Tock Seng said.

'What were you thinking? Why did you bring me here? What made you think that I would *enjoy* this? I mean, you're totally out of touch, not only with the way I feel, but with . . . reality.' I made a face. 'All that stuff about me being jazz or grass or sea – that's just bollocks. Nobody can be a peacock. They can only be themselves. The problem is that you've decided to cathect me and so –'

'I've done what to you?'

'Cathexis. Psychologists use it to describe what happens when a patient's ego boundaries collapse, and he merges his self with an image of another person. This freedom from self, the flooding of himself into this person makes him feel like his soul is one with hers. He feels ecstatic, almost mystically so. Loneliness evaporates, and joined with his soul-mate, he feels that he needs no other and he can climb any mountain and cross any ocean – you know, all that wank you hear in songs. You're not in love with me, but with an ideal of me. You're not in love with this hairy skeleton –' I tapped my head, 'but with some opalescent goddess who shimmers in your head.'

'You think too much,' Tock Seng said. 'You can't just box how I feel into a Greek word. Why try to analyse the sublime, mysterious way we feel about each other, instead of just –' His hand reached out.

'Don't touch me,' I said.

We walked down the rest of the way in silence, joining the solemn procession creeping downwards, the deathly march of hundreds of chests made hollow by the hope-killing sight in the crown.

We boarded the ferry and the ship ironed its way over the wrinkled water. The copper woman would not miss us, for she could not even see us, her icy eyes, sightless, bored at the clouds, as if willing the sun to burst forth from behind the white foam to illuminate her blind eyes. Her verdigris skin made her look nauseous. She stood, her feet glued to her concrete pedestal, like a mob victim about to be pushed towards a watery death by Vinny and Guido.

93

I turned towards Gotham, but there was nothing there to cheer me. The city looked like a cushion overcrowded with pins, sticks of iron, copper and steel stuck recklessly here and there, high and low. The architecture of angles and anguish. Unlike trees which grow towards the sky, these rootless buildings rise lifelessly, casting their dead shadows on the squirming shoal caught in Mammon's mesh.

I felt like a fish writhing in that net. Tock Seng had promised to cut me free, so that I could dive towards a city free of ATMs and Jumbotrons, to castles where knights with golden locks would feed me from a sweet cup – my Atlantis. But my dream of liberty from Mammon was just a fantasy, Tock Seng was no Percival on a white horse, and freedom was as dead as the metallic woman who loomed behind me.

'You have to live in the real world,' I said. 'You have to stop chasing illusions. Some day, if you're truly fortunate, you'll be a home owner with a Toyota, a dog, and kids who are private-schooled. Maybe you'll even attain central air-conditioning. To wish for anything more would be unrealistic.'

Tock Seng just 'humphed' in disagreement. So we just sat next to each other, like newly weds sharing a speechless meal in a cheap diner.

Then it happened, something I could never even dream of.

The sun spurted at the edge of the horizon, igniting the waves. Divining the coming darkness, zillions of windows flickered to life and the torch unfroze its copper flame. The red-tipped whitecaps skipped like tongues of fire over the molten mercury sea, enflaming the cold waters until a candlelight fog rose from its phosphorescent body. In that moment when the world was caught in that vaporous light, everything suddenly flared into an incandescent glory.

Never had I ever seen such a sight, the perfect fusion between artifice and nature. Whitman's city of spires and masts. Tongues of fire, Pentecostal, like the spirit descending on the apostles. The obelisk towers of the Brooklyn Bridge. The seagulls oscillating above, confusing the sky with white rings of chaos. The Chrysler Building, its silver spear piercing the soft rose mist. It was a perfect marriage between the man-made and God-created: the metropolis, the sea, Liberty's baton, the fish birds, the sun, the stars, the moon – all luminous in unison. In front of the chained city, the starry waters trembled under the mackerel sky, an undulating mirror shaken joyfully by the dance of the exultant birds, chasing their breeze-borne cries.

'Holy hat of Confucius!' I exclaimed.

'This is It,' Tock Seng said. 'I knew you would like this. I brought you to the crown because I knew you would hate it. Because whenever you're travelling, there are going to be long periods when you'll be tired, pissed off and bored. But just when you think things can't get any worse, something happens to make it all worthwhile. This is It. When you see something beyond your imagination. Something so beautiful, your brain explodes with insight and your heart with awe, like an ecstatic epiphany.'

Then he asked me again to marry him.

'This is amazing.' I looked at the view before me, surprised at what I felt. Tock Seng *really* did know my heart, showing me something I never knew that I could love. 'But I can't go with you.'

'But why not? Isn't finding this –' he spread his arm at the magical landscape, 'much better than what you usually do on Saturdays? Isn't this so much more fulfilling than reading *Cosmo* and agonizing about whether it's better to get a foundation with SPF 15 UV protection, or one with a light-diffusing formula?'

'Just because I like to take care of my skin doesn't mean that I'm a shallow person. It doesn't mean my greatest concerns in life revolve around dieting, nail polish and perpetually doomed attempts to give up smoking. I have hidden depths to my personality,' I said, frowning as I tried to think of some proof. 'I write poetry. And not just free verse, but elegiac pieces which follow a strict rhyme scheme. Like sonnets.'

'Well, come with me,' Tock Seng said, 'and we can explore those hidden depths together.'

I shook my head. 'I can't. I won't be happy. What's the use of seeing a great sunset if you can't share it with someone?'

'But if we get married we'll always have each other,' Tock Seng said.

'But just having a spouse isn't enough,' I said. I remembered what Dr Sidious had told me about the instinctoids. 'I need the whole tribal unit – friends, relatives, neighbours. I need to live in a community, and not just be an alien all my life.'

Tock Seng shook his head. 'You're wrong. That's what the Lot was trying to tell us. We don't need a tribe, we only need each other. In Eden, all Adam had was one Eve, but his whole world was Paradise. You just need one soul-mate, someone you know is like the flesh of your flesh, bone of your bone. If we're together, we'll never feel alone.'

'It won't be enough.' The gap in my soul felt so dark and large that it would take more than one person to fill it. This lonely hole needed Steve, my sister, Professor Ad-oy, and maybe even more people than that – for sometimes this black hole felt infinite, like some mysterious vortex unfathomed by astronomers.

We reached the dock and got off the boat.

'I'm sorry, but I just can't go with you.' I let go of his hand. 'Please don't follow me, just leave me alone.'

I expected him to put up a fight, but Tock Seng just stood there, frozen in silence. He looked like a statue, like those men who were turned into stone by the demon Medusa. It was as if my words had killed his heart and turned it into a tombstone, and all he could do was stand there lifelessly. Was this what I was becoming – a member of Mammon, a woman who could petrify men with just a toss of her serpent hair?

I turned my back on him and followed children with Mickey Mouse earmuffs back into the garden of electrified trees and everlasting neon.

10

When I woke up, the bulbs were still blinking. From my balcony, you could see that it didn't matter whether it was day or night, the city burned in an eternal neon. The bulbs glowed even in the bright morning, red lights guiding the children with the Mickey Mouse earmuffs to the Disney megastore on Times Square, red lights that flashed like cold fire in the devil's playground.

I rang Steve to find out if he would do the Test.

A metallic recording answered. 'Hello, nobody is at home, not even the answering machine. This is the toaster speaking. Leave a message after the beep and I'll try and remember it.'

'It's me,' I said. 'Pick up.'

'So how was it?' Steve's voice came on the line. 'Did they pour on the posh dosh? Did they offer you loads of lolly?'

'Uh-huh,' I said. 'You won't believe the hotel bed.' I rubbed the shiny sheets. 'It's got metallic velvet sheets. I look like I'm lying on top of a really soft Porsche.'

'Cool. Do you have a mirror above your bed so you can see yourself having sex?'

'Of course,' I said. 'But the key thing is not what's above the bed, but who's been on it.' This was no ordinary bed, but one which had been used by globobosses, Euro fashion-Führers and Wembley Stadium rock gods. 'I can now honestly say that I've been in the same bed as Rupert Murdoch, Helmut Lang and Bono.'

'So when are you coming back to take me out for a celebratory dinner at Le Petit Blanc?' Steve said.

'It's not that easy. There are a couple of Tests I have to pass.' I told Steve about the *Gen Vex* party. 'How on earth am I going to pass that Test? I'll never get in. The minute I step into the *Gen Vex* party, I'll probably set off the dork alarm and get ejected by the fashion police.'

'Ach, don't stress about it,' Steve said. 'Keep your knickers on. Granted, you might not be the High Priestess of Hip, but you're cool, sort of. You read the glossies. You track the Top 20 hits. You know what last year's Best Supporting Actress wore to the Oscars.'

'So what?' I said.

'You've got your finger on the pulse of pop culture. And you're fairly fanciable. If you got into this season's hot dress, I'm sure you'd cat-walk your way into the party, no problem.'

'You don't get it. This is no ordinary party, at no ordinary club. The venue is like the Oxford of glamour, exclusive to the brightest of the glitterati. They're holding the party at Utopia. Just listen to this . . .' I read Steve the description of Utopia in *Time Out New York*'s 'Club' section:

UTOPIA
11 p.m., $50
Poseurs unite at this high drama fashion club, which entertains a beautiful, jaded but decadent crowd. Media hot-shots, yummy trust-fund babes, Wall Street $$$-makers, and other Masters of the Universe do their weekly rendezvous here to air-kiss among the nocturnal lounge-flora of pretty boys, drag queens, and whip-toting fetishists.

This Saturday, Utopia hosts the *Gen Vex* party, a must for any dedicated heat-seeker. DJ Mother Teresa works the wheel of steel tonight, chewing up a big wad of dubcentric music and blowing a big bubble of spaced-out beats.

Entry is supervised by style sheriff Timmy Timmy, the most discerning doorhag in Gotham, who ensures that Utopia is safe from ugly non-Manhattanites: Eurotrash, rednecks and the Bridge and Tunnel mob. You're unlikely to get in unless you look like a member of the international fashion fabulosi, worthy to hang out with the supermodels, Hollywood megamonsters and rock gods who frequent the club. To pass through the golden gates, weirder is always better. If you don't get in right away, just leave. At this altitude of chee-chee, attitude can be sky high.

'Fuckenell,' Steve swore. 'You didn't tell me it was *Utopia*.'

'So you know it?'

''Course I do. The people in my office, they talk about Utopia like it's some magic temple that they might get into someday when they reach the nirvana of cool. Like, "If I got promoted to Head of Entertainment, blew my raise on an Armani, and shagged a Hollywood starlet, maybe they'd finally let me into Utopia." My boss's boss's boss's boss managed to get on to the List once.'

'The List?'

'When you go to a club, they usually ask if you're "On the List". If you say "No", then the doorman will usually say, "Sorry, but it's a private party," but that's just a polite way of telling you that you're not cool enough.'

'How do you get on the List?'

'Nobody knows. One day, when word gets around that you're an It girl, you'll get a phone call from Utopia saying that you're on Rochelle or Erykah's list. It's like they give you the code word, you go to Utopia and say it, and the doors just open sesame before you.'

I groaned. 'I'll never get on the List.' My life revolved around staring at the OLIS database and poring over vellum manuscripts. And even worse, I did all these geek freak things wearing second-hand khakis from Oxfam. 'If they ever needed to build a nerdy robot, scientists would study me. I am like the nerd prototype.'

'Never fear, Steve The Cool-Meister is here – willing, ready and able to help transform you from swot to hot.'

'How?'

'By giving you the Glam-O-Meter. Usually, if you've scored enough points on the Glam-O-Meter, you'll be able to get into any club even if you aren't on the List.'

'The what?'

'It's a sacred device, passed on to me by Chief, one of the assistants in our office. He used to work security at Utopia and other hot clubs in New York. I'll fax it to your hotel tomorrow.'

I stared at the fanged fish slithering around the glass tank. 'There's another Test that I need help with,' I said.

'What?'

'They want me to make you Singaporean.'

'Why?'

'They want to see if I can make people blend in,' I said. 'So I have to teach you how to be Singaporean.'

'But what does that involve? What would you do to me?'

'I'd teach you how to dress, talk like a Singaporean,' I said, 'and you'd learn about various Singaporean customs.'

'Fantastic. Does that mean I get to learn kung fu?' Steve made these strange sounds which I could only presume were Bruce Lee battle cries.

'Don't be ridiculous,' I said. 'People don't do kung fu in Singapore.'

'Aren't you all Chinese in Singapore? I just thought it was part of your culture. Everyone in Chinese movies knows kung fu.'

101

'I don't believe this,' I said. 'We've known each other for three years. Have you ever seen me do kung fu once?'

'No.'

'Have you ever seen me watch a kung fu movie?'

'No,' Steve said. 'But I just thought it was a part of your heritage that you could not express while you were in England.'

'Believe me, if it was part of my heritage, I would have done a flying somersault and kicked your ass by now.'

'So what Singaporean customs would you teach me?' Steve said. 'I wouldn't have to do anything weird, would I?'

'What weird things do you think you'd have to do?'

'You know, non-European customs. Weird shit like tongue-piercing or walking on coals or forcing someone to live in the outback without any food or water for thirty days.'

I sighed. 'Singapore's an ultra-modern city state. It has a higher GDP than Britain. Thirteen-year-old kids in Singapore are having web conferences with their peers in Australia, while St L'leh hasn't even got round to computerizing its library catalogue yet. We're not exactly a bunch of primitive cannibals running around in loincloths. We don't do kung fu or any weird shit.'

'But I know you eat a lot of weird shit. I've seen the stuff your sister sends you. Bird's nest and shark's fin. I could never eat that. And I know that in China, they make mothers eat their own aborted foetuses.'

'Maybe,' I said.

'I read that in the *Guardian*, so it has to be true. Doctors sell the foetuses for a quid,' Steve said. 'I'm not eating any dogs or dead babies.'

'I'm sure we can work around that,' I said. 'Those are delicacies anyway, not standard Singaporean fare. The Test is about you being a typical Singaporean, so you'd probably just have to eat chicken rice or prawn dumplings. Normal stuff. And beef curry. I know you like that.'

'Right, OK,' Steve said. 'But I'm just warning you. I'm a fish-and-chips, bangers-and-mash, baked-beans-on-toast kind of lad. I don't really want to eat anything else.'

That would be something I would work hard on. I recently persuaded Steve to expand his diet to include Italian food, which meant making his pasta with pesto and sundried tomatoes instead of ketchup. But even that minor culinary improvement took a few months of nagging before he caved in.

'What sort of TV shows will I have to watch?' Steve said.

'Why is that important?'

'All I do is work and watch TV. In fact, the only reason to get a job is so you can make enough money to get Sky. Will I still get to watch *Neighbours*?'

'We don't get any Australian soap operas in Singapore,' I said. 'And I don't see why we should.' England is the only country I know that's so addicted to Australian soaps they actually show them twice a day. It's quite bizarre.

'Yeah, scoff all you like,' Steve said, 'but at least we don't show programmes called *The 24 Filial Piety Puppet Show*.'

I subscribed to *Eight Days* to keep up with what was going on in the entertainment scene in Singapore, and Steve often made fun of the titles of the shows listed in the magazine, even though he had never even seen them.

'You've got movies called *Haunted Karaoke*,' Steve said. 'There's no way a show with a title like that can be any good. Oh, right, will I have to do karaoke?'

'I don't know,' I said. 'Maybe.'

'Well, I don't do karaoke,' Steve said. 'The only time I sing in public is when I'm in a stadium and pillocking the referee.'

'Yes,' I said, 'I'm familiar with your fine rendition of "The referee's a wanker."'

'By the way, will I get to watch soccer in Singapore?' Steve asked.

'Yes, we get English soccer there.'

'So I'll still get to see Watford?'

'Uh, no,' I said. 'We get mainly Premiership soccer.'

'Now wait a sec. If I do the Test, would I have to change my team? Who does the typical Singaporean support?'

'Manchester United,' I said.

'Agh! I knew it. Everyone supports those bastards. I'm sorry, but I can't do the Test. There's no way I'm going to support some arrogant, paranoid, Merchandize 'R Us club.' Like most English football supporters, Steve nurtured the kind of revulsion for Manchester United that one usually reserves for paedophiles and necrophiliacs. 'They're not a football club, they're a stock-exchange-floated, shirt-manufacturing factory.'

'It's not like you'll have to support Man U for life,' I said. 'The Test only lasts for five minutes.'

'What do you mean?'

'You'll have to go into a group of Singaporeans and persuade them that you're exactly like them. But it's only going to be for a couple of minutes. It's just like acting. You were always great at improv while you were in OUDS.' Steve had a lot of the actor in him, so I thought flattering the side of him that loved hamming it up might do the trick. 'You'll get a free trip to Singapore,' I said. 'I know you always wanted to travel. Do you want to spend the rest of your life never going further east from London than Norwich?'

'I guess you're right,' Steve said. 'They'll pay for everything?'

'Yes. Accommodation, food, everything.'

'How long will the whole thing take – the Test and the preparation?'

'Maybe a month.'

'I can't take that much time off work,' Steve said.

'I'm sure you can. Your company is owned by Mammon anyway, and I'm sure they will be able to persuade them to give you paid leave.'

'Right. But how difficult is the training going to be?' Steve said. 'Will I have to learn Mandarin? I'm crap at languages. I endured five years of French and all I remember from it is Evian, café au lait, croissant and bagel.'

'You mean baguette.'

'Oh yeah, you're right. Bagel is Italian, isn't it?'

'Jewish,' I said.

Steve groaned. 'You see what I mean? It just seems like a lot of work. It's like going back to college. I killed myself studying so hard at Oxford, and the only reason why I did that was because I knew that if I got my First, I would never have to take another test again. I hate studying. Just thinking about it makes me want to sleep. In fact, I think I'll go and lie down now.'

'Oh yeah, I forgot,' I said. 'You're King of the Skivers.' Steve's idea of doing his laundry was turning his underwear inside-out. He never washed the bottom of his plates because he claimed that he never ate off that side anyway.

'Can't you get someone else to do it?' Steve said. 'Why do they want me?'

'They asked me who was the most British person I knew, and I told them about you.'

'Well, just tell them that you made a mistake,' Steve said. 'Anyway, I'm not that British.'

'That is so not true.'

'Yes it is. I've never felt that English, anyway. There are a lot of things people do here that I don't. I've never bought a lottery ticket. I've never played rugby or cricket. And I think I'm the only person in England who has a TV and *didn't* watch Diana's funeral. Just tell Mammon that you want to find someone more British than me to do the Test.'

'Look, you're my best friend,' I said. 'If you won't do it, how am I going to persuade anyone else to do the Test?'

I heard the sound of a ring pull and beer fizzing.

'Well, there is one thing that might make me change my mind,' Steve said.

'What?' I said.

'I'll do it if you can get me the money to make *Beyond Good and Evil*,' Steve said.

Beyond Good and Evil: the Movie was Steve's pet project. Though he graduated with a First, he had rejected offers from City lawyers and Euro banks to work at Zog!, hoping to use his job to slip his screenplay to one of the many Hollywood superstars it regularly interviewed on its hit breakfast show, *Wakey Wakey! Beyond Good and Evil* was what Steve called 'a Tarantino for intellectuals', which basically meant that it was a Nietzschean gangland thriller with allusions to Bergman, Antonioni, Schopenhauer, Dostoyevsky and other European smartypants who had unpronounceable names with at least three syllables. Steve hoped his screenplay would be the magic wand that would change him from a council-estate anorak to a Tinseltown Armani. 'The screenplay is great, all I need is money to make a short film. It'll be like a sample, sort of a calling card so that producers will give me money to direct the film.'

'How much money would you need?'

'About fifteen thousand quid.'

'Ouch,' I said.

'But once you get the job with Mammon, with the kind of obscene wages they'll be paying you, you should be able to afford it.'

'I guess you're right.' It was a lot of dosh but I was attracted to the idea of kickstarting Steve's Hollywood career. 'If I give you the money, will I get any screen credit?'

'Of course. You'll be the executive producer.'

I smiled. I could see my name up on the silver screen – bold and in CAPS – for all the world to see. Singapore had never produced an internationally famous movie producer before – this would be a historic first – Chiah Deng Gan, Hollywood power broker. 'You know, if I get in the *Gen Vex* party, I might be able to slip your screenplay to some mcMovies executive.'

'Yeah, yeah,' Steve said excitedly. 'Hey, Gotham is the land of the D Girls –'

'Who?'

Steve sighed. 'God, you have a lot to learn before you try to crash that party. "D Girl" is industry slang for "development girl", since most movie producers' assistants are female. I'll fax over the Glam-O-Meter to you tomorrow, and we can work on turning you into a tasty totty.'

I put down the phone. My TV beamed out the latest Mammon Company ad: a family laughing over a glowing grill – cut to dinky (dual-income-no-kids) couple grinning over cappuccinos – cut to a man on a mountain bike, plunging down a narrow ridge towards an orange canyon floor.

'Since the turn of the millennium, people all over the world have turned to the Mammon Company,' the faceless voice announced, 'which is what makes the Mammon Company – the Company you keep.'

I couldn't figure out which mcProduct the ad was trying to sell, but I guess it didn't matter, since Mammon sold everything, and this ad was aimed at raising the generic value of the Mammon brand.

I pondered the slogan – 'the Company You Keep'.

When you bought a mcProduct, you weren't just buying a commodity, you were buying into an identity. All you had to do was drink mcCola, and you could become like those

rich poseurs, part of a new global community of pretty
people who glided through life with a bright, clean smile.

I looked at those white, wholesome faces on the TV.
Was this the company I wanted to keep?

11

To prepare for the party, I spent the next couple of days immersing myself in the contents of *Generation Vexed* magazine. It was like injecting consumerist crack. Instantly, I was hooked on those lustrous photos, addicted to the aesthetic that mixed urban cool and multi-cultural ennui. *Gen Vex* was full of celebrity models closing international deals on tiny Motorola mobiles, while lounging on Jacobsen's sensuously futuristic Egg chairs, circa 1957, like the ones in Alexander McQueen's Paris apartment.

I looked at a photospread entitled 'Go Orient Yourself':

If you live on the Upper West Side, in the Western Cape or the West End, go East to master the science of high-rice living in a small space. A smiling Buddha and a lacquered screen might make your local sushi den look Asian, but here at *Gen Vex* that just doesn't cut the wasabi. Forget the futon and ditch the bamboo prints. Mod-Asia is all about the energy and eroticism of the urban east. Venetian blinds play with the shadows across the room and increase the rectilinear divisions of the space. Hazy fluorescent lighting drifts up to the tenth floor – perfect for the complexion of the millennium Madame Butterfly, who kicks off her Jimmy Choo heels and sparks up a Mi-Ne cigarette. Out on the terrace, the violet panorama of the city seems ethereal. She stares out at the horizon, wondering if she's lost her Orientation.

Since the turn of the millennium, there's been a sudden explosion of affluence for a number of under-thirty-fives, whether they're a West Coast snowboarder, a copywriter for a cutting-edge advertising firm in Stockholm, or a grunge kid working in an independent record shop who suddenly signed a film contract. There's a young international group that grew up moving around without any possessions – the global nomads – and they used *Gen Vex* to show them how to live a sophisticated lifestyle. But *Gen Vex* surpassed rival magazines by not only showing its readers what was hip. It also told them where to buy hip.

Next to the photospread entitled 'EastEnder', readers were told of the '*Chaise longue*, from $1,895, by Claire Fisher, upholstered in Dragonfly fabric, $1,125. Brush pots, from $500 each, from The Beagle Gallery. Shinto bed, $8,155, from Noel Henessey. Ambient Perspex wall light, $750, by Elizabeth Hirens.' *Gen Vex* listed the phone, fax, address, email and website of the stockists, so you had to be a right idiot if you were unable to get hold of the products.

Gen Vex was not just a lifestyle magazine, it was a 288-page full-colour I Ching. *Gen Vex* told you where to sleep and what to sleep in ('*Good in the Shack*. The beach house comes home to Brisbane'), what to eat ('caviar and sour-cream blini'), and what to eat it on ('Arne Jacobsen dish'), what to surround yourself with ('"Dim Some" lights, Y3K Powerbook, and three best friends'), where to vacation ('Roland Barthes said plastic was "the first magical matter that is ready for the commonplace". Tel Aviv Museum of Art's Plastics Exhibition proves that plastic's fantastic'), cataloguing every minute detail of life, right down to what font you should use for your business documents ('Just Your Type: Lessons in Bare Face Chic').

I hate to say it, but I genuinely loved *Gen Vex*. I loved the trend-savvy aesthetic of it, but my fascination with the magazine also filled me with fear. Before *Gen Vex* came along and told people where to buy hip, being hip actually came from something *in* you. You were trendy because you had an eye for style, a gift from Apollo, a creative sensibility that could instinctively spot the sexy, fabtastic thing *au moment*. But now that *Gen Vex* had made cool a commodity, even fashion morons whose taste naturally gravitated towards big hair, tartan and nose-digging could be cool, as long as they were rich. *Gen Vex*, like many of Mammon Inc.'s commodities, had changed the world in the last ten years by making the unbuyable things of the world buyable. But I *really* liked the magazine. I felt a pang of guilt – was I just acting like a crassly materialistic geisha girl? When I flipped through its shimmering pages, was I simply ogling high-quality capitalist porn, being seduced by a shallow value system that put style over substance, a lifestyle that was a subversion of that old Sprite slogan – 'Thirst is nothing, Image is everything'?

I returned to the hotel to find this fax from Steve:

Planet Zog

tel: 44 207 725 3871
fax: 44 207 725 3892
86 South Quay London SE4 7RJ

FROM: Steve Lucas	TO: Chiah Deng Gan
Pages: 1 of 1	Fax: 1 212 876 5435
Re: Glam-O-Meter	cc:

☐ Urgent   ☐ Please reply   ☐ Please recycle

Glam-O-Meter (Copyright © Chief)
Slip Chief's heat thermometer between your lips and see if you're hot enough to sashay past the brass stanchions.

Add the appropriate points to your score for every tick you have in the following boxes:

☐ Female (10)
☐ Asian (10)
☐ Homosexual (20)
☐ Look indie-star grunge (10)
☐ Black AND look hip-hop AND in a group of < four (35)
☐ Look freaky (e.g. Dominatrix, Gender-Hacker, Sexy Robot) (20)
☐ Wearing the Look of the Moment (if I have to tell you what it is, honey, then you're not wearing it) (80)
☐ Work in the Industry, e.g. a career in fashion, publicity, clubs, photography, the fine arts, the performing arts (film, TV, music, dance, theatre), architecture or design (20)

☐ Know an Insider (Club Promoters, Security) or a Celebrity (50)
☐ Are a Celebrity (150)

Deduct the following points from your score whenever you check any of these boxes:

☐ Male (10)
☐ White (10)
☐ Male, white, with big muscles and over six foot two (80)
☐ You are/look like a redneck and have a Southern accent (20)
☐ You are/look like you're from New Jersey (a.k.a. Bridge and Tunnel) (20)
☐ Khakis and tennis shoes (20)
☐ Abuse the Security (100)
☐ Drink in line (80)
☐ Skip the rope (50)
☐ Do/sell drugs (100)
☐ Black and look hip-hop and in a group of > four – could you *look* more like drug dealers? (50)

Results:

You need to score above 100 in order to be on the right side of the velvet rope.
Todd Chandler, despite being a white male wearing khakis (hence announcing 'Look, I have no penis!') (–10 –10 –20), manages to get into clubs because he is a celebrity photographer (+150). His total score =110.
MC Puffy, despite having a Billboard Top 5 R&B single (+150), went to Utopia once with an entourage of ten that swore at Security (–50 –100), and was given the 'private party' line. His total score = 0.

I calculated my score – Asian (+10), female (+10) – and came up with a measly 20. I was 80 points short of the magic number.

I had to drape myself with the Look to bridge the points deficit.

Finding the Look wasn't difficult – all I had to do was turn to p. 154 of *Gen Vex* to find paparazzi photos of five different celebrities voguing the Look at various premieres/launch parties. The captions helpfully mentioned that I would find those clothes at Donna Lauren on Madison.

I stood outside the Donna Lauren store, a 100-year-old Rhinelander mansion. It looked like every grand building that I've seen in Europe – columns and classical statues – only when I'm visiting a posh residence in Europe, I'm usually around elm-framed bowers, deer and gurgling fountains. Here, the manors are stuck right in front of bus stops, regularly visited by shuddering MTA buses that announce their arrival by vibrating so loudly that they drown out the construction workers who are drilling the pavement.

I stepped into the store, passed the grandfather clock and ascended the grand staircase, gliding past oil portraits that displayed the representatives of old money. There was a frowning man in Pilgrim clothing, a child sailor pouting next to his pet bird, and various smaller frames memorializing a range of anorexic dogs that belonged to the *faux*-family.

I arrived at the Ladies' Collection. There was a fireplace that crackled with a real fire. A chandelier with electric candles dangled its crystal earrings at me, while admiring its reflection in the blank TV screen. Someone had left a zebra-skinned boot on the coffee-table, which held books that showcased the architectural talents of Mondrian and Prits Penitz, giving the impression that the shoppers were in a living-room that belonged to a millionairess who enjoyed the urban culture of the Museum of Modern Art *and* the primitive passion of the African safari.

A moneyed mum pushed her stroller into the room. She wore a denim shirt, black Spandex pants and Nikes, as

114

though she had just left the gym. But one look at her face left you in no doubt that, despite her casual attire, she would inspire any roughneck to want to become a Gatsby-style millionaire, so that he could buy a mansion on a blue lawn and stretch his arms towards the green light across the dark bay. Talk about affluenza alert.

All the clothes hung from armoires, giving you the feeling that you were rummaging through some rich aunt's wardrobe. Donna Lauren certainly gave a whole new meaning to the concept of 'home shopping'.

'Hi, I'm Holli. Do you need any help?' A sales assistant approached me and smiled solicitously, as though she was inviting me to join her college sorority.

I pulled out a white leather dress that looked like a nurse's uniform. All the clothes looked germ-free and Chloroxed to death, following an austere, sterile hospital aesthetic: Lab Chic.

In the fitting-room, I shoved my body into the dress. I gawked. I looked nothing like the model in the *Gen Vex* magazine, who wore this number to the Mammon Inc. Breast Cancer Ball. In fact, the garment made my usually discreet bulges look like giant goitres. I was not born with designer genes. Some people can look svelte and babelicious in just a T-shirt and shorts, but even if you put me in an eight-thousand-dollar outfit, I would still look like I was trying to hide a lawnmower beneath my dress.

But I had to get into this dress in order to get into Utopia. I had to turn my belly of blubber into abs of steel. I had to diet.

'Do you know the best way to diet?' I asked my sister on the phone.

'*Ai-yah!* I knew this would happen. Remember the last photo you sent me? I showed it to Mummy and Daddy and Aunty Gwek and your ex-class-mate Lei Wan and our neighbour Azidah and even the woman waiting next to me at the wet market, and they all said you look a bit *pwei*.' My sister said '*pwei*' slowly, like she was blowing up a balloon, drawing out the syllables to emphasize my pudginess.

'I was in subfusc,' I said. 'The Oxford gown always makes me look ten pounds heavier.'

'You *pwei* never mind. I still love you just the same,' my sister said. 'You mustn't stop eating. I always read about these girls in New York, they want to be models, want to be skinny, vomit all their food out and become anaerobic.'

'Anorexic,' I said.

'But I can teach you a safe way to diet. A way passed down from your great-great-grandmother.' She paused for dramatic effect. 'The foot-binding diet.'

'The what?'

'You remember last time in China, you need to have small feet, if not no man want to marry you?' my sister said. 'So all the women bind their feet – very painful. And if your feet pain pain, then you got no mood to eat. You eat less, you lose weight.'

But I didn't want pain. I guess I was *pwei* due to an unhealthy combo of a high sedentary level and a low pain threshold. I never believed in no pain means no gain. My philosophy has always been no pain means no pain. The only exercise I got was climbing the stairs in the Oxford towers, since although we were well into the millennium, most of the University buildings were still elevator-proof. I used to visit the gym down at Iffley, but I stopped because all the other exercisers made me feel guilty by pedalling furiously and reading *Beowulf*, while I cycled leisurely and painted my nails.

I asked Steve on the phone, 'Do you know a way I can lose a lot of weight without having to diet or exercise?'

'Sure. Get gastric flu,' Steve said. 'The last time I got that,

I could hardly eat, and anything I did eat, I vomited immediately. I lost five pounds in two days.'

'Be serious.'

'Why don't you get Mammon Inc. to fly you to Ethiopia, and drink from some dodgy stream there? You'd get bacillary dysentery, and lose lots of weight in no time. I don't know any friend of mine who *didn't* look well skinny after a trip to the Third World.'

'I'd like a method that isn't a medical hazard,' I said. 'No suggestions that might cause near death, please.'

'Hey, you said you needed to diet to lose weight quickly, you didn't say you wanted to diet so you could be *healthy*. Those two things require completely different plans. You want it fast, or good?'

'Preferably something in between.'

'The Aristotelian Golden Mean. Very well. You know, of course, that I am partial to the "Beer Me" diet, which involves drinking so much one day that you can't eat anything the next day; the food-free day is punctuated by some vigorous lean-over-and-puke stomach crunches. But I can sense that you're looking for a slimming gimmick that is slightly more sensible.' Steve hummed briefly. 'The presenters on my show say that Prozac makes you lose four, five pounds during the first few months. Cigarettes suppress your appetite. Caffeine draws water from fat-cells, and is used in many anti-cellulite creams. The style experts around London eat nothing but tofu salad, which gives them their proteins and minerals. They wash it down with a double espresso and calm any anxiety cravings with the Prozac. And they all smoke *while* they're eating – it reduces their calorie-per-minute intake, makes them eat slower, eat less.'

'What sort of fitness training do they do?'

'Multiple orgasms,' Steve said. 'They claim that an orgasm burns four hundred calories an hour. Like it burns more calories than swimming or rowing.'

'Steve, if I had the type of body that could have an orgasm for an hour, I wouldn't need to do *anything* to improve it. I'd keep it the way it was, and after I died, my children would donate my body to science.'

Since no one I knew could suggest any convincingly feasible diet plan, I decided to apply my research skills to discovering the safest, least 'ouch' way to lose fifteen pounds in four weeks.

In the next few days, I did an exhaustive survey of all the latest slimming strategies. I read advice from medically qualified MDs and homeopathic faith healers, listened to talk-show interviews with celebrity stylists, soap actors, gym owners ('How I went from Chunky to Hunky'), borrowed books by Nobel-Prize-winning biologists and scientologists, I even perused those colour newspapers that you find near the supermarket check-out lanes announcing with many '!!!!' the discovery of the love child of the President and a Venusian alien.

Nearly everyone agreed that keeping a health journal was a good idea, thus:

DAY I

I decide to adopt Dr Abram's Revolutionary Blood Type Diet, which is (allegedly) 'based on research that has already won the Nobel Prize for Medicine'. I hope the diet is not based on Nobel research in the same way that West Side Story *was based on* Romeo and Juliet.

Though Dr A explains for 400 pages why the diet is good for me, I don't really understand anything he says. However, his use of Latin-sounding terms like 'protein lectins', 'agglutinate' and 'blood type antigen' reassures me and makes the diet sound scientifically proven and Surgeon-General sanctioned.

Since, like many Asians, I am a blood type 'O', I should relish fish, avoid dairy products, and nosh on most vegetables except tomatoes. Ketchup, oddly enough, is like poison to me since it 'agglutinates' my blood cells and screws up my insulin production and hormonal balance. Hopefully, if I follow the diet, I will end up looking as beautiful and fit as those people you see in cigarette ads.

DAY 5
So far so good. I have obeyed the laws of proper food combination religiously for five days, e.g.:

> *New Diet:*
> *Breakfast = Orange juice and high-fibre bran cereal; Lunch = Salmon on rye with lettuce; Dinner = Poached cod with baby carrots and new potatoes.*

This is an incredible improvement over my old diet at Oxford, which went like this:

> *Breakfast = Sleep through breakfast; Lunch = Kentucky Fried Chicken Mega Value Meal – eat the chicken, but leave the coleslaw; Dinner = Eat the coleslaw furtively in the food-forbidden Bodleian Library while reading the* Incendium Amoris.

I do not miss the high from consuming chocolate or alcohol very much, since that has been replaced by a new buzz that one gets from leading an ascetic lifestyle – e.g. 'Look at me, I'm so disciplined, I am a model of righteousness and restraint, canonize me now!'

DAY 7
I am so depressed.
   All this virtue and I have only lost one pound. What am I doing wrong?

119

Is fidgeting not enough? Do I really need to exercise? I saw in Reader's Digest *that fidgeting actually burns calories, so all week I have been swaying from side to side like a metronome. Maybe I should replace it with an aerobic activity that raises my heart rate substantially for at least an hour.*

That thought makes me so tired I have to sit down.

But I have been so good. I've even switched from Coke to Diet Coke. I can't believe how much Aspartame I've consumed this week. This must be what it feels like to be a lab rat.

I figure that though I am eating correctly, I am still eating too much. I need to find a way to make myself skip at least one meal a day.

I squeeze some lime into my Diet Coke and stir in some vindaloo curry powder. I drink it and nearly pass out. But the brew makes me so nauseous that I can't eat dinner. So mission accomplished.

DAY 8

I am so sick of eating fish over and over again. It's like chewing the white flaky skin that falls from lepers.

Oh shame, shame, evil demon-possessed soul that I am, I broke down and got a chicken-and-bangers fry-up from the local chippy, followed by some low-fat Tiramisu yogurt ice-cream.

I finally admit that basically, I have less will-power than a para-alcoholic. I not only act like, but also look like, a human fridge magnet.

I need professional help, a licensed expert who knows how to turn sofa slugs into supermodels.

I need to hire the services of the ex-American Gladiator, Latifah 'Iron' Belle.

I first saw Iron Belle in a Nike TV ad, where she explained how she balanced her life as a single mother, Olympic sprinter and ballet dancer.

So I set up an appointment with Iron Belle at Jerk & Pull!, a gym famous for being the first 'sexercise' club in New York, a temple for body beautifuls who believed that the quality of ass-grinding dance music was as important as the selection of available muscle machines. The club had strip-club-like diffused lighting, with back-lit mirrors and walls with rosy hues – strategies normally used to make erotic dancers look good.

I walk past the unisex changing rooms, the 'swim with dolphins' class and the yoga basketball court, to Iron Belle's studio.

A stunning figure steps into the gym, with pedicured feet that are squeezed into towering plexiglass heels that even drag queens would deem excessive. Every feature of her carefully sculpted body – those rock-hard shoulders, the cobblestone abs, the razor-wire hamstrings, the taut, gravity-impervious breasts – is highlighted by her tight Spandex suit, which, if not inhabited by Iron Belle, would probably shrink to the size of a condom.

'So you want Iron Belle to turn you into an Iron Maiden?' she asks me.

I nod.

'First, instead of indulging in your usual lard fest,' she says, 'you'll have to replace your meals with my scientifically advanced formula – "Iron Brew".'

She gives me an orange can, and I take a swig of the fuchsia-pink sludge. Surprisingly, it doesn't taste bad. It just tastes weird, like pork-flavoured milkshake.

'Do you know why diets don't work?' she says.

'No, Mrs Belle.'

'Because diets are all about counting calories. And women suck at maths. I bet it takes you half an hour to figure out how to double the tax so that you'll know how much tip to leave the waiter.'

'Yes, Mrs Belle.'

'My brew does all the calculations for you, giving you the optimum calorie intake per day.' She rattles off all the essential vitamins and minerals it contains – B, C, iron, folic acid, etc. – I feel healthier just listening to her. 'It has a low glycemic index, the "G" protein, which helps shrink fat cells, along with cangzhou root, forming a unique combination of antioxidants to help neutralize the body's free radicals.'

She brings me to a shimmering grove of chrome machines.

'Get on the Road Runner,' she says.

'Beep beep,' I say, but she does not smile.

'Run,' she says, and presses a red button.

I am only on the treadmill for ten minutes, but I'm getting tired. I normally don't hear my heart pounding this hard unless I've had three gin and tonics down at Jude the Obscure's.

Iron Belle flashes her vampire teeth. 'I said "run"! You're trotting slower than an anaemic chicken.'

I inform her that chickens don't trot. 'The word "trot" describes the gait of a horse or any other four-footed animal in which diagonal pairs of legs move forward together.'

'If you've got enough breath to speak,' she says, 'you're not working hard enough.'

She presses the red button again.

Shit, I think.

I am sprinting away on the Road Runner. I must look like one of those cartoon characters, trapped in a monstrous factory. Like there's a giant piston in front

of me, ready to stomp me to death, and I'm on the
conveyor belt that's hurtling me towards pancakehood,
so I look like I'm fleeing for my life, sprinting on the
black belt of death.

DAY 10

'You're half an hour late,' Iron Belle says.

'I can't help it,' I say. 'It took me that long just to tie
my shoes.'

'We'll take it up a notch today,' she says. 'And after
that we'll do some spot reduction exercises – crunches,
reverse crunches, cross-knee crunches, vertical leg
thrusts, hanging knee raises.'

I get back on the treadmill. After an hour, I wiggle
my fingers weakly at her to tell her that I can't take it
any more, but she just presses the red button again and
says, 'Faster, faster.' The treadmill inclines another five
degrees. 'Feel the burn,' she says.

My legs are on fire and I'm about to asphyxiate at
any moment, if I don't choke on my spit first. It's hard
to see how exercising can actually be good for me,
especially since it makes me feel like I'm being burnt
at the stake while being strangled by a homicidal
maniac.

Those are my last thoughts before I black out.

DAY 16

I've spent the last week running painfully to nowhere.
Today, my grinding routine is interrupted when Iron
Belle presses the red button once too often and the
treadmill flings me off and sends me hurtling into a
management consultant.

I have been consuming nothing but Brew all this
time. I really miss eating, the sensations of crunching
into crisp skin, the spurts of flavour as you chew

delicately spiced food. I hate drinking my meals. I never ever want to have to drink my food until the day comes when I've lost all my teeth, and even then, that would provide sufficient cause to make me approve of euthanasia.

'I saw your blood and urine test results today,' Iron Belle says. 'You had fried beef dumplings and pecan pie yesterday.'

Damn, busted.

'You are only allowed to drink the Brew,' she says. 'No burgers, no pies, no Doritos, just Iron Brew. Remember, what you eat today, you wear tomorrow.'

I get on the scales. Happiness! I have lost five pounds!

I am well on the way to the kingdom of slimdom, and feel stupid for jeopardizing that with my dumpling-and-pie binge yesterday.

DAY 23

I hate Iron Belle more than I've ever hated any human being. I would hit her but there is no part of my body that is not in excruciating pain.

'Get on the scales,' she says.

I do.

'You've lost another six pounds this week,' she says. 'That's eleven pounds in all.'

Elation! I love Iron Belle.

DAY 26

I hate to say this, but the more I've exercised, the easier it has got. Now I can get to my target heart rate without looking like a Vietnamese refugee fleeing through a minefield in a pink Lycra suit.

Iron Belle still wants to push me to the limit, though. Fortunately, it's less painful than a week ago. This

*time, when the treadmill flings me off, I land on a
petite blonde publicist, who is much softer than the
management consultant.*

DAY 31
I feel totally transformed.

I've lost fifteen pounds. Euphoria.

*I don't even mind not eating crap any more. I have
gone from snack-o-matic to über-woman, complete
with a new fascistic, contemptuous attitude towards
junk food, e.g. 'My body is a superhuman, finely tuned
machine, and I am not going to pollute it with Mars
bars. I shall only consume top-grade fuel.'*

*I am so psyched, after my usual training session with
Iron Belle, I go running around Central Park. There is
nothing as satisfying as the sanctimonious feeling one
gets when speeding past someone who is sitting on a
bench eating pork rinds.*

Now that I had the Body and the Dress, all I needed was
Gen Vex Hair to achieve the complete *Gen Vex* Look.

A quick glance at the italics that captioned the magazine's
centrefold revealed that a Lucien Frederike of Shear
Pleasures Salon was the mane magician responsible for the
poseurs' hair.

Unfortunately, the notable features of my hair are that its
shape and texture make it the perfect tool for scrubbing
those hard-to-reach spots of the pisspot. My hair didn't just
need work, it needed witchery. So I placed my faith in
Manhattan's Lord of the Locks, hoping that he could
transform my bristles into something fantastic. Then I could
step out confidently every evening, into the night air, my
tresses shining with the magic sheen of the panther's
moonlit gleam.

However, when I tried to book an appointment at Shear

Pleasures, a bronze statuette gave me her standard receptionist smile and explained to me in that slow, 'special' tone that
one reserves for drooling children with advanced learning
disabilities, that 'Monsieur Lucien is very busy. He will not
be available for . . .' She flipped through her appointment
book, page after page after page. Then she shook her head
and gave me a slight, wistful smile. 'Monsieur Lucien is not
available.'

'I'd like my hair done this Saturday,' I said, 'for the *Gen
Vex* party.'

'That will not be possible,' she said. 'Monsieur Lucien is
very famous.'

As if that explained it all. But in a way it did, for Lucien's
stardom among the hair needy was due to the fact that he
had all the specifications that one required from a top
celebrity stylist, i.e., he was gay, with the neurotic
temperament of an artiste, and possessed such classically
sculpted statue good looks that he could only be described
as being utterly luurvely. When quizzed by an adoring
Oprah as to the secret of his success, he replied, 'Other
stylists, they do hair. Monsieur Lucien does . . . *coiffure*.'

'Now, Madame Chi Chi Poo Poo,' I said to the
receptionist, 'I know you think I'm a style idiot, hopelessly
out of the fashion loop. You think, "Who is this naïve
enfant who thinks she can walk off the street like some Miss
Average Joe and gain an audience with the maestro?" I'll let
you know that I'm fully aware of how famous Monsieur
Lucien is. I know that he glamour-groomed Cindy and
Christy into the supermodels that they are today. I know
that his hirsute *haute couture* has appeared on countless
covers of *Vogue* and *Harper's*. I know he was the one who
gave the Secretary of State her Washington power helmet.
And, of course, I've been notified of the recent scandal in
La-La land, when two rival Versace-leathered publicists got
into a catfight, scratching and clawing over whose actresses

got to hire Lucien's services for Oscar night. I know Monsieur Lucien is the star snipper of the decade, which is why I want him to fix this walrus on my head.'

I took out a hundred-dollar bill and scribbled a figure on the top left corner. 'I've written a single digit on the top of this note. I want you to take this piece of paper to Monsieur Lucien, and tell him that he can add as many zeros after the digit as he wants. Then you can charge that figure to my expense account.' I handed her my Mammon Inc. credit card.

The receptionist picked up the phone and whispered in French for about five minutes. I looked at the Mammon Inc. credit card, plastic gold against the moon-white table. The receptionist put down the phone and said, 'Monsieur Lucien will see you at six o'clock on Saturday.'

I smiled to hide my relief, and slid her a green twenty-dollar bill. 'I'm glad the green light has illuminated your eyes so we were able to come to an understanding. *Au revoir* till Saturday.'

I left the salon, gloating in the sunlight that glistened off the ivy-covered buildings. Everything looked soft in the afternoon's emerald haze. I walked along the tree-lined Central Park West, still smiling, but deeply disturbed by this new euphoria I felt, shocked by how much pleasure one could receive from a show of wealth – that intense, momentary flash of the green light.

'This is Lucien's private chamber,' the receptionist said. 'He will be with you shortly.'

I stepped into a salon that was completely different from the low-budget hair shacks that I was used to. Unlike my usual salon in Singapore (Ping Pong's Hair Snips Snips), there were no back issues of *Woman's Own* (circa 1992) scattered on the counter tops, no hairdryer cords trailing haphazardly along a floor moustached with tufts of hair. No, this room was pristine, washed by the liquid beams that streamed from the glass ceiling, cleansing everything to an impeccable sheen.

The décor was all metal and mirrors. The walls were coated with a grey paint usually used for Porsches, then subtly lit to emphasize their dull shine. I had never seen an interior that was so *reflective*, with its slick walls and glinting tables, all the surfaces textured like a silver lake, having a soft grey hue that mirrored an undulating, purified image of anything that looked at it.

A rack of test tubes showcased the most phantasmagoric displays of chemicals that I had ever seen. There were sinister vials of blood-thick red, sparkling potions in sapphire and azure, viscous concoctions that smelt like Mediterranean olives, but stung like green venom, and other tubes filled with clear juices, beerish brews, candy-striped swirls, and by far the most fascinating, a vessel filled with what looked like pearls melted in milk. Lucien's expertise meant that he went far beyond your standard herbal shampoo and conditioner – he apparently dabbled in the more arcane arts. His whole set-up looked like a high-tech alchemist's lair, like Merlin meets *Battlestar Galactica*.

Monsieur Lucien Frederike entered all in white, robed in what looked like a cross between a dentist's coat and a priestly surplice, but with hip Helmut Lang detailing. He rubbed his head, smooth and hair-free as a newly initiated monk's, and said, 'Sit.'

He gestured towards a Dali-inspired chair that was so sensuously, obscenely curved I felt I was committing an act of fornication just by sitting in it.

He ran his fingers through my hair, and recoiled. '*Mon Dieu*, did no one inform you of the invention of conditioner? It is so dry, so damaged, tangled . . . My hands are sensitive, I cannot touch this, or I might get rope burns. This is not hair, this is hay. And you know what happens when you blow-dry hay?'

I shook my head.

'The best you can get is a hay bale,' he said. 'And do I look like I need to feed cows?'

'Uh, no.'

'Then do not come to me with this.' He averted his eyes from my head. 'I am not a farmer, I am a musician.'

I told him that I had always been under the impression that he was a hair stylist.

He shuddered. 'Must I explain this to everyone? My patron god, Apollo, strung his lute with his hair. The true hair stylist strings hair to create a mood, an aura of music, such beauty and sexiness that you can draw a man with the pluck of a single string.' He plucked a strand of my hair. 'Then you know that you have achieved *coiffure*.'

'Fair tresses man's imperial race ensnare,' I said, 'and beauty draws us with a single hair.'

'Ah, so you know Alexander Pope.' He smiled for the first time at my quote from *The Rape of the Lock*. 'I see you are not as ignorant as your mop suggests. Most of my clients do not appreciate the power of the *femme* locks, but I see that you are different.' He walked over to his rack of test tubes. 'Let's see what I can do to heal this disaster.'

He poured out a milky salve on to his hands and rubbed it into my hair. 'Let this balm seep to your roots. I shall be back in half an hour.'

He left the room, leaving me to survey the surroundings yet again.

The room was bereft of any greenery; the only botany on display were the Georgia O'Keefe paintings, surprising explosions of colour against the sterile white walls, close-ups of magnified orchids that looked like an exhibition that could be entitled 'Red Giant Vagina', 'Blue Giant Vagina', 'Pink Giant Vagina', etc.

I passed the time listening to some hidden stereo that leaked an ambient mix of electronica into the airy room.

129

Gregorian chants, distorted guitars, computer-generated thuds and the dance-inducing wail of a black woman lamenting the infidelity of Man to her sistahs melded into a surreal song that swirled in a semi-club atmosphere in the astral-lit space.

Lucien returned and brushed his palm against my hair. 'Ah, much better. The texture is much softer, more manageable. Now your hair is dark, but gentle, almost like the dusk.' Lucien proceeded to cut my hair, waving his steel wand through it, like a star-bright blade whistling through the twilight gloom. After that, he misted my locks with Vitaspray ('For extra support,' he explained) and winnowed my hair dry with a diffuser, my strands soft-lifted by the hot air.

When he was finished, he stood back, sighed with satisfaction and said,

> *'Sur ta chevelure profonde*
> *Aux âcres parfums*
> *Mer odorante et vagabonde*
> *Aux flots bleus et bruns.'*

'Yes, I am a genius,' Lucien said. 'Baudelaire could write about hair, but I have created what he could only see in his mind's eye.'

Lucien's boast was no exaggeration. I never imagined I would look like a phantasm from *Les Fleurs du Mal.*

> On the deep ocean of your hair
> Where perfume laves
> Odours and vagabond sea
> Of blue and brown waves.

But as I sat before the mirror, mesmerized by my own image, the sight of my hair reflected in the soft glass was magical, rippling like black fire against a silver cloud.

I had achieved the Look. For the first time in my life, when I looked in the mirror, my instant reaction was, 'Oh my God, I look so cool.' I slid my hands down the sexy white-leather dress, skin-tight against my finely honed body, which, for the first time in my life, bulged in all the right places. I never thought I could ever feel that way about myself – the Queen of the Nerds, the Girl Scout from Camp Homely – to be able to see myself and think – 'Hello, cover girl. *Gen Vex* this month, *Vogue* the next.'

'Yes, these velvet ropes,' Lucien lifted my hair, 'will get you past any velvet rope.'

I was giddy with my success. If the American dream was all about the reinvention of self, then I had achieved that dream – and all it took was money. Every time I looked in the mirror, I received a jolt of pleasure at my glorious transformation, but as that ecstatic emotion seeped through me it quickly turned into a dark poison, leaving me feeling chilly and disturbed. My hair swayed like divine serpents, and whenever I saw my own reptilian locks in the looking glass, like Medusa in Perseus' mirror, I could feel my heart turning as cold as stone. For the first time in my life, I had to admit that the bad guys were right all along. Mammon Inc. was right and I was wrong – money can make you into the person you've always dreamed of becoming. To be a star, I didn't have to be intelligent or industrious or virtuous or well-connected or God-fearing – all I had to do was stand beneath the green light. All you needed in America was the right plastic, a Green Card, the right kind of Visa.

12

I descended a slick, incandescent staircase into the stainless-steel catacomb of Utopia. The foggy glass ceilings enhanced that secret-agent cave feeling: drivers on the road above saw, through the moonlit mirrors, a hypnotic image of the happenings down below – the distorted, alluring, even decadent reflections of flashing red lights and shadows dancing, while inside, I stood entranced by the hazy flickering of limos and lights zooming on top of me.

When I turned my attention to the other guests on the floor, I suffered wave after wave of celebrity jolts – the involuntary zap that you feel through your back whenever you spot someone world famous. You step forward and straight into the all-American smirk of – Oh my God! Tom Cruise! – turn right – Oh my God, it's Mariah Carey! – look ahead – Oh my God! It's the boy who's in all the CK ads! And I was like, OK, be cool, act like it's no big deal, don't gawk like it's the first time you've seen someone famous, as if your nearest brush with fame was shaking the hand of an actress from an Australian soap who was in Oxford doing a Christmas panto of Dick Whittington. I rested my hand on my hips and lowered my eyelids, trying my best to affect an air of cool, blasé, 'been there' decadence.

Forget about the décor (the kitsch yet cool soap-bubble

walls) and the pulse-raising music, the essence of Utopia was
not *what* was there, but *who* was there. The List included
names that frequently bold-faced the gossip columns, guests
whom everyone knew by their first names (look, there's Julia,
Brad, Sharon, Mariah, Lauryn!). I had never ever seen so
much star-studded furniture. What I mean is that since it was
unlikely that I would have any deep, meaningful interactions
with them, their presence seemed highly impersonal, almost
decorative, and as I weaved past Whitney Houston towards
the topless bar boys, it seemed the celebrities were like
pieces of furniture, just part of the interior design, no
different from the fireplace or votive candles or chandeliers
or blinking trees that filled the room with a burnt-orange
mood light. The celebrities were *the* essential furnishing of
Utopia though, because without them the club would just be
an underground warehouse with brothel-red strobe lights
and odd-looking furniture that you wouldn't even be able to
flog at a Sisters of Perpetual Devotion jumble sale. But with
a Hollywood A-list actor draped over a puke-green sofa and
a Soul Diva leaning her tight buns against a sewing-machine
table, the celebrities acted like starry jewels, turning the set
into a treasure trove of glamour and sophistication.

Most people in the room seemed to be jiggling their bits
in a sexily acrobatic fashion, which caused me a great deal
of anxiety since my knowledge of bodily movements was
severely restricted to those used in normal, everyday
activities, e.g. walking, showering, raising my right hand to
reach the baked beans on the top shelf, etc. I had no idea
what to do with my limbs when black voices commanded a
white boy to play that funky music. So I did my best and
swayed from side to side, hoping that I didn't come off
looking like a dysfunctional pendulum.

I was also trying my best not to become *too* sexually
aroused. Utopia was jammed so tight that you couldn't
move more than an inch without bumping into someone,

which was how I ended up dancing wedged between a teeny bopper band member, Brad Pitt and two gorgeous male models I had seen on the sides of many buses. Now I'm not a celebrity junkie, not one of those people who subscribe to *People* magazine so that they can keep track of the ever-spreading branches of the Hollywood dating tree, but at this moment I found it impossible *not* to be star-struck. It's hard to keep your mouth from drying up if four strikingly handsome, internationally renowned men are gyrating their crotches two inches away from your hips. I suspected that I would never get this close to so much beauty again, flesh grooving against flesh. These men were the gods of our generation, idolized by millions across the globe. A week ago, when I was just an ordinary citizen, if I had got as close to these guys as I was now, a burly guard would probably have grabbed me and flung me across to the other side of the street.

It was then that I realized that Mammon CorpS had managed to fulfil one of my deepest wishes – to be part of the élite. I guess I went to Oxford because I wanted to be one of the Top Guns, but they never accepted me there. I had always dreamed of being with the bright young things, and now here I was, grinding my hips along with the glitterati. I felt that joy of relief, of having made the List, reached the final destination – not only was I among the beautiful people, I *was* one of the beautiful people.

'Oh damn, I'm sorry, I nearly got my drink all over you,' the woman said, swinging her ceramic coconut away from my jacket just in the nick of time. Then she grabbed my left lapel and said, 'Oh my God, where did you get this from? It's fantastic, brilliant, it's just absolutely *sex*. Is this a genuine vintage Fifties doctor's coat?'

'Yes,' I said.

'Get out of here!' She slapped my shoulder. 'I've been

134

scouting all the vintage stores downtown, but once that *Vogue* article came out about Lab Chic, all these coats were snapped up.' She rolled her eyes. 'I nearly didn't manage to get the right Look for tonight's festivities. Since I couldn't do Lab Chic, I had to wear these slutty hot pants instead, since the slutty look *never* goes out of style.' She patted her bum. 'These hot pants are fantastic. They go right into the butt crack to really lift and separate, like a Wonderbra for the caboose, if you will. But where *did* you get that absolutely sex coat?'

'My cousin is a doctor,' I said. 'This was her first coat, which she had chucked away in her store room. That's one of the few good things about being Asian. You'll probably always have at least one MD in the family.'

'Oh, it's *great* being Asian, especially in the next few months,' the woman said. 'Being Asian will be the new It thing during the summer. We'll be going through a "Glad to be Geisha" phase.'

'How do you know?' I said.

'Oh, that's my job, to figure out what the new It thing is going to be. I'm a trendspotter.'

'A what?'

'A trendspotter. I read lots of magazines, watch TV endlessly, talk to the clubbies in action and the other young ones on the street and in the malls, that sort of thing. I keep my finger on the pulse of pop culture, so when Fortune 500 companies want to know what angle to use in their ad campaigns, they come to me.' She sipped the flaming virgin from her coconut. 'By the way, I'm Tamara. So what do you do?'

'I'm an Adapter,' I said.

'That's absolutely sex!' Tamara said. 'I know millions of my friends who would kill for a job like that. Why don't you come meet them? They're in the VIP room.'

'Sure,' I said.

*

135

Another celebrity jolt. Oh my God, it's Marcus Evans! My favourite indie director, master of metaphysical thrillers set in gothic European cities, oozing with beautiful, brutal violence and tough boys in gleaming tail-fin cars, spouting Sartre and blowing silent, profound rings of smoke.

I very much wanted to construct an intelligent sentence that would express (via allusive nods to Bergman and Truffaut) my thoughtful, sensitive appreciation of his art-house *œuvre*, but realized I was so awe-struck that the best course of action would be silence, since anything I might say in this nerve-stricken state would probably sound like it came from an epileptic yak.

'Happy New Year, darlings! Michiko, meet Chiah Deng, she's a CorpS.' Tamara introduced me to the woman next to the famous director. 'Michiko's a fashion designer. So help me out here, Michiko – what's going to be the It colour next season?'

'Black,' Michiko said.

'Seriously Michiko, don't kid me,' Tamara said. 'New Yorkers wear black all the time, it's our default colour. Are you telling me the new black is going to be black?'

'It's black, but not just any black,' Michiko said. 'It's coffee black, like the beans produced by the Mozikanazum Indians.'

'Didn't they just become extinct a few months ago?' I said.

'Yes, and many in the fashion industry were absolutely outraged. I'll let you in on a semi-secret – Donna, Tommy and Calvin are going to do mainly black lines for their coming Fall collections, to commemorate the demise of the Mozikanazum.'

'So the word on the street is that next season, all-black is going to be red-hot?' Tamara said. 'Stellar!' Then she turned to the African man on her right. 'Chiah Deng, meet Housain. He designed Utopia.'

136

'I like it, it's very cool, love the Fifties Scandinavian chairs,' I said. 'I like the way it's built underground like a bomb shelter. You know, it helps you live out all your airline-lounge-cum-CIA-agent fantasies. Are you working on a new project at the moment?'

'Yes, I'm working on a new club on Bleecker, called Dynasty,' Housain said. 'Persian rugs, Ming vases, Cuirassier armour, velvet cushions, commodes veneered in seawood marquetry – all the treasures of a decadent aristocracy vibrated by the pounding bass of the latest hip-hop hit. I'm thinking Louis XIV meets Fresh Prince of Bel Air.'

'Like a house party held in Versailles,' I said.

'Exactly,' Housain said.

'It must be really interesting work,' I said.

'Usually it is, though lately I've been stuck at the site all day shouting at the contractors,' Housain said. 'I really wanted to catch the Whistler exhibition at the Met. but I think I've probably missed it. Did anyone get to see it?'

'I saw it a few weeks ago,' Tamara said. 'I particularly liked the "Nocturne in Blue and Silver", how the magic of the night transforms the Porte Binet and its grotesque towers into a translucent enamel that assumes a certain grandeur. It was intriguing, how the retrospective placed Whistler in the tradition of Degas, Monet and other painters bent on capturing their impressions of light and air. Like Baudelaire, Whistler rejected realism as a negation of the imagination which was able to see all in one synoptic glance.'

I never imagined such discourse could come from a blonde in hot pants drinking out of a coconut. But it seemed that Tamara probably buried a MFA behind that ditzy, Ab Fab persona.

'Damn, yes, I wanted to catch the exhibition too,' Marcus Evans said. 'But I've been stuck editing my film all this month. I think the exhibition's moved to the National Gallery in London. I thought I would catch it next month when *Prague Nights* premieres there.'

'Hey, I'll be in London next month as well,' Housain said. 'Maybe we can hook up and go see Whistler. After that we could go to that new restaurant that Vong's just opened.'

'Oh yes, the Thames Kitchen is excellent,' Tamara said. 'Their black sea bass with eggplant caviar is an absolute devil delish delight.'

Marcus Evans looked at me. 'So where are you from originally?'

His question startled me. I thought I'd done a pretty good job of integrating with this group, but I was wrong. Why else would he ask me that question, a question solely reserved for outsiders, for people who obviously stuck out from the in crowd?

'What makes you think I'm not from New York?' I said.

'None of us are from New York originally,' Marcus Evans said. 'I arrived in the Big Apple via Minneapolis, Boston, Prague, Jo'burg, London, then here.'

I felt relieved. For the first time in my life it was normal not to be a native.

'I was just trying to place your accent,' Marcus Evans said. 'It sounds British but not really.'

'I came to New York via Singapore through Oxford,' I said. 'I guess while I'm here I should work on my American accent.'

'God, no! New Yorkers love an English accent,' Marcus Evans said. 'I've dated a couple of models. They're gorgeous, of course, but the problem is when they talk they get so boring they could put to sleep a gnat that's drunk ten espressos. However, I dated this English model once and it was great. I loved her accent. All she had to do was say something and it would make me laugh. It was like going out with a Beatles movie. Are you going to be in London next month?'

'Maybe,' I said. God knows what Mammon CorpS had in plan for me after this.

'Well, if you're free, maybe we could have dinner some time,' Marcus Evans said.

At which point it suddenly registered that a Palme d'Or winning director was asking me out on a date and I nearly fainted. A sudden attack of groupie fever infected me.

'Okey dokey macaroni,' I said. *Us* magazine reported that this was the new catchphrase among the Manhattanites, lifted from *Lara*, the number-one comedy sitcom in America.

Tamara waved madly at someone on the other side of the room, and the object of her frantic semaphore squeezed through the crowd towards us.

'Wolf, I haven't seen you in eons,' Tamara said. 'Let's play catch-up.'

'Well, my deal finally cleared with mcFilms,' Wolf said, 'so I moved out of my shoebox in the East Village crosstown to Chelsea – yesterday. I found my dream apartment, a three bedroom in a doorman building with the full dressing – air-conditioning, a fireplace, and you know, most importantly, a washer dryer. A washer dryer, not just in my building, but actually *in my apartment*. I'm dizzy with excitement.'

Michiko hugged Wolf. 'I'm so happy for you,' she said.

'That's because you live in New York,' Wolf said. 'My ex in the Philippines was like – why are you getting so excited about a *washer dryer*? And *then*, you know, he found out how much rent I was paying for this place, and he just flipped – like for that rent in the Philippines I could get a ten-room mansion, and have more than enough money left over to start a military coup to take over the country.

'But anyway, you should have seen the crowd going for this apartment. It was like a wrestling match. Everyone had to put down their bids, and bring in all their credit history and tax returns and bank statements. Man, it got really ugly. Like this guy went up to the landlady and said, "I'll put down the twenty-thousand-dollar deposit in *cash*," and he flips open this black suitcase full of Ben Franklins. Then five other people ran up to the landlady and said, "We brought the deposit in cash too," and I'm like – this place is a nut house.

'It doesn't help that the landlady's totally weird. She has this thick southern accent and is ancient, like a dinosaur version of that chick in *A Streetcar Named Desire*! Anyway, she's insane, but you know, she inherited this building from her parents, who had it since the beginning of the twentieth century, so that's how she earns her living: by collecting rent and being insane. Subjecting her potential tenants to whacko behaviour.

'So she starts interviewing me, and she asks me what I do.

'I tell her I'm a screenwriter, I'm twenty-two and I just signed this huge deal with mcMovies. Like it's the most money they've ever paid for a first screenplay. So I'm working this whole "I'm Hollywood's new wunderkid" angle. Then she asks me where I'm from originally, and I tell her I'm Swiss-German.

'She gets totally ecstatic about this info, which is slightly creepy. She goes on about how Swiss-German is her favourite combination.'

Then Wolf started mimicking the landlady's southern accent. '"I had a German gardener once. He was gay. I liked him very much. He handled my roses with a Teutonic efficiency, but because he was a ho-mo-se-xual, he had the necessary flair and creativity to imbue the garden with an imaginative extravagance. My garden was both neat and pretty. I like the Swiss. It's a very tidy country. I'm sure

140

you'll keep the apartment clean. They were A-fri-cans. Those people are not as clean as the Swiss. And I'm sure you'll pay the rent on time as well, since you make such good clocks in Switzerland."'

Wolf went back to his own accent. 'And then the old bat goes on about how the problem with gay men is that they're too flamboyant and have too many parties and drugs and anonymous sex, but it's good that I'm Swiss, since the Swiss don't like to have parties, so she won't have problems with me shooting up and screwing around. In any normal situation, I would have zapped her for being homophobic, but I wanted this apartment so badly I would have let her blow me. I'm thinking – OK, this old bat is crazy, but at least all the stereotypes are working in my favour, and I see the forty other people behind me all crazed, fevered, foaming for this apartment. So I get sucked into this mob frenzy, and will put up with Hitler levels of abuse to get this apartment since I have visions of myself lying in front of the fireplace naked in front of those huge bay windows. So I tell her that I'm not like most ho-mo-se-xuals, and that I have a boyfriend who lives three blocks from this apartment and we've been together for two years. That we're very quiet, and all we do at night is order in General Tsao's Chicken and listen to some Mozart.

'So she tells me, OK, I can have the apartment. But I need to give her twenty thousand dollars, in cash, today.

'And I'm like, it's two-thirty p.m., and the banks close at four, so I'm running really tight. And I'm like I don't even know if they'll allow me to take that much money out in cash in one day. So I ring up my boyfriend and my two best girlfriends, and ask if I could borrow cash from them.

'We all go and withdraw five thousand dollars each. We put the money in a gym bag. But then my friends point out that I've got twenty thousand dollars in a gym bag and I have to go crosstown with the bag. They're so scared that

I'll get mugged, which is stupid, since I've never heard of anyone getting mugged in the afternoon in New York, but I guess if you're carting this much money around it makes you *really* paranoid. So my friends insist on coming along with me, and they grab their *baseball bats*. You know, to beat up anyone who might try to mug me. But they also put on their Yankee caps so people will think that we're going to play baseball instead of going on a mission to transport twenty thousand dollars in a gym bag.

'So I'm walking along the street with my friends, in Yankee gear and baseball hats, and thinking – this is getting *way* too bizarre and ridiculous. But I finally get the money to the mad landlady, and she starts counting the cash out in front of her.

'She points to Romesh and asks if he's my boyfriend and I say yes.

'Then she asks me if we're going to sing show tunes, since she heard that ho-mo-se-xuals like show tunes.

'I tell her that I'm not a big fan of musicals.

'Not even *The Sound of Music*? Isn't that the music of your country?' she says. And then she looks at me real suspiciously, like she has serious doubts about the honesty of all the answers that I've given before.

'I tell her that I'm Swiss, and that the Von Trapps were Austrian. She smiles and says good, she hates show tunes. Then she tells me that I got the apartment.

'And that's how I got my Chelsea pad.'

Everyone laughed.

'Fantastic story, Wolf,' Tamara said.

Though I had just met the Gen Vexers, I felt I could have more in common with them than with any other clan that I'd ever met. I had never felt so attracted to a group. It was like, after endless years of exploration, scouring the obelisks of Singapore and the cottages of England, lost on a lonely voyage in quest of a community that I would want to call my own but finding nothing, I had finally found my tribe here in Manhattan. These Gen Vexers were young, creative geniuses in glamour jobs, with nerd-high levels of education but a hip sense of humour. Like me, they had no cultural fixed identity. The Gen Vexers were cosmopolitan citizens of the world, equally at home in a 212 or 0207 area code, equally well versed in the work of George Lucas and Joseph Campbell to be able to analyse the mythological archetypes in *Star Wars*.

'I'm going to get another zombie. I love those bamboo cups,' Marcus Evans said. 'Do you want to accompany me to the bar?'

'Sure,' I said, thrilled that he had opened a door for us to have some personal one-on-one time.

'So where do you live in the City?' Marcus Evans asked me as we walked towards the bar.

I only had a basic knowledge of New York neighbourhoods, so I said, 'Soho,' hoping that it would be vaguely like its namesake in London, so that I might be able to bluff my way through any grilling.

'Oh, is it on Broadway?' Marcus said. (I felt I had now interacted with him on a sufficiently intimate level to be able to think of him by his first name.)

'Yes.' Hurgh, what else could I say about my non-existent apartment? Something that sounded typically New Yorker. All I had gathered so far was that they seemed to enjoy exchanging horror stories about their apartments, in the way Vietnam vets swap tour-of-duty tales. 'It's in a great location, but I wish I had more space.' That seemed to sum up the typical New York stance on apartments.

But Marcus looked at me as if he expected me to say more. But what – what more could I say?

I blurted out a 'Poetry in Motion' ad that I had seen on the subway. '"We hammer wood for a house but it is the inner space that makes it livable!"'

143

I wasn't fully certain what that really meant, but hoped it would sound aptly profound for this topic of conversation.

'Very true,' Marcus said. 'I love that poem from Lao Tzu: we shape clay into a pot, but it is the emptiness inside that holds whatever we want.' He touched my elbow. 'While we're on the topic of needing space – it's getting really crowded in here. Do you want to head out, get some air? I could walk you home. I love walking at night in New York, don't you?'

I smiled to hide my panic. What could I say to stop him from walking me to my imaginary apartment without looking like I was blowing him off? I glanced at my watch – it was past one. 'It's kind of late. Is it safe to walk at this time of night? Won't we get mugged?'

Marcus gave me a funny look and said, 'You don't really live in New York, do you?'

'What makes you say that?' I said. Damn, he had twigged that I wasn't a real New Yorker. I was in danger of flunking the Test.

'For one thing, only tourists worry about getting mugged at night. Only people who don't live here think New York is all crack dealers and serial killers. And nobody here actually says "Okey dokey macaroni". It's just a TV phrase, but all outsiders think it's something that New Yorkers say. So where are you really from?'

'I'm based in Oxford,' I said.

'Are you really a CorpS?' Marcus asked. 'I thought all CorpS had their base here in New York.'

Ugh, busted! 'I'm sort of undergoing their Test at the moment,' I said, trying not to stammer. 'If I pass then I'll get my full Mammon CorpS colours, with the New York apartment and all.'

Marcus touched his pocket. 'Umm, I feel my phone vibrating.' He took out his phone and said to it, 'Uh-huh, sure, I'm on my way.' He turned to me and said, 'Sorry, but something's come up. I have to run. I'll give you a call when

144

I'm in England.' Then he nudged his way through the crowd, away from me.

Since he didn't ask me for my number, I supposed that he had no real intention of ever calling me.

'Don't worry about it. I messed up the first time too. We all do.'

I turned around to see who was talking to me, and shot the man a 'do I know you?' look.

'I'm Baron Soontir Fel, I'm a CorpS,' he said. 'If you need some help, I could give you a crash course on how to act like a *Gen Vex* New Yorker.'

'Help!' I said.

'The key is to go into a group and tell an interesting anecdote,' Baron Soontir Fel said. 'Make it intimate and personal. The crowd here tends to be remarkably . . . open. A lot of times I'm hearing relationship angst stories from a complete stranger at a party, and think – God, she's *really* sharing – but I suppose Americans have a much more confessional culture than the rest of the world. Which explains the flood of talk shows – but I digress. Your story doesn't have to sound true, or even realistic – it just has to sound like it's something they've seen on TV. The crowd here love telling stories about how such-and-such happened to them, and how it was exactly like the Soup Nazi episode from *Seinfeld*.'

'What do New Yorkers usually talk about?' I said.

'Oh, real estate. The stock market. Visitors. Like how you have a constant flood of visitors that you have to chaperone around every weekend, and get annoyed with them because they always walk at an ultra-slow tourist pace. Sports – the Yankees, Knicks and Rangers. Ranting about lower-income ethnic groups, like cab drivers who drive like they're still in Delhi and take you to the wrong place because they don't understand English. Pets – since cats and dogs are often child substitutes for New Yorkers. Therapy – parties are

145

great for swapping advice that your shrinks gave you. Make sure your story includes something random and weird. New York is just such an off-kilter place. The stories should include chaos, a dash of urban grittiness, and definitely some aggravation.'

'So basically, it's a story about stress?' I said.

Baron Soontir Fel laughed. 'Yes. The rant is the favourite genre for a New York conversation. However, at this party, you should focus on glamour stress.'

'What's that?'

'Stress caused by too much fun and success. Like having too many multi-million projects to work on and too many parties to go to. Remember, a Gen Vexer is not just harried, but fabulously harried.'

'I think I can pull that off. I watch *Lara* every week.'

'Good. Now, if you're ready, I'll introduce you to another cosmopolitan coterie of Gen Vexers.'

'Happy New Year, one and all. This is Chiah Deng, she's a CorpS.' Baron Soontir Fel introduced me to his stylish salon. 'This is Jose, he's the art director for *Gen Vex*.' He pointed to a Spanish man. He turned towards a Chinese woman and said, 'This is Mei Ying, she's a photographer, next to her is Paolo. He's an interior designer, and his most famous client is the Barbie doll. And I'm sure you know who my other two friends are.'

I nodded. There was Danny Cohen, creator of *Lara*, and Dominique Dawn, literary critic *du jour*, trendy because of her extreme minority status – she was a wheelchair-bound African-Jewish-Chinese lesbian who suffered from dyslexia, so she could speak for most groups that felt othered.

I noticed it was impossible for the Gen Vexers to introduce themselves without mentioning their jobs, which was slightly odd, as if Danny Cohen wasn't just an

146

individual human who produced TV shows, but he *was* a producer, like his career = his essence.

'We were just saying how great this party was,' Mei Ying said. 'If it wasn't for these gatherings, I'd probably never get to see any of my friends.'

'Yes, it's ridiculous,' Jose said. 'I work two floors above Mei Ying but we haven't had lunch for two months.'

'We've just been working like maniacs on parallel floors,' Mei Ying said. 'Work, the New York disease. Our voicemails experience more frequent and intimate contact with one another than we do.'

'I guess it's partly my fault since I'm never here during the weekends anyway,' Jose said. 'Ever since I got my mountain cabin upstate . . . you know it's half the price of my apartment but about 500 per cent bigger.'

'I don't blame you for fleeing to Ulster County during the weekends,' Dominique said.

'My apartment is like my hotel suite, you know, if I had to think of it as my home, I would just totally freak,' Jose said. 'The only thing I like about my apartment more than my cabin is my doorman. I'm seriously tempted to hire someone to stand outside my cabin just to receive packages.'

'Where do you live?' Danny asked me.

'Downtown,' I said tentatively.

'I heard it was crazy down here this morning,' Danny said. 'Did you get stuck in the demo?'

I had seen the demo on Channel 11 this afternoon, so I launched into my fictitious New York story.

'Yeah. I woke up this morning and went out to do some errands. So I step outside and see this mega protest against police brutality. All sorts of groups – African-Americans against Police Brutality, Arabs against Police Brutality, Mothers of Victims against Police Brutality – just everyone who's ever been pissed off by the police, you know. I was half-expecting to see the Left-Handed Jews against Police Brutality, and the Microwave Owners against Police Brutality.

'So I try to push through them – going "Excuse me, excuse me, but I need to cross the street to buy some hair dye." And the people look at me like I'm *so* shallow, because they're out on the street doing their bit to wrestle justice for humanity, while I'm out here shopping for beauty products. But I was like, *whatever*, just get out of my way.

'As I'm pushing through the crowd, I elbow this guy who screams "Ouch!" and guess who it was?'

'Who?' Baron Soontir Fel said.

'Todd. My ex. He dumped me by email and I hadn't seen him for two years. He's an investment banker, and I thought he must have moved upstate or got posted to Tokyo or died scuba diving or something, because he lived just five blocks from me but I hadn't bumped into him for two years.'

'Wow, like how random is that?' Danny said, using one of his *Lara* catchphrases.

'So I ask Todd where he's been,' I said. 'And he says he's been living in New York all the time, same address, got a promotion at Morgan Stanley, but other than that, still doing exactly the same thing.

'And I say, "Oh, when you say you're doing the same thing, I take it that you mean that you're still a type A, highly insecure, neurotic control freak."'

I paused for dramatic effect and looked around at my rapt listeners. 'You know, kids, the moral of this story is that, no matter how small the errand, you should *always* wear make-up when you go out, because you never know when you'll bump into your ex.

'Like I was so glad that I looked fabulous and was wearing a great outfit, so when my ex asked me how I was doing, I said, "Fabulous," and I did genuinely look as if my life was great – even though I've recently upped seeing my therapist to twice a week since I've just been dumped by another neurotic control-freak banker, and *really* need help to break this self-destructive pattern.'

'That's a great story,' Paolo said. 'Danny, you should use it for *Lara*.'

'I sure will, that story is just totally *Lara*,' Danny said.

'I've got lots of stories like that,' I said. I took Steve's screenplay from my bag. 'A friend of mine wrote this. It's great, absolutely the Bomb.'

'Sure, I'll have a look at it,' Danny said.

Baron Soontir Fel smiled at me. Love me, hug me, take me to dinner – I finally did it! Everyone believed that I was a real Gen Vexer. I wanted to leap up on the stage, where Vampyros Lesbos Ewidge was doing her strip-hop routine, and jig my victory dance, waving Ewidge's panties like pom-poms.

But as with all things Mammon, after I felt the surge of triumph, I felt a seeping of unease. My victory was almost *too* easy. I had never been in a society that was so easily impressed by superficial details. The *Gen Vex* existence was all about bright surfaces, an identity formed from outside in. You *were* what you wore, as if your inner worth could be determined by whether you knew this was the season to wear cargos or capris or denim cargo capris.

The internal personality of the Gen Vexer was created purely by external details: their jobs, quips, zip codes, CD collections, choice of gyms, Palmpilots and other consumer products. Their lives seemed to be separated from any quest for meaning, God and the deeper mysteries of faith, issues that formed the core of *my* identity. The Gen Vexers were the New Power Generation, the epitome of the global under-35 dream, but was there anything beyond their Eames chairs and Bali beach houses, or were they just completely shallow, as depthless as the image of an actor on a flat movie screen?

'You did a great job,' Baron Soontir Fel said to me, after we left Utopia.

'Thanks,' I said. 'I couldn't have done it without your help.'

Baron Soontir Fel smiled. 'I hope you remember that when you become my boss.'

'What do you mean?'

'The CorpS know that Draco Sidious is planning to retire soon, and that he's looking for an heir. He's very excited about you, because we haven't had a recruit that's been so similar to him in temperament since you came along. Chances are, if you pass the Tests, he's going to groom you for the top.'

13

'When is your sister arriving?' Steve asked. He picked up *Time Out* from the floor. For a moment, I stared at him, mildly stunned at what he had just done. Like, oh my God, Steve was actually *tidying* the house. Why? This was so bizarre. Steve had never picked up a magazine from the floor in his life – our living-room was carpeted with magazines – and now he was actually putting the magazines on the *shelf*.

'She just called from Gloucester Green,' I said. 'Her cab should be here any minute now.'

Steve picked the fag butts out of the dinghy.

'What are you doing?' I said. 'Are you . . . *cleaning?*'

'I know what a big deal she is to you. I want to make a good impression. She's just come from Singapore. I'm sure she's used to everything being very clean.'

'I come from Singapore,' I said. 'I'm not very clean.'

'Yeah, but you've lived with me for three years. I've corrupted you.'

'True.'

Steve got an eraser and started rubbing out the phone messages that we had pencilled on the wall.

'Everything's going to be fine. You don't need to be

nervous. I'm sure she'll like you.' I said those words to make me believe them. 'I'm sure you'll like her too.'

'Has she seen the new you?' Steve asked.

'What do you mean?' I said.

'You look totally different from pre-New York. You look like a magazine cover. Like every time I see you I feel that I should be talking to you about "fifty ways to have orgasms in the office" or that kind of stuff that appears on the front of *Marie Claire*.'

'Thanks, I guess,' I said. 'I sent my family a photo of me at the *Gen Vex* party, the one that appeared in the *mcTimes* the next day. They went all weird.'

'What happened?'

'They put the photo in a frame and surrounded it with candles and flowers.'

Steve laughed. 'You've become their Madonna.'

'Maybe. I'm right next to their altar to Guan Yin. They have a statue of her, and a bowl of oranges.' I shuddered. 'Personally, I think their behaviour is kind of creepy. I hope to God they don't start putting fruit offerings around my photo.'

I sat in the dinghy and waited for the doorbell to ring, the 'briiiing!' that would bring about the point of impact, the moment when my worlds would collide. Previously, my two worlds coexisted peacefully in separate orbits. When I was with my sister, it was like I was on Planet X, talking about mooncakes and putting up trigram mirrors to deflect the evil spirits from our bedroom. When I was with Steve, I would be on Planet Y, drinking tea and obsessing about politeness and protocol, e.g. discussing the institutional greeting issue: if you see people every day in college, and you have 'met' them, should you greet them? Should you greet them every time you see them? If I was on any other planet, nobody there would even *care* about when and how often you should say 'hi' to someone. And now those two worlds, hovering at two opposite ends of the universe, were zooming towards each other.

'So what is she like?' Steve said.

'She's very Chinese.'

'Oh, so she's completely different from you.'

'What do you mean?'

'Well, you're not very Chinese. You never do any Chinese things.'

'What Chinese things *don't* I do?'

'Plant rice.'

'What?!' I went ballistic. 'I can't believe you said that! You think that's what my sister does all day? She gets up every morning and takes a ride on our water buffalo to our local paddy-field. There she puts on her little triangular straw hat and plants rice. And in the evening, she goes for kung fu lessons.'

'I didn't mean it that way.' Steve reddened. 'You know what I mean.'

'No, I don't.'

'I mean, you don't have any Chinese friends. You dress like any other student. You don't have any Chinese art in your room. You don't even use chopsticks. You don't do *anything* that's Chinese. All you've done for the last three years is study English books and loiter in the pub with me.'

'I do Chinese things,' I said, 'only you don't know they're Chinese.'

'Like what?'

I paused to think. I couldn't think of anything Chinese. What *was* Chinese, anyway? 'That's not the point. Being Chinese isn't just about eating sweet-and-sour pork, and hanging calligraphic scrolls in my room.' I stood up. 'God, this is going to be such a disaster.' My sister probably had a similarly warped cultural stereotypical image of Steve, wearing a bowler hat and pinstripe trousers. 'My sister probably thinks you spend your weeks going on grouse hunts on heathery moors. And your weekends drinking tepid amber ale and waving a Union Jack.'

Briiiing!

'How are you adjusting to the weather?' Steve enquired, as he helped my sister trundle her suitcases into the living-room. This was a cue for my sister to go off on an extended whinge. Complaining about the weather was a traditional British ritual used for bonding with strangers. Whenever Steve met anyone new, he would warm up to them by making moaning noises about how crap the weather was.

All my sister said in response was, 'It's very cold.'

'Are you getting used to it?' Steve said.

She shrugged.

'What's the weather like in Singapore?'

'Hot.'

I couldn't blame her for being monosyllabic. She probably thought Steve was incredibly boring. I don't know of any other nationality apart from the English who have such a passionate interest in talking about the weather.

Since the weather tool wasn't helping break the ice, Steve tried 'the trip' angle. For reasons that are still beyond me, British people love going into intricate details about how they managed to get from one place to another – how long it took, the best route, the various disasters that happened on the way, etc.

'So how was your journey?' Steve said.

'OK,' my sister said.

She sat on the couch. I sat on the kitchen chair. Steve sat in the dinghy. Nobody said anything for a year-long minute.

'Was your flight terribly long?' he said.

'Fifteen hours.'

My sister looked at me. I didn't know what to say. I tried hard to think of a common topic for them to talk about, but couldn't. They simply didn't know anything about each other's worlds. Steve switched on the TV. We feigned an interest in *The Antiques Roadshow*, like we were all *so* fascinated in discovering whether that wooden cabinet really belonged to Henry VIII.

After ten minutes of cold silence, and having run out of ways to resurrect the corpse-like state of the conversation, Steve stood up and said, 'Are you hungry? I am. I'll go get some fish and chips.'

'I hate potato,' my sister said.

'My sister has to eat rice with every meal,' I said. 'Why don't you get us some food from the Chinese take-away?'

'You like Chinese food?' my sister asked Steve.

'Not really. I don't like most Chinese food, apart from sweet-and-sour pork, which I love. But Chiah Deng says the sweet-and-sour pork from our local Chinese take-away isn't real, whatever that means.'

'Yah, it's *ang mo* sweet-and-sour pork, not Chinese sweet-and-sour pork,' I said to my sister. 'The batter they use – very funny one – not like the one you use. And the sauce – yeech – they put so much cornflour in it, it's like jelly.'

'I like it. I'll go get some.' Steve left the house.

Steve came back with the food. We opened our cartons.

Both Steve and my sister automatically started removing the red peppers from their cartons and putting them in mine.

They looked at each other and laughed.

'Red peppers are her favourite,' Steve said.

'I know,' my sister said.

'If I don't give them to her, she'll just take them from my carton anyway,' Steve said. 'If I refuse to give them to her, she'll throw a tantrum fit until I submit.'

'I know. She's so bossy. She got to have everything *her*

155

way. Like when we watch TV that time, if there's something on TV that she doesn't like, she'll stand in front of the TV until I change channels.'

'Unbelievable!' Steve looked at me. 'You are *so* selfish.'

'Yeah, but those Taiwanese soap operas are really bad,' I said. 'Like the dialogue – ugh – it doesn't move the narrative forward, it's full of clichés, it's loaded with expository info. Like, "Look Leng Ying at the glorious sunset overlooking the Panda Park where we are now sitting. You are looking deceptively happy even though you just found out that your boyfriend wants you to abort your baby." I mean, who talks like that? I'm just protecting my sister from bad art.'

'Yeah, like you were protecting me from Terry Pratchett?' Steve turned his head away from me towards my sister. 'Chiah Deng actually goes into my room and burns any book that she doesn't approve of. I bought this Terry Pratchett book – harmless comic fantasy stuff – but it was published by HarperCollins. And that was the week Murdoch killed the Patten book from HarperCollins on China.'

'Murdoch's move was a threat to freedom of speech,' I said. 'I can't understand why anyone *wouldn't* want to boycott HarperCollins.'

'You burnt his book?' My sister was so appalled that she stopped chewing. 'I don't know how you can live with her for three years. She so difficult to live with. Especially just before she going to have her period.'

'Oh, Jesus, tell me about it. You really don't want to be around her when she's PMSing,' Steve said. 'She gets really hungry and really horny. I always know when she's going to have a period, because I'll wake up in the morning and the fridge is empty and there's this really ugly bloke sleeping in my boat. You should see how ugly they are. She has no taste when she has PMS. She'll sleep with anything with a dick

156

and legs. I mean, it's mad. If I knew I had her problem, during that time of the month I would make sure I didn't sleep with *anyone* because whoever I chose would be a big mistake.'

My sister laughed so hard she spat the sauce all over the table. 'Maybe that explain why she boyfriend Tock Seng for such a long time.'

'Tock Seng was good-looking, very good-looking,' I said.

I told them how Tock Seng wanted me to go travelling with him.

'What, just disappear with him and go bum around the world?' Steve said. 'How did you ever get to go out with a nutter like that in the first place?'

'Maybe it was because Tock Seng looked like Encyclopedia Brown.'

'Who's?' Steve said.

I told him about this series of children's books about a boy detective called Encyclopedia. His dad was a police chief, and whenever he had a case he couldn't solve, he would tell it to Encyclopedia over dinner, and Encyclopedia would solve it. Tock Seng looked like the drawings of Encyclopedia in the books. 'I thought if I was friends with Tock Seng, then my life would be filled with murder and intrigue.'

'Did that happen?' Steve said.

'Well, we didn't come across any corpses, but we did do lots of weird things together. He got me into so much trouble.'

'Yah, lucky she got such a good sister to protect her,' my sister said. 'Every time she do something naughty with Tock Seng, Daddy would try and cane her.'

'Your Dad tried to cane you?!' Steve said.

'Oh yeah, I got caned all the time when I was in Singapore.' It was the normal way to discipline kids. Just thwack them and they'd never do the naughty thing again. Much more efficient than all the touchy-feely, Dr Spock, reason-with-your-children stuff. As a concession to compassion, my parents would tie a rubber band round the end of the cane. They hit me so often that the wood used to split at the end, but the rubber band held the cane together so the splinters wouldn't get into my leg.

'Yah, but I got always protect her,' my sister said. 'Every time Daddy try and cane her that time, I go and hug her, so he hit me instead.'

'Jesus, what did you do to provoke that?' Steve asked me.

I told Steve about how Tock Seng had the dream with the angel that told him to xerox food. 'We broke into our school office. We put a plate of fried Hokkein noodles on the photocopier. We xeroxed about twenty copies until the gravy from the noodles got into the copier and blew it. A teacher caught us. My principal told my Dad about it. After that, I got caned.'

'Does she do the same evil things to you that she does to me?' Steve asked.

'What evil thing she do to you?' my sister said.

'Hey guys, I'm glad that you're bonding and everything,' I said, 'but could you do it some other way than playing "Let's Take the Piss out of Chiah Deng"?'

Steve ignored me and ranted on. 'She always tanks up on coffee so she can study all night. Well, when she's done studying, she can't sleep because she's still on a caffeine high. The only thing that will put her to sleep is reading a book while soaking in the bath. She sits in the bath, reading, until she falls asleep. But get this – she never reads any of her own books. Because when she falls asleep, the book drops into the water and gets soaked. So she always takes one of *my* books. So all my novels are ridiculously swollen.'

My sister starts waving her hand excitedly. '*Ai-yah*, she does that to me also. Only she don't take my book, she take my Tetris! She play my computer game until she sleep. Then the computer fall into the water and get spoilt.'

Steve shook his head. 'Unbelievable. If there was any justice in the world, she should have got electrocuted when the computer fell in.'

I was about to defend myself when Steve turned his eyes to me and said, 'You abuse us *so* much.' My sister had the same look in her eyes. That shut me up because I had never seen so much affection as I saw in those different eyes, love in blue and brown. I guess that was what true love was, someone who knew you in all your depravity, and still loved you in spite of it, and, in a weird masochistic way, because of it. What other people might find disgusting or annoying about me, they found attractive in a joky anecdotal way. Though they complained about these things, deep down they found them endearing, or they wouldn't have put up with me for all these years.

My sister went to her suitcase and took out some videos. 'You like kung-fu videos?'

'Yeah, I love action movies,' Steve said.

'All these got Michelle Yeoh in it.' She gave him the videos – *Heroic Trio*, *Wing Chun* and *Supercop*.

'Fantastic,' Steve said. 'I love Michelle Yeoh. She kicked ass in that Bond movie. Does she fight in these movies?'

'A lot.'

'Does she fight any women?'

'Yes.'

'Fantastic.' That's one of the things he picked up from working in children's TV, their catchphrase is "fantastic". He turned to me. 'Your sister is the greatest. Thanks a lot.'

He got up and gave her a hug.

'So when are we going to get married?' she asked Steve.

'I beg your pardon?' Steve said.

'*Ai-yah*, Chiah Deng didn't tell you?' my sister said. 'In Singapore, if you touch a girl, you have to marry her! You hug me – you make me not a virgin. You have to marry me!'

Steve just sat there, silent, his eyes wide open.

I rolled my eyes. 'Be nice,' I told my sister.

She giggled. 'You don't have to be so scared. I just having fun with you,' she told Steve. 'It was a good joke, ha ha. You see your eyes – they're as round and big as our Daddy's buttocks.'

Steve laughed. He turned to me. 'I like her,' he said. 'She's funny.'

'I like him too,' my sister said to me. 'How did you both become good friends?'

'Five-course nouvelle cuisine at fast-food prices,' I told my sister. 'That's what I remember best about Formal Hall – that's where I first met Steve.'

Why did I go? Well, my St L'leh scholarship restricted my grocery list to items in Tesco's economy range, so I always grabbed this weekly opportunity to enjoy a black-tie dinner in the Great Hall, with silver cutlery and waiter service. Formal Hall injected a dose of civility to my grunge lifestyle, since I usually missed Hall meals due to late nights in the Bod, and supper usually meant eating tuna-and-sweetcorn pizza off paper towels. For once, it was nice to eat off a plate that I *didn't* use to wipe my mouth with.

For one night, I could feel like royalty, dining in a huge Hall that married medieval and classical styles, with Doric pilasters along the bone-yellow stone walls, and tall arched windows breaking into a frieze. You know that a place is grand when the windows are above eye-level, looming above your head. There were paintings of nobles in curly wigs, dons in black gowns and bishops in red robes, all wrapped in feminine attire, but trying their best to look powerful, manly and well hung.

I entered the Frideswide Room, where they were serving pre-dinner cocktails. Everybody seemed to have found their own comfortable cul-de-sac, huddled in their little cliques, swishing crystal glasses. There were the boaties, the physicists, the Cherwell news hacks, the Union politicians, the rugger buggers, the cricketing Blues and the fey OUDS thespians. I stood by myself in the middle of the room, looking like some social leper with VD and halitosis.

I looked around for some group, any group, that I might penetrate.

William, Hettie and Richard stood by the velvet drapes. We were all in Ad-oy's tutorial group together, so I figured that gave us some common ground.

'I wish Christ Church would stop ringing that bloody bell,' Hettie said. 'It always comes on during the nine o'clock news. I can't hear anything in my room apart from seven tons of "bong bong bong". What do they expect me to do? Lip-read Peter Sissons?'

William laughed. 'Now that's a challenge.'

I had no idea what they were talking about because I had no TV. The licence was worth about three months' groceries, so there was no way I could afford to pay the BBC.

'I can't believe my life is being wrecked by some statute designed for students in the seventeenth century,' Hettie said. Originally, there were 101 students at Christ Church, and ever since then, the bell has been rung 101 times at five past nine to summon the students back to college. 'But it's bloody typical. Ever since I arrived here, I wake up every day to discover yet another senselessly arcane custom that has no purpose other than to make my life inconvenient.'

Richard nodded. 'I couldn't agree more. I just found out that we're supposed to do our exams in subfusc.'

'Surely you jest,' William said. 'We have to wear a gown and a jacket during the three-hour exams?'

Richard nodded. 'Yes. In the height of the summer heat, sweating in a hall with no ventilation and no air-conditioning. We'll be buttoned to the top of our necks,

161

trying to translate Aristotle, while our bow ties slowly choke out our will to live.'

Since the group seemed to be bonding by bashing archaic Oxford traditions, I tried to join in the slag-fest by saying, 'I think the most outrageous tradition is the one to do with our degrees. Did you know that if you stay on in Oxford for more than seven years, even if you screwed up all your results, if you pay them twenty-five quid, you can graduate with a Master's?'

I thought this was a pretty interesting Oxford trivia tit-bit, but nobody in the group even made eye-contact with me. You'd think I'd just offered them some irrelevant information on the joys of train-spotting in Milton Keynes.

'Isn't that Chen?' Hettie said, gesturing at a Chinese student who had just walked into the room.

'Yes,' I said.

'He's from China, isn't he?' Hettie said.

'Yes,' I said, wondering how that would be relevant to what we had been talking about so far.

'Why don't you talk to him instead?' Hettie said. 'I'm sure you have many things in common.'

Since Chen and I are the only two Chinese students in college, everyone presumes that we're going to have this auto twin-like bond. Since I was being told to fuck off, I downed my Merlot in a gulp and walked towards the scout to get a refill.

Tom was in the line in front of me, so I asked him, 'So, how was your week?'

'OK,' he said.

'Are you doing anything fun this weekend?' I said.

'No,' Tom said.

This continued for about two minutes, with me trying to start a conversation, and Tom killing every attempt with bland monosyllabic answers to my questions.

I had encountered many students like Tom, students

whom I found very odd, since they always seemed to be at social functions, yet made no attempt to be sociable at all. I couldn't figure whether their inability to make small talk was due to social incompetence or snobbishness, but in any case, my awkward attempts to kick-start a conversation always sputtered out, until we just stood there looking at our drinks, trapped in a Siberian silence.

Tom suddenly broke the ice by looking me in the eye and saying, 'Were you in the computer room last night?'

'Uh, yes,' I said.

'How many pages of your essay did you print out last night? Did you print more than fifty pages?'

'No,' I lied.

'Nobody is supposed to print more than fifty pages at a time,' Tom said. 'We ran out of toner again, even though I only put some in the printer three months ago.'

Tom is the computer room Nazi. Nobody is officially in charge of the JCR computer room, but Tom spends all day there emailing discussion groups and designing signs in Word that say things like 'NO FOOD AND BEVERAGES' and 'NO UNAUTHORIZED INSTALLATION OF SOFTWARE'. Someone once changed the desktop background from 'Windows Standard' to 'Wheat', and from the way Tom freaked out, you'd think that they had installed a screen-saver featuring naked photos of his mother.

A white bloke entered the room. He picked up a glass, then walked over to the fireplace, where he stood alone, sipping his champagne. I had noticed him before, because he always stood by himself at these shindigs. I'd never bothered to talk to him, because I figured that since everyone ignored him, he was probably psychotic or a wanker or just insanely boring. But I needed to escape Tom's Gestapo interrogation, so I smiled at the bloke like he was my best friend and walked over to the flames.

'Hi, I'm Chiah Deng,' I said.

163

'Oh, I know you. I mean, I've seen your name on lists and stuff,' the bloke said. 'You're the other person on the St L'leh scholarship. I'm the other one – um – I mean, other from you.'

I found his whole Hugh Grant stuttering thing rather endearing.

'Chiah Deng. That's such a top name,' he said. 'Much better than Sara or Tamsin. All the girls here, their names are either boring or poncey. Or just plain ridiculous. There's a student here whose parents wanted a boy they could call Edward. But they got a girl instead, so they named her Edwardia. Why did your parents give you that name? Does it have any special meaning?'

I was slightly shocked. Was he actually trying to start a friendly conversation? Nobody in college ever bothered to chit-chat me.

'When I was a baby, my parents brought me to a fortune-teller to help choose a name for me,' I said. 'In order to get an auspicious name, you need to factor in your binomial, the Five Elements, the Yin and Yang. It's very complex.'

'What's a binomial?' he said.

'It's a Chinese character, sort of like the Chinese equivalent of the English alphabet, the ABC. According to the lunar calendar, time is determined by two different sets of Chinese characters. One set is called the Ten Heavenly Stems, and the other set is called the Twelve Earthly Branches. Thus every moment in time has two characters, one from each set. The combination of these two characters is called a "binomial". So, if you look at the time of your birth, you'll come up with the two characters that make up your binomial.'

'So how does this affect your fate?'

'Your binomial is linked to the Five Elements and the Yin – Yang system. These two systems affect and control your life, the universe and everything.'

'What are the Five Elements?'

'The world is made up of Five Elements – Wood, Fire, Earth, Gold and Water,' I explained. 'They're kind of like the building blocks of life, the fundamental things you need in order to get things to work. Usually, if something isn't working in your life – your boyfriend dumped you, or your tutor is never there during office hours – it's usually because there's one of those elements missing in your life.'

'So how did that affect the choice of your name?'

'If you look at all the astrology stuff, I was born in the Year of the Ox. That year is linked to the binomial Kui Chou, which is linked to the Wood element. But looking at my time of birth, the fortune-teller saw that though I had the Earth, Gold and Water Elements, I was missing one Element.'

'Fire,' he said.

'Yeah, so unless I add some Fire to my life, my life will never be complete. Without Fire, everything I do will fail – I'll never get married, and I'll be miserable at school. Hmmm – that sounds like me now. But anyway, so the fortune-teller told my parents to add a "Fire" element to my name, to add balance to my life.'

'How did they add fire to your name?'

'By calling me "Deng". Writing a Chinese word is like painting a picture.' I took out my lipstick, and wrote out 'Deng' on my napkin:

火丁

'You see the right side of this character?' I said. 'It looks like a flame.'

'What does it mean? Fire?'

'No, it means "lamp". But obviously, it has a "Fire" element in it.'

'Fascinating. But what has this to do with the Yin and Yang? I've heard it mentioned pretty often but I don't know much about it. Apart from the fact that you're supposed to balance it.'

'Right. In the beginning of time, the Great Ultimate gave birth to two forces, Yin and Yang, which also underpin your life, the universe and everything,' I said. 'They're directly opposite to each other, like Yang is male, linked with Heaven, the sun, everything that is bright and good, while the Yin is female, and linked with darkness and everything that's passive and evil.'

'It's not a very feminist concept, is it?'

'That's one of the burdens of being a Chinese female,' I said. 'But anyway, you need both Yin and Yang in equal amounts in your life. They need to be in harmony or you'll experience the usual general catastrophe stuff – poverty, infertility, spinsterhood, etc.'

'So your name must also have a balance between the Yin and the Yang?' he asked.

'Right.'

'How do you know if your name is Yin or Yang?'

'By calculating the number of strokes in your name,' I said. 'You add up the number of strokes in your first, second and third names to get the Zong Ge, or "character" of your name. All even numbers are Yin and all odd numbers are Yang.'

'But where did "Chiah" come from?'

'It's my generation name.'

'What's that?'

'Traditionally, each Chinese family has a poem associated with it,' I said. 'As each new generation is born, it takes the next word of the poem as the generation name. This way, during family gatherings, you can tell just by their names who's your uncle, cousin, etc. My father started a new generation series with the poem "Chiah He Wan Shi Xing".'

'What does that mean?'

166

'Literally, it means "family-together-ten thousand-things-happy",' I said. '"Chiah" means "Family". All the girls in my generation, like my sister and cousins, we all have "Chiah" as our second character. Which is why my sister is called Chiah Chen. So if you came across someone from our family called "Wan" something, you'd know that she's from the thirty-first generation.'

Steve leaned against the mantel. 'Fuckenell. Being Chinese sounds bloody complicated. You'd think you'd need a computer to coordinate all those different bits of data.'

'That's why people usually hire a fortune-teller,' I said. 'The tellers have thick almanacs, and walls plastered with red charts. Come to think of it, some of them *do* use computers nowadays to cross-reference all the lunar dates and binomials.'

'Would you get a fortune-teller to name your kids?' he asked.

'Are you kidding? Of course not. Fortune-tellers charge a couple of hundred dollars for a baby-naming, and I'm not *that* superstitious. Anyway, I think the names of children tell you more about their parents than the kids themselves. You know, they're like a symbol of the parents' aspirations, what they want their kids to be.'

'What did your parents want you to be?'

'"Deng", or "lamp", is a symbol of fertility. So, you know, they want me to grow up to be sort of a baby-producing machine, spurting out grandchildren for their playing pleasure.' I remember this conversation because it proved that Generica was wrong about the world. People are attracted to the special, and you can only be special if you're different. In that moment, I became friends with this bloke because he was the first person I'd met at Oxford who liked me *because* I was so different.

'But what's *your* name?'

'Steve.'

167

'Does it have any special meaning?'

'Yeah. When I was born, my parents saw that Uranus was passing Jupiter, and so they got an astrologer to make up a five-letter name for me that means "diamond geezer and all-round sex god".'

'I suspect that you just made that up,' I said, laughing. Then I frowned. 'You know what I don't get? Why doesn't anybody like me? No, it's not that. I don't think they even dislike me. You have to know someone before you can dislike them, and nobody here even knows me.'

'It's more like an apathetic disdain. Like they can't even be arsed to get to know you. Like they wish you were dead.'

I shook my head. 'If they wished I were dead, that means that they hate me. But I don't think I'm worthy enough to arouse such a strong passion in them. It's weird, but it's almost like they don't mind me living – they just don't want me to exist.'

'It's because we're St L'leh scholars. We're the only two in college on a full scholarship, so we're always going to get the invisible-man treatment.'

'But I thought being a scholar would be a good thing. You'd think it would bring prestige and honour, rather than the treatment one usually reserves for flesh-eating viruses.'

'We're only here because we make the college look politically correct,' Steve said. 'St L'leh has always been accused of being too élitist, of only letting in rich public-school types, so a couple of years ago, they came up with this scholarship for two poor students. I went to a comprehensive school, my dad's a plumber and my mum works at the deli counter at Tesco's. I'm the token state-school lad to show people that St L'leh believes in diversity, and really *doesn't* discriminate against kids who say "tea" instead of "dinner".'

'And I'm the token foreigner from a poor under-developed country?'

168

'You've got it,' Steve said. 'Welcome to the English class system.'

Steve told me about how he went to the Freshers' reception, the first get-to-know-you do for first-years. It was super-poncey, out on the croquet lawn with Pimm's and strawberries.

'I spotted this girl who was so hot, she nearly broke the glass capillary on my sex thermometer,' Steve said. 'This ex-Eton tosser spotted her too, so we both started chatting her up.' The boy got bonding with the girl – Georgina (known as George) – because both their fathers were law partners at Slaughter and May. Eventually, Steve found out that they were all reading English Literature, so he tried to move the conversation towards common ground by asking George what her favourite book was. 'George said James Joyce's *Ulysses*, and immediately the public-school tosser starts talking out of his arse. He was going on about how it was amazing that Joyce was able to transplant the theme of Homer's *Iliad* into the Ireland of his time.' So Steve pointed out that Joyce based *Ulysses* on Homer's *Odyssey*, and not the *Iliad*. 'But instead of being impressed, George gives me a weird look. She said, "What book is that? I've never heard of it." "The *Odyssey*. You know. The *Odyssey*. O-D-Y-S-S-E-Y." I finally spelt it out for her after she kept looking at me as if I was making gorilla noises. "Ahhhh . . . the *Odyssey*," she said. "It's pronounced Aw-the-sea and not Oh-die-say." It was an easy mistake to make. Steve was the first Lucas male to go to university. He couldn't pronounce a lot of big words correctly, even though he knew what they meant, because all his education, like mine, came through reading books by himself, rather than hanging around posh people who used those phrases at cocktail parties. 'Nobody I grew up with had ever read the *Odyssey*,' Steve said. 'I don't think anyone on my council estate could even *spell* "Odyssey". I mean, it's complete bollocks, but at

169

St L'leh, class is everything. No matter how witty or charming I was, the girl looked at me like I was reciting her pages from *Glenn Hoddle's Psychic Guide to Soccer*. And no matter what bag of shite the public-school tosser came up with, she listened to him like he was Alfred Kazin resurrected from the dead.'

'You know what the irony is?' I said. 'We're here because we're smart and not because we're rich. But we're treated like idiots by students who are here because they're rich and not because they're smart.'

'It's always been like that, though. We're part of a grand Oxford tradition. Back in the old days, they would have called students like us "servitors". And as Samuel Johnson once said, the difference between us servitors and gentlemen commoners is that we are men of wit and no fortune and they are men of fortune and no wit.'

14

'The theatre is where you'll start the first stage of the Adaptation process,' Draco Sidious said. 'Sit.'

We obediently swung down the seats and parked our butts on the velvet cushions.

'You'll be working on that set,' Dr Sidious said, pointing at the stage.

There's no such thing as a typical Oxford room, but it seemed like the set was designed to be one. On one hand, there were all the symbols of an ancient age. The pointed lancet windows bathed the air with liquid light, while dead white men in dark Holbein hues cast their shadowy gaze from their giant frames.

However, the set didn't look like it came off a BBC Jane Austen production, because it was also dotted with Generation X paraphernalia. Pint glasses, stolen from the college bar, sat in beer puddles on the precious furniture. A TV sat beneath the gloomy portraits, its main function being to present the latest Tarantino flick rented from Blockbuster. A coke machine, luminous in red, hummed its chilly tune in between two oak bookshelves. All in all, the effect was that of an English nobleman's chamber decorated with American slacker grunge.

Dr Sidious smiled his approval. 'What we're going to do

is to put your sister into a typical Oxford scene. In this case, it will be tea in the Junior Common Room.' Dr Sidious turned to my sister. 'I want you to act like your usual Singaporean self. Don't try to fit in. Then Chiah Deng will be able to see when your normal behaviour prevents you from being approved. After you've finished performing the scene, Chiah Deng will be able to decide what Adaptations you'll need to make.'

When my sister entered the set, she came upon two cliques standing at opposite sides of the room (as there always were in the JCR), namely the haves and the have-nots, those on subsistence-level scholarships that they won on merit and those with PPMM (Papa & Mama) scholarships that gave them a bottomless fund by which they could pay for two-hundred-quid balls and dinners at the Randolph Hotel. My sister naturally gravitated towards the rich group, and I didn't blame her. The other group (an Indian and Japanese male, and a Mexican female) just stood there not talking to each other, staring into their mugs as if they were engrossed in reading the tea leaves at the bottom.

The rich group, on the other hand, beamed with the satisfied smiles of those who knew they were the centre of the universe, radiating their magnetic brilliance like the sun. And my sister, like myself in the past, walked towards their light in the way a bug is drawn to a flame, not realizing that their warm glow was not an invitation to intimacy, but a warning that any inferior being would be scorched upon contact with their splendid incandescence.

How did I know that this group was at the top of the food chain? Their faces and clothes were not that different from those of any other middle-class student, but their superiority was expressed in the way they carried them-selves. It was all in the way they arched their eyebrows, their elegant accents, the way they always spoke with their chins raised to a forty-five-degree angle, so that they looked down at you with their colourful eyes. And those eyes were well trained, eyes which could, with the slightest dilation, silently convey supersonic volumes of contempt. Steve's nickname for the group like that in our college was 'the Poncey Dolphins', because whenever they laughed, they would raise their noses and make the 'haw haw' noises one associates with the marine cetacean mammals from the Delphinoid family.

'Is it true that the dons are thinking of shifting the tutes on the scholastics to Magdalen during Hilary?' the blonde asked the copper-haired male.

'What you talking about?' my sister said.

Explain to her all the obscure lingo, I wrote in my notebook. Oxford had a complete inability to use normal words for ordinary things. It was like there was this whole bullshit process of trying to create this élitist tradition, some false hallowed past, that's completely artificial. When I first arrived and found out I had to take a 'Prologomena', I freaked out because it sounded damned intimidating, and then I found out that all it meant was 'Introduction'. That was so Oxford. It didn't have introductory classes, it had 'Prologomenas', as if that made the classes sound more difficult and unique. But then it was like this whole place was run on the principle of *quidquid latine dictum sit, profundum viditur* – everything in Latin sounds profound.

Also, unlike most universities, they didn't call their terms Autumn, Spring and Summer, but inexplicably still stuck to some obsolete calendar that made them Michaelmas, Hilary and Trinity. And they didn't even pronounce words the same way as the rest of the country did. Everyone else in the world pronounced 'Magdalen' as 'Mag-de-lin', the way it should be pronounced, but for some inexplicable reason, people in Oxford called their college 'Maudlin'. It was one of those little things, I supposed, that was invented to separate the tourist from the native. You know someone doesn't belong there if they stop you on the street to ask for directions to Mag-de-lin College.

The Dolphins just ignored her question. 'No, I think Scary Carey is going to lecture on Aquinas' *analogia entis* at Teddy Hall,' the copper-haired male said, using Latin, nicknames and other Oxford codewords to keep my sister out of the loop.

A guy walked into the room, wearing a Columbia sweatshirt and a Yankees baseball cap, and carrying a brown paper bag. He looked like an American exchange student, Johnny, from my college, who dealt with the anti-American feeling in college by amplifying his Americanness, becoming super-US, like some cartoon version of a Yank. The Johnny look-alike picked up the *Guardian* from the coffee table, and glanced at the headlines on the front page. He flung it down and picked up the *Independent*. 'Unbelievable,' he said. 'This is so sucky.'

The Yank walked over to the Poncey Dolphins, waving the newspaper in the air.

The brunette flung open her arms. 'Hello, Jack sweetie! How are you?'

Now I am going to tell you about an odd phenomenon: the Poncey Dolphins had a way of uttering words that, if you just read them, would give you the impression that they liked you and wanted you to be their best friend. But at the same time, with their tone and their body language, they vacuumed all sincerity from those chummy words. So it's always a rather odd experience talking to the Poncey Dolphins, because it's like you're seeing them behind this force field, this plexiglass shield. You see this smiling face that makes all these buddy-buddy noises, but you still get the feeling that they would rather hang out with an obscure strain of an incurable virus than with you. So, even though the blonde and brunette exchanged air kisses with Jack, and

174

enquired about his health and general wellbeing, it was clear that an Aids-infected toilet brush had a better chance of getting intimate with them.

And, frankly speaking, I had no idea how to adapt my sister so that she could penetrate the force field. At St L'leh, I had tried to assault the shield with charm and intellectual wit, all to no avail. Finally, I gave up trying to use any of those things, because I knew that the force field could not be penetrated by any of my stunning personal qualities, but was induced solely because I had been born to the wrong set of parents. And I certainly didn't know how to adapt my sister so that she would be able to turn on a force field as well. Even if I tried, I wouldn't know how to say nice things to someone and still convey a fuck-off subtext. I guess it was all down to breeding. The Dolphins had been trained since infancy to add subtle layers to their personal interactions which we less evolved social species have yet to pick up.

'Yeah, hi Tamsin,' Jack said to the brunette after they exchanged air kisses. Then he turned to the man. 'Tommy boy, could you get the committee to put in a motion at the next JCR meeting to replace one of the British newspapers with the *Herald Tribune*?'

'Why?' Thomas asked. By Jack's question, I deduced that Thomas was probably the JCR President, another inexplicably odd Oxford appellation.

'Why do we need two British newspapers, especially since they're both so provincial? I don't understand this country. I just read the *Washington Post* on the Web, and the front page was about this massive flood in India that killed eight hundred people. All you have on the front page here –' Jack tapped the newspaper, 'is the results of the Test Match against the Australians, and a report on a new breed of sheep being developed in Norfolk. I mean, eight hundred people died and all the English care about is cricket and things that go baa baa? Why don't we get the *Tribune*, so some of us can read some *real* news?'

'I'll bring the matter up at the next meeting,' Thomas said unenthusiastically.

'And do you know when BT is coming to install my phone? I've been waiting for two weeks. Does College seriously expect me to contact people solely via pigeon post? It takes a week before anyone gets any of my messages. This place is so stuck in the Dark Ages. I don't know how any of you manage to communicate with each other.'

'I'll chase the technicians from British Telecom for you,' Thomas said. The three Dolphins exchanged glances, eyes that expressed irritation at having to deal with the typical tendency for Americans to need to talk loudly, frequently and voluminously (resulting in a tedious addiction to phones, that the Brits had to learn to tolerate).

'If I was at Columbia, I would have gotten a phone by now,' Jack said. 'I don't know how you get anything done here. I had to photocopy the reading for the Prologomena last night, but all the shops had shut by five. When I was at Columbia, I could go to Kinkos at two in the morning and copy a whole novel if I wanted to. And after I'd finished photocopying, I could get some Vietnamese food delivered to my apartment.' Jack turned to Gemima. 'Could I borrow your copy of Donne's Holy Sonnets for the Prologomena?'

'The Holy Sonnets are a sequence of metaphysical poems that enact a witty deconstruction of the Pauline dialectic regarding the flesh and the Spirit,' my sister said.

The Dolphins stared at my sister, stunned at this unexpected display of lucidity and intelligence. When I was at home, whenever my sister bugged me about spending too much time reading the Holy Sonnets rather than watching some Taiwanese soap opera on TV, I would tell her that I had to because they were 'a sequence of metaphysical poems that enact a witty deconstruction of the Pauline dialectic

176

regarding the flesh and the Spirit'. I guess that line got drummed into her head after frequent repetition. And for the first time in this scene, she stopped being invisible. I'd found that most of the racism I encountered at Oxford didn't come in the form of verbal assaults, but through the process of negation, where people treat you as if you weren't there. I suppose that was why people like Jack tried to be as annoying as possible, as a way to gain attention and get the Dolphins to acknowledge his existence.

'Oh, are you reading English too?' Jack asked my sister. 'Who's your tutor?'

'I don't know,' my sister said.

Jack laughed. 'Neither do I. It's typical of Oxford. We're halfway through Michaelmas and my tutor suddenly decided he wants to go to Prague for six months. So College replaced him with some first-year graduate student from the Australian outback who knows even less about the sonnet *volta* than I do. Oxford really sucks.'

'If Oxford so bad, why don't you go back to Columbia?' my sister asked.

Jack stared at my sister, surprised that she had no idea about the premise for complaining about Oxford. *Explain to sis that people come to Oxford not because it is a great academic institution,* I wrote, *but because they want some of the élitist mystique to rub off on them. Only a stint at Oxford can give them that world domination aura that the Poncey Dolphins possess.*

Jack didn't want to admit his desire for the aura, so he just said, 'I think I'll go get some tea,' and left the group.

Thomas rolled his eyes. 'I don't know why they let *him* into College. He's obviously a few fries short of a Happy Meal.'

'Oooohhhh, I *love* Happy Meal!' my sister said. 'I collect Happy Toys. They're so fun! I got the Wedding Rapunzel Barbie, the Tamagotchi, the Winnie the Pooh plug head.'

177

'I have no idea what a plug head is about but it sounds appalling,' Gemima said.

'Yah, it's very appalling, it's so cute!' my sister said, obviously not knowing what appalling meant. 'Each plush head has a plastic clip on the top. You can clip them on everything and anything! I got all eight!'

'You know what's amazing,' the brunette said to Gemima, gesturing at my sister. 'She's so dense, I'm sure light bends *around* her.'

'So where are you from originally?' Thomas asked my sister. And I knew that the question, which on the surface seemed to be an attempt at polite small talk, was in reality designed to emphasize my sister's difference from the Dolphins, her otherness, because beneath that question was the implication that she was alien, that she didn't belong in this room.

'Singapore,' my sister said.

'Oh, Singapore is Chinese, isn't it?' Thomas said. 'I think Yoshi is from China.' He pointed at the Asian man in the other group and said, 'Have you talked to him yet?', which was a not-very-subtle attempt by him to exile my sister to the foreigners' group.

'No,' my sister said.

The Dolphins looked at my sister, expecting her to leave. But she didn't.

'I'm surprised there aren't more Americans here for tea today,' the blonde said. 'You'd think they'd never pass up an opportunity to scoff down the cream cakes and free biccies.'

'I believe the *posse* –' the brunette said mockingly, 'went to watch the latest Hollywood production. And I must say, Gemima sweetie, I fear the worst.'

Gemima widened her eyes in fake horror. 'You don't mean?'

'Yes, I suspect it might even be a Disney movie.'

'Oh, Disney,' my sister said, finally finding a reference that she understood. 'I like Disney. *Mulan* very good.'

'But didn't you find the transformation of your culture's icons into singing animals with Judeo-Christian bourgeois values at all sacrilegious?' Gemima said.

Teach sister, I wrote, *only to extol the virtues of art-house European film-makers like Bergman or Antonioni.*

My sister just stared at Gemima stupidly. 'I like Mushu the dragon. He's one of my favourite Happy Toys. You know, all the Mulan action figures are wrapped in Cello Wrap with safety warnings in over thirty languages!' My sister grinned. 'That's my hobby – collecting Happy Toys. You got hobby or not?'

'I'm the President of the Oxford Union,' Gemima said. 'Recently we invited Thorstein Veblen and F. Scott Fitzgerald to discuss the relationship between the concept of conspicuous consumption and *The Great Gatsby*.'

'It was a fascinating debate,' the brunette chipped in. 'Marx was in the audience and argued that his theory of surplus value was much more useful in the deconstruction of the novel.'

'Sounds interesting,' my sister said, completely not getting that all these 'guests' were dead. 'What other hobbies you got?'

'Gemima also enjoys fox hunting, show jumping and mocking uncouth members of the *hoi polloi*,' Thomas said with a smirk, enjoying the fact that my sister had no idea that they were making fun of her.

'Yes, I think you're a fascinating specimen,' Gemima said to my sister. 'You should consider drawing up a will to donate your brain to the School of Physics. I hear they're trying to come up with a perfect vacuum.'

I couldn't bear seeing my sister being mocked any longer, so I asked Dr Sidious if we could end the scene.

Dr Sidious nodded, and my sister left the set with the other actors.

15

So I had three months to turn my sister from a Chink hick
to a posh chick. I tried not to panic. I love my sister, but I
had to admit it – the Poncey Dolphins were right – my sister
had an intellect that was only rivalled by lint. When we first
bought a radio, it took her six months before she realized
that she could listen to AM radio in the afternoon as well.
In order to impress the Dolphins, she would have to acquire
an A–Z knowledge of Western intellectual history, be
familiar with academic icons ranging from Aristotle to
Nietzsche's Zarathustra. My sister really didn't know very
much about any of that. She really didn't know very much
about *anything*. There was definitely quite a lot of yardage
between her goalposts.

Not that I'm being a hypercritical snob. My sister actually
relished her ignorance. When we were growing up, when
she saw me reading Baudelaire, she would shudder and say,
'*Wah*, I don't know why you like reading these *cheem*
things so much, it just makes me blur. Don't read so much.
You'll sprain your brain and hurt your eyes. By the time
you're thirty you'll be blind and always have a headache.
Why don't you come to the OK Lounge to sing karaoke
with me?' She could never understand why I liked being
cheem – cultured, intellectual. You know, I believe my sister

actually *enjoys* keeping her head empty of thoughts. Sometimes I think that if she blew up a balloon her head might deflate.

But hope springs eternal. I just needed to get the right books: manuals that condensed intricate concepts like ennui, Darwinism and Keynesian economic theory into digestible, *Reader's Digest*-sized bites.

I logged on to Amazon and was immediately bewildered by the confounding array of books available.

You wouldn't believe the number of books launched by the publishing industry whose *raison d'être* was to educate the unwashed masses on the rudiments of every topic under the sun. For example, there was *The Complete Idiot's Guide to Opera* (Macmillan), *Absolute Beginners' Business French* (Hodder & Stoughton), *Postmodernism for Beginners* (Icon Books), *The Internet for Dummies* (IDG Books) and *The Bluffer's Guide to Champagne* (Oval Books).

Now, if I were an insecure individual, this confusing variety of titles would be just the thing to precipitate a minor identity crisis. For one thing, you had to decide whether you wanted to be a beginner or a bluffer. Were you a 'complete idiot', or merely a 'dummy'? And what was the difference, really? Such questions usually generate an unpleasant surge of existential angst, thus I logged off and decided to write my own series of guides.

Swank Up Your Speech –
The Talking Cheem *Guide for the Blur*

by

Chiah Deng Gan

To talk *cheem*, you don't have to memorize every word in the *New Oxford Dictionary of English* (ed. Pearsall and Hanks, OUP, 1998). You just need to know the few special words that have that *je ne sais quoi*. These words – like your Maggi Cook-It-Right sauce – if sprinkled in the conversation at the right moment, will make you an instant member of the *cognoscenti*.

1) AFICIONADO
Definition: Use when you want to say that you like something.
For example: A dumb, uncultured Ah Lian would say, '*I like Rambo*.'
An intellectual snob would say, '*I am an aficionado of Rambo*.'

Editor's note: If you use this sentence around other intellectual snobs, they would probably think you were talking about the French Symbolist *poète maudit* Rimbaud rather than the Hollywood action hero.

2) SLOUGH OF DESPOND
Definition: Depression or general blah-ness.
For example:
If you're feeling low . . .
A dumb, uncultured Ah Lian would say, 'I feel very *xian*.'
An intellectual snob would say, '*I am stuck in the Slough of Despond*.'

Editor's note: By making an allusion to John Bunyan's *Pilgrim's Progress*, you'll sound like an *aficionado* of seventeenth-century allegorical narratives and *voilà*! – attain instant membership of the *intelligentsia*.

3) PERNICIOUS/ABOMINABLE/REPREHENSIBLE
If you want to sound *cheem*, you can substitute 'very bad' with any of those words.
4) FOURTH ESTATE
Definition: Reporters.
For example:
Any normal person would say, 'I heard about (*insert news event*) on the TV last night.'

182

An intellectual snob would say, 'According to the Fourth Estate, the (*insert news event*) might have a — impact on the global economy.'

5) SEX WORDS

Nothing makes you look more *cheem* than using these phrases when talking about bonking.

a) Fornication
Definition: *King James Bible* word for bonking.

Editor's note: Makes you look as if you've read the whole Bible in sixteenth-century prose.

b) prurient
Definition: Something that makes you feel like bonking.
c) Saturnalia
Definition: A lot of people bonking.
d) *in flagrante delicto*
Definition: When someone comes into the room and sees you bonking.

Editor's note: This word is from the medieval Latin.

Posh Talk Rule 1: Anything you say in Latin will make you sound *cheem*.

Posh Talk Rule 2: Anything you say in French will make you sound *cheem* and sexy.

e) *pièce de résistance*
Definition: French word for something very amazing, e.g. 'His penis was a *pièce de résistance*!'

EXTRA TIP:

Freud's theory of Eros and Thanatos
Definition: (Unnecessary)

Editor's note: You don't have to understand the theory, you just need to know how to insert it in your conversation.

EXAMPLES:
i) If the *cheem* chatterers are talking about books with sex, say:

> 'That book has been attacked by some members of the *Fourth Estate* for being pornographic, but I disagree with them. As an *aficionado* of erotic literature, I find that (*insert title of book*) does not arouse *prurient* interest, only sadness and despair.'

Editor's note: You can say this about any posh book with sex in it, from *Lady Chatterley's Lover* to *Lolita*.

ii) Movies.

EXAMPLE:
Memorize the following dialogue so that you can say it when you hear the smart snobs talking about Stanley Kubrick's *pièce de résistance*, *Eyes Wide Shut*:

> 'All the acts of fornication demonstrate *Freud's theory of Eros and Thanatos*. When Tom Cruise catches the masked couples *in flagrante delicto*, he disturbs their *saturnalia* and they threaten him with death.'

I stopped tapping on my keyboard after I came up with a list of twenty words. I didn't want to overwhelm my sister. After all, her brain waves did fall a little short of the beach.

*

I went into the bathroom with my *Guide for the Blur*.

My sister was scouring the tiles with bleach. '*Ai-yoh*, your floor so dirty. When was the last time you scrubbed the floor?'

'I'm supposed to scrub the floor?' I gave her a slightly confused look, like she had just asked me when was the last time I went yodelling. For me, the idea of scrubbing the floor was like watching *Pet Rescue* or playing indoor bowls. I knew that quite a few people did it, but it just never occurred to me that I should be getting into it as well.

She slapped her hand on her forehead. '*Wah leow*, I can't believe it. You know how dirty your house is?'

'I'm sure you're about to tell me,' I said.

'Your house is so dirty I have to wipe my feet before I go outside,' my sister said.

'OK, so I'm not Mary Poppins.' I shrugged. 'So sue me.' I gave her my *Guide*.

My sister looked at it and frowned. 'Am I suppose to read this? I don't like to read. Can you record this on tape so I can listen to it when I sleep?'

I shook my head. 'Not only do you have to read this, you have to memorize all the words.'

She shrieked. 'There are twenty words!'

'Exactly. See how easy I've made it for you? Normally, in order to talk *cheem*, you would have to have undergone at least ten years of rigorous scholarship. But I've rigged it such that you only have to learn these twenty words to sound smart.'

She flapped the *Guide* in my face. 'This is your idea of making my life *easy*? What other *easy* thing you want me to do next? Find a cure for cancer? Start an orphanage in India? Give up rice and eat only mashed potato?'

'It's not that difficult. You can take the whole week to learn this. That's just three words a day.'

*

Two days later, I asked my sister, 'So have you learnt any of the words yet?'

'Yah, yah,' my sister said. 'I've been studying. I'm just taking a break now.' She tossed a root into the stew.

'Did you even *look* at the *Guide*?' I said.

'Yah, yah. The thirteenth word in the *Guide*. How you pronounce it?'

'Sprezzatura,' I said. 'Spret-sa-tour-uh.'

My sister giggled. 'Is it a sex word?'

'No,' I said. 'It's an Italian word used by Castiglione in *The Courtier*. If you use it, it'll make you look *cheem*, as if you've read Italian Renaissance literature.'

'Spray-sar-too-ah,' my sister said. She giggled again. 'Sounds like a noise a man's ding dong makes when he's having sex.'

I marvelled at the gentle, white geese-float of the steam. Ordinarily, I would have ordered her to memorize the word list, but the pungent aroma made my mouth water, rendering it impossible for me to ask her to stop cooking to go and study.

In the days that followed, even though her educational progress had been less than satisfactory, I found it difficult to tell her to get down to some serious learning. Whenever I was about to scold her, she would say, 'Try this jelly, it's really good,' or 'Don't disturb me now, I'm trying to get the stain out of the carpet,' or 'Do you have any other clothes you need me to wash?'

It was amazing. By the end of the week, our bathroom smelt of Zen sandalwood, our kitchen was filled with pots bubbling with gourmet delight, and I could actually walk around my bedroom without stubbing my toe on some junk on the floor.

For the first time, our chairs and table weren't buried under a pile of underwear and magazines circa 1999. 'Wow,' Steve said, the first evening he came back from work after my sister's mass cleaning. 'So this is what our furniture looks like. I didn't even know we had a stereo in that corner.'

However, by the end of the week it was also obvious that my sister had not learnt a single word in the *Guide*.

So I read her the riot act. 'You know what your problem is? What you lack in intelligence, you more than make up for in laziness. You really have to knuckle down or you're never going to pass the Test.'

'Hah! Lazy? Me?' my sister said. 'What about you? You're so lazy you never ever clean your place. Your house so dirty, when cockroaches want to go on holiday, the tour bus brings them here. What do you think I've been doing all week? I been knuckling down, cleaning for you. And you still scold me, so ungrateful.'

'Don't try to guilt me,' I said. 'You only scrubbed the pots because it's less painful than pounding the word list into your head. I'm going to give you another *Guide* to memorize. I expect you to have learnt both this *Guide* and the word list by the end of this week.'

THE GUIDE TO BEING AN OXFORD IT GIRL

by

Chiah Deng Gan

Here are the Top 10 questions that people might ask you at social functions.

Memorize these answers so that they'll think you're a posh socialite.

Questions about your:

I) NAME

Your name: Sophie

Names of your best friends: Sophie, Tara, Sara, Cosmina, George, Robert, Prince William, Tom.

2) CHILDHOOD AND EDUCATION

You were raised in Egypt. You could see the pyramids from your mansion terrace. Unfortunately, your family had to flee after Daddy's warehouse was burned down by the ungrateful natives. When you returned home, you were shipped off to the Sherborne School for Girls.

3) CAREER GOALS

You want to be a cultural critic in either academia or the media, but only if you can be successful enough to be a star on telly (cf. Germaine Greer) and get to appear in Gap ads (cf. Andrew Sullivan).

4) STYLE

Think *Vogue* meets *TLS*. Think Ab Fab Genius. You want to have the brains of Marie Curie, and the body of a Victoria's Secret knickers model. Your credo: Smart is sexy.

5) FAVOURITE HOBBY

Karaoke.
But you enjoy it in an ironic postmodern way. When asked why you like karaoke, you always say, 'Because it is a pandemic "vox pox" participatory performance art.'

6) MAJOR SOURCE OF INCOME

Trust fund which you will inherit from your grandfather, who founded a £1.6 billion paper and packaging business.

7) BOYFRIEND

Ben, a Philosophy major at Yale. You met during a fundraising event for your favourite charity held at the Armani emporium in Knightsbridge.

8) FAVOURITE CHARITY

The Refugee Project. Founded by hip hop artiste Lauryn Hill to help disadvantaged urban American youth.

9) TYPICAL WEEKEND PLANS

Shopping at Harvey Nicks, skiing at Klosters, launch parties at St Martin's Lane Hotel, visiting your country estate in Hampshire.

10) NAUGHTIEST SECRET

You used to sniff coke at the K-Bar in London, and when Daddy found out, he sent you to the Meadows clinic in the Arizona desert for two weeks. There you were also treated for drink-related problems and a minor eating disorder.

'I'm not going to learn this.' My sister tossed the paper on the table. 'It's useless.'

'What do you mean?' I said.

'I can't even understand it. Why don't you write it in simple English, in Singlish? This *Guide* is like those magazines you always read, like *Cosmo*. Too *cheem* for me.'

I couldn't believe my sister thought that the lingo in *Cosmo* was too complex for her understanding.

'I wrote it this way, so you would get the tone of the discourse. You'll have to learn how to speak the way the *Guide* was written, if you know what I mean.'

'I can talk like the *Guide*, but nobody will believe me,' she said.

'Why not?'

My sister laughed. 'Look at me. I like to wear Versace but I know that doesn't make me look white. It just makes me look like an *Ah Lian*. And I like looking like an *Ah Lian*. I look so Chinese. I can tell people I do all these white-people things – skiing, shopping in London, but they'll still see me as Chinese. Sometimes you can be so stupid.' My sister walked to the shelf and pulled out Milton's *Paradise Lost*. She shook her head. 'I warned you last time, you read too many books, strain your brain, make you stupid. You think just because you read *ang mo* books, then people will think you're *ang mo*? What you do is not important. Only what you look like. You're like banana. Outside you're yellow, so when people see you, they only see yellow. Inside, you can be really white, but people will still treat you like you're yellow.'

I opened my mouth to disagree, but nothing came out.

189

Maybe my sister was right. In my years at Oxford, I had totally immersed myself in the British lifestyle, drinking tea, reading the *Guardian*, watching *Match of the Day*, but at every cocktail party I went to, every new person I met still kept asking me when I was going back to my own country. I sat down in the dinghy, shoulders slumped. 'So there's no way we can pass the Test. The Dolphins will just take one look at you and they'll reject you. It doesn't matter what you say or do.'

My sister sighed and patted my head. 'I don't know what you ate to make you this stupid, but it's working. You're using the wrong way to make people like you. Let them like you not because you're like them, but because you're you.'

'So how are you going to do the Test?' I said.

'I'm never going to learn how to be a *cheem ang mo*. So I'm just going to be me. Do you love me?'

'Of course,' I said.

'I like being Singaporean,' my sister said. 'It's fun. If I go do the Test, be very Singaporean, I think they'll like me too.'

'But you were yourself in the first Test, and they utterly rejected you,' I said. 'If you do the same thing again, you're going to fail for sure.'

'Ah, but I not going to do the same thing,' my sister said. 'This time I prepared. I know what Singaporean thing to do to make them like me.'

'What are you going to do?' I said.

'I don't want to waste time explaining it to you, I got to go cook now. You very blur, it take too long for me to explain it to you.'

'You can't expect me to let you take the Test without knowing what the hell you'll do!'

'Just trust me. I always been very popular. Everywhere I go people like me. In school people like me. I come to Oxford, Steve like me. Everywhere you go, you always don't know how to make friends. I remember at kindergarten, you always sit by yourself reading Enid Blyton. All your other friends playing Pepsi Cola 1–2–3, but you always like bookworm under the pong-pong tree. Then you come to me and complain you don't understand why nobody want to friend you.' My sister rolled her eyes. 'Sometimes you can be such a blur face. I always better at being popular than you. My friends' IQ higher than yours.'

'You're so clueless,' I said. 'You have no idea how badly you did when you were talking to the Dolphins. They were making fun of you all the time and you didn't even know. If I let you go in like you are, they'll destroy you.'

'Don't worry, I have Special Plan. Trust me, I know how to pass the Test. I don't even need three months to train. I can take the Test tomorrow.' My sister sighed. 'You know how many episodes of my Taiwanese drama serial I've missed since I've been here? Thirteen! I want to go back to Singapore as soon as I can.'

So the next day I rang Draco Sidious and said, 'We're ready.'

'Are you sure?' Dr Sidious said. 'You've only been training her for two weeks. Most training periods take at least three months.'

'My sister wants to take the Test,' I said. 'Nothing I can say will make her change her mind.'

When my sister walked on to the set, she found the Poncey Dolphins discussing one of Oxford's pet pop-culture conundrums, which is, 'What did Mulder do when he was at Oxford?'

'I think he only did an undergraduate degree in Psychology,' Thomas said. 'I read somewhere that Chris Carter didn't want to give Mulder a doctorate, to make him more like a normal bloke.'

'I beg to differ,' Tamsin said, 'I think Mulder did a doctorate at Oxford. You need a doctorate in order to become a profiler at the ISU. Also, Mulder's always described as a psychologist, which implies that he must have at least a Master's.'

'Maybe he received his doctorate from another university,' Gemima said. 'But it's all a mystery, really. The only thing we know for sure is that he was at Oxford in 1983, because in *Fire*, Phoebe says to him, "Did you leave your sense of humour in Oxford ten years ago?" But what did he do after that?'

'I think he did an undergraduate degree, then went on to work for the FBI,' Thomas said. 'In *Pilot*, he says he was recruited by the FBI straight out of Oxford.'

All this time, my sister had been standing there silently, unable to join in this bonding-by-pedantry ritual because of her total ignorance of the Oxford system. Ugh! She said she had a plan. I hoped it involved more than just standing there like some drinks trolley.

'Maybe he did his Master's at Oxford,' my sister said.

Ugh! That was definitely the wrong thing to say. You proved yourself to be an Oxonian insider by correctly listing the esoteric name for your graduate degree, e.g. the MSt (which the hip called a 'M Stud'), MPhil, Mjur, MSc, MLitt, MTh, but you never said that you were doing a Master's.

My sister's words immediately branded her as an outsider. The Dolphins acted as if her suggestion was a huge white dollop of pigeon shit that had dropped out of nowhere, and the most sophisticated, civilized response would be to ignore it.

'Yes, that episode bothers me,' Tamsin said. 'In *Pilot*, Mulder says that he's skilled at applying behavioural models to criminal behaviour, which everyone presumes is something he learnt at Oxford. But the Psychology degree is not psychiatry. Mulder would not have done any practical work on criminal behaviour even if he had done a doctorate.'

A man walked on to the set towards the Dolphins, wearing his scholar's gown.

'Hi, I'm Richard,' he said. 'I'm visiting from Merton. My tutor invited me for dinner at High Table.'

'We were just talking about Mulder and what he did at Oxford,' Thomas said.

'Hmmm, yes,' Richard said. 'Some times I wonder if Mulder really studied here. For one thing, his diploma in *Dreamland II* says "Oxford University", rather than "The University of Oxford", which is the correct nomenclature.'

'How sharp of you to have picked that up,' Gemima said.

Richard grinned. 'It would be a pity if Mulder *didn't* study at Oxford. Sometimes, when my brain wearies of metaphysics, I amuse myself by thinking how Spooky Mulder might have been inspired to investigate the paranormal during his sojourn at Oxford. Dun Scotus allegedly glides round the old library at Merton, feetless.'

'Why's that?' Tamsin said.

'They raised the floor a few centuries ago,' Richard said, 'which is how that great Scholastic thinker misplaced his feet.'

Since they were totally ignoring her, my sister decided to barge into the conversation. She took something out of her bag – a plastic statue of the Merlion, a creature with the head of a lion and the body of a fish.

'I got bring present for all of you from Singapore,' she said.

'Goodness, what *is* this monstrosity?' Gemima stared at the green knick-knack.

'I know you all like old old things. Let me tell you an old, old story, since I know you Oxford people like that. Long time ago, in the thirteenth century, there was a prince called Sang Nila Utama. He was very rich but very bored, so one day, he thought, "Oh, I very bored, I want to adventure." So he sail on his ship, sail sail sail sail sail, then suddenly one day, got big storm! They throw their food away, but the boat still sinking. They throw their clothes away, but the boat still sinking. Everyone very frightened, thought they die for sure. Then the captain beg Sang Nila Utama, "Throw away your crown!" Sang Nila Utama throw away his heavy crown, and then, like magic, the storm stopped.' My sister grinned at the Dolphins.

Tamsin yawned. 'Keep talking,' she said. 'I always yawn when I'm interested.'

'After the clouds go away, they saw this island – Temasek. Sang Nila Utama like the island a lot – got birds, and fruit and many pretty flowers! Then suddenly –' My sister roared and Gemima nearly jumped out of her Jimmy Choo pumps, 'he saw this BIG animal. It was so fierce, so strong, he never saw anything like it before. He asked his advisors what the animal was, and they said, "It's a lion." So Sang Nila Utama decided to call the island a new name, "Singa-pura", which means "Lion City". That's how my country got its name.'

I finally saw what my sister's plan was, and it made me ill. When I first arrived at Oxford and complained about how no one took an interest in what I had to say, she would tell me, 'Your problem is that you try to get them interested in you by talking about English things. But they're always going to know more about English things than you, so you will always lose out. But you know more about Singapore than them. If you tell them all the interesting things about you and Singapore, then they will become interested in you.'

My sister waved the plastic Merlion. 'I got a Merlion each for all of you. It's such an interesting name, and you Oxford people like old, old names. Merlion is from the old language – Sanskrit. It puts together the Sanskrit word "Singa Pura" and "Temasek", which means "sea town".'

The Dolphins acted like my sister was this Mongol at the

gate, who was making loud and annoying noises. It was like they thought that if they ignored her and stayed on the right side of the moat, she would eventually go back to the wilderness whence she sprang.

'Well, it's always pleasant to meet a fellow scholar from another college,' Thomas said to Richard. 'So what did Merton give you for receiving a distinction for your Prelims? St L'leh gave me a hundred quid and the privilege of dining at High Table once a month.'

'I received a book prize – gift certificates from Blackwells,' Richard said. 'They also gave me an odd historical right. I am proud to announce that as a result of my notable results for my Prelims, I now own the perpetual right to pasture one cow on Christ Church Meadow.'

I looked at Draco Sidious. He stared at the stage, his face inscrutable. I wondered if I should tell him to stop the Test. My sister looked totally calm on stage, but I was on the edge of despair. Maybe I should just pull the cord and eject my sister from her tailspin dive before she crashed and burned.

My sister flipped open her basket and pulled out a dumpling.

'Try this,' she said to Thomas. 'You'll love it.' The dumpling was wrapped in green bamboo leaves, tied with twine. My sister swung the triangular dumpling from its string, chanting, 'Try it, try it,' like she was trying to hypnotize Thomas into eating it.

Thomas realized that my sister was probably not going to leave him alone until he ate it, so took the dumpling and unwrapped it. He took a tentative nibble of the sticky rice and raised his eyebrow. Then he took a larger bite.

'This is amazing!' Thomas said.

'See, I told you that you'll like it!' my sister said.

So that was her secret weapon. I had never met anyone who could resist my sister's rice dumplings. As you sank your teeth into her culinary masterpiece, you would encounter the sinfully oily ooze of the marinated pork belly, tempered with the mushy sweetness of the green beans. The softness of the beans was perfectly balanced with the pleasure of grinding the roasted peanuts, and the salty duck egg yolk made the dumpling a sensational mix of contrasting flavours and textures – sweet, sour, salty, mushy, crunchy – all combining into a taste explosion.

'This dumpling also got interesting story,' my sister said. 'You eat it during the dragon boat festival. There was a poet called Qu Yuan. He did many good things for the people, but the bad people in the King's court didn't like him, so they kicked him out. After that, he went round China, writing about all the bad things he saw. But one day, he was so sad about all the bad things he saw that he jumped into the Mi Luo River and killed himself. When the fishermen found out, they got in their boats to look for him. That's how the dragon boat festival started. But they couldn't find his body. So the people threw the rice dumplings into the river to protect Qu Yuan, so that the fish would eat the dumplings and not bite his body.'

My sister passed round the dumplings to the rest of the Oxonians, who devoured them like piranhas.

'Mmmmm, this is quite heavenly,' Thomas said. 'We haven't see you around here before. Are you from another College?'

'I just came from Singapore,' my sister said. 'Where do you come from?'

'My father is Welsh and my mother is English,' Thomas said.

'Is he a sheep shagger?' my sister said.

'I beg your pardon?!' Thomas said, stunned that my sister would suggest that his father enjoyed sexual relations with livestock.

'My sister tell me in Wales the weather very cold. And it's

very boring there, nothing to do. So all the men go and shag sheep.'

Draco Sidious laughed. 'Did you really tell her that?' he said.

I smiled weakly. I never really explained to my sister that sheep shagging was actually a form of bestiality, and I guess she mistook sheep shagging for some quaint British hobby, like bell-ringing or Morris dancing. I felt bad. My sister had finally made some progress towards acceptance with her stunning dumplings, and I had screwed it up with some careless comment I made two years ago.

This was getting way too painful to watch, so I yanked the cord.

'Could we stop the Test now?' I said to Dr Sidious. 'I think my sister's done the best she can.'

Watching the Test was like seeing both sides of my soul act out against each other. It was like my soul was divorced, East from West. Cause: irreconcilable differences. I didn't realize this until I saw it on stage, but for the first time, I could see how much contempt my Western side had for my Eastern side. I felt guilty, hating myself for hating myself. I ejected my sister from the Test because I knew it would be impossible for her to pass. Racism in Oxford was immovably embedded in everything around me, you could hear it in the clipped accents, taste it in the vintage wine, see it in the medieval battlements – those proud war-like stones, protecting the noble English from barbaric invasions. I could feel myself sinking into the Slough of Despond, for I suddenly realized that there would be no place for me among the élite in England. If I really wanted to soar to the starry heights, I would have to go elsewhere. But where? Not to Singapore. I had too much contempt for the stupidity and cultural cluelessness that I saw in Singaporeans like my sister. Even if I became Singapore's answer to Milton, I wouldn't value that. It would be like becoming Queen of the

197

Slugs. You might be the ruler of your habitat but you're still at the bottom of the food chain. Satan's words from *Paradise Lost* echoed in my head:

> Me miserable! which way shall I flie?
> Which way I flie is Hell; my self am Hell

16

Dagobah Hall sat in the city centre, sedate in her monastic calm. In a city where homicidal bus drivers, suicidal cyclists and brash Italian motorists did their best to cause deaths while navigating the baffling one-way traffic system, the Hall's creamy citadel was a sanctuary where leisurely immortals dreamt.

This afternoon, Dagobah filled the floral air with her special music. Her towers, bell-swarmed and lark-charmed, sang an orchestral melody that calmed my soul. Dagobah Hall was the place in Oxford where I went to see beauty that would heal me. It was the place where I first saw the blue shadows. We never had blue shadows in Singapore, it was a wondrous British sight, blue snow glowing in the moonlight. Oxford looked so magical that night, like a city of aquatint. On that night, the snow fell on me like star dust, and I felt like an angel, stretching out my moon-silvered arms to the sky.

I entered the St Cassiodorus room. Beneath the branchy roof, the sunlight poured in from the clerestory windows like a white stream, proving that this was indeed the dwelling place for the 'learned imps' in Spenser's *Faerie Queene*.

Professor Ad-oy emerged from an alcove like one of those

allegorical creatures. He looked startled. 'My, you do look different.'

'This morning I woke up and I was scared to look in the mirror,' I said. 'I was afraid I might find that I have no reflection. That I might have turned into a devil like them. I don't know if I can keep doing the Tests any more. I don't like the way it's changing the way I feel about my sister. I don't like the way it's changing me.'

'Come, come, try this cup of tea and we'll see what we can do to make you feel better,' Professor Ad-oy said, pouring the tea into a shining cup. 'I've slightly modified this blend since the last time I saw you. Now it has Gotu Kola, one of the most important Indian Ayurvedic rejuvenating tonic herbs.'

I stared out of the window, not wanting to see my new image reflected in the silver teapot.

'You know that you are still welcome to join me as my assistant,' Professor Ad-oy said. 'What is holding you back?'

Today, from the tower top, Oxford looked like a city in decay, her ancient walls stained by coal smoke and pitted by acid rain. From this pinnacle, I could see the emperors' heads on Broad Street. Those magnificent stone faces, worn by time and harsh weather, now looked, as John Betjeman once said, like 'illustrations in a medical textbook on skin diseases'. I sighed, feeling as worn down as those eroded stumps.

'I can't give up my friends and family,' I said. 'I wish I had the strength but I can't. They would freak out if I turned down the Mammon job.'

The last time I looked out of this window, the Thames raged in Fall's fury. I had watched the punts drift by as the sunset burned the river red. The waters became a wet inferno, the river crimson with autumnal foliage, leaves like floating flames, burning in the sun-sparked water like liquid light. But the events in the Fall had brought about my fall, and now winter glazed the river, turning the Thames into a rich, cold, silver chain.

'Have you ever tried praying about this?' Professor Ad-oy said.

I shook my head. Just off Broad Street was a small church, with an empty graveyard where cold yews leant wearily against the tombstones. 'I don't know how,' I said.

'Let me teach you how to pray as the mystics did,' Professor Ad-oy said. 'Hesychasm is a method of prayer that our Order has adopted from the Eastern Orthodox monks. It is deceptively simple. You focus on a passage in the Catechism, and when thoughts enter to distract you, you gently let them go and float your attention back to the Word.' He frowned. 'How can I explain it in a way that your generation can understand?' He stared at the candle swinging overhead, its flame casting dark figures against the stone walls like Plato's shadow show. 'I have it! Your mind is like a movie screen. As you progress in life, you collect more and more images. Pictures of friends, lovers, mentors, enemies, footage of successes and failures. And you also build up a sound track, for example, of memorable conversations, and . . . songs you love. These images and sounds occupy your mind, and shape who you are. You need to let go of all these images if you want to find peace.

'It is only when you empty your self, let go of all the pictures and noise that clutter your mind, that you can be filled with something beyond what you can achieve by your own effort.

'Put your thoughts to death, kill your self, and enter the dark night of the soul. Become black, like a blank movie screen. Then you can hear what you never knew you never heard.

'Prayer is not talking to God. It is being soundless in God. Contemplative prayer is inner silence. The Eastern divines understood this – as Lao Tzu once said, "Silence is the Great Revelation." Hesychasm comes from the Greek *hesychia*, which means "state of quiet".' Professor Ad-oy got up. 'Let me leave you alone to your meditations.'

I opened the Catechism and read:

Q. What is the kingdom of heaven like unto?
A. As saith the LORD in the Gospels: the kingdom of heaven is like unto a merchant man, seeking goodly pearls: When he had found one pearl of great price, he went and sold all that he had, and bought it.

I closed my eyes and meditated on that – the pearl of great price. *Pearl of great price. Pearl of great price.* My mind started drifting, in and around it, and I saw . . .
. . . those teeth. The Mammon logo rushing towards me. The Red Dragon, his fangs bared, glowing white like pearls. I shook my head. Focus on the reading, I told myself. I turned to the next page:

Q. What need I sell to enter the kingdom of heaven?
A. As saith the LORD in the Gospels: If any *man* come to me, and hate not his father, and mother, and wife, and children, and brethren, and sisters, yea, and his own life also, he cannot be my disciple. For what shall it profit a man, if he shall gain the whole world, and lose his own soul?

So Christ was like Mammon. He demanded that I give up my friends, family, my life itself before he would give me the kingdom, the pearl of great price. But what a painful price to pay . . .
I shut my eyes and contemplated His words – *hate his brethren and sisters* – my mind drifted into how . . .

*

202

My sister was the only person I could, literally, talk shit with. Every Saturday afternoon after lunch, I would sit on the toilet and give my sister a complete description of what came out of my ass, e.g. colour, size, texture and density (i.e., whether it floated or sank straight to the bottom), the full spec. Our conversations revolved around catching up with the various types of dumps we had had during the week. Like six months ago, I was sitting in the bog, moaning to my sister on the phone, 'Oh God, oh God. This is so painful. I'm definitely going to chew my food better from now on.' I was having one of those dumps where the turd lacerated my anus as it crawled its way out.

'What does it look like?'

I got up and looked into the toilet bowl. 'God, it's so long it sticks up out of the bowl. I've even left a skid mark down the side. It's as thick as my toe and a foot long. It's a Python Poopie.'

'Hah, but it's not as bad as the shit I had yesterday,' my sister said. 'Yesterday, I shit like dry vomiting. It was all different colours – a little red, a little brown, a little yellow. Very watery. If I wasn't sitting on the toilet, everyone would think I just vomited in it.'

'That is strange. Most of the time your shit is pretty small and dry. You normally shit like a gerbil.' My sister usually plops tiny round turds that look like hamster pellets and make delicate splashing sounds when they hit the water. I call them 'Cork Crap' because the little poops float on top of the water and refuse to be flushed. 'Most of my shit this week has been pretty good. I've been having all these *Star Wars* dumps. The crap is green and looks like Yoda. And I felt so good afterwards, it was like it had given me special powers.'

At this point, Steve walked past and complained about me shitting with the door open. He said – believe it or not – that it's gross.

'Like you fart theme tunes from TV sitcoms and piss out of the window, but *I'm* gross?!' I said.

'What I do is endearing. It makes people laugh,' Steve said. 'What *you* do just smells bad.'

One day, when Steve was rehearsing his favourite party trick – drinking beer and farting the tune from *Friends* – he said, 'I just had an epiphany. I don't know why.' He paused dramatically, and looked straight into my eyes. 'People read books for the same reasons that they make friends.' Then he went back to farting.

You read to hear someone express feelings that you thought only you felt. Feelings about the shit in your life. You read because it reminds you that you are not alone.

The first time my sister killed a live chicken, she chopped off its head but it wouldn't die. It just ran out of the kitchen and flew around the living-room, spraying blood all over the walls.

I shook my head. This was impossible. I was going round in circles like a decapitated chicken – my sister, Steve, Mammon, my sister, etc. My brain was like an MTV video gone berserk, a montage of photos, lightning cuts, flashing one after the other, bombarding me, until I couldn't even see what was in front of me any more, just this jumble of images and music. I couldn't hear, couldn't think, couldn't breathe, all I could do was sit there, paralysed, as these movies came crashing down, wave after wave.

When I was seven, during school assembly, I got a detention because I forgot to wear my name-tag.

When my sister found out that I would have to stay back after school, during recess, she folded her shirt sleeves up three times (we were only allowed to fold them up once) and took off her school badge. The prefect booked her for those two offences and gave her a detention too.

When I asked my sister why she broke the rules on purpose, she said it was because she didn't want to spend the afternoon without me.

I pushed my sister's face from my mind. I looked at the book before me and read, *For what shall it profit a man, if he shall gain the whole world, and lose his own soul?*

We placed two white mice, Leo and Kate, on a sponge and floated them in our bathtub. Steve threw an ice cube at the sponge and shouted, 'Iceberg! Abandon the *Titanic*!' I threw a cube at Kate. It hit her and she fell off the sponge. I shouted at Leo, 'Look, your girlfriend's drowning! Don't just stand there, you useless rodent. Jump in and save her!'

I unplugged the bathtub, creating a vortex that sent the mice spinning towards the plug hole.

Celine Dion was playing on the stereo, on volume level nine (the stereo goes up to ten). We sang 'My Heart Will Go On' as the mice drowned.

Whenever we tell our friends what we did, they always say that one day we'll end up as serial killers.

I smiled. But then I shook my head, and let go of Steve. I murmured, *For what shall it profit a man, if he shall gain the whole world, and lose his own soul?*

When I was sixteen, my sister and I went to the hawker centre. The hawker was chopping a duck and putting the slices on to some fragrant rice.

'I'd like to order a Man-Well-Hung,' I said.

'No Man-Well-Hung,' the hawker said. 'Only got chicken lice, duck lice and fried lice.'

'I'd like a bowl of the Come-Of-Some-Young-Man,' my sister said.

'No Come-Of-Some-Young-Man,' the hawker said. 'Only got chicken lice, duck lice and fried lice.'

I stifled a giggle and blanked my sister from my mind. The mantra echoed in my head: *For what shall it profit a man, if he shall gain the whole world, and lose his own soul?*

Finally, all the images faded, dimmed by the Word. Images still flickered across my mind, but they were dim, like twilight shadows dancing across a smooth wall. For the first time in my life, my soul was filled with sepulchral silence, empty of the voices of those I loved.

I opened my eyes, and saw the emblem of St Cassiodorus hanging on the wall – the bronze asp curled around a wooden stake. Suddenly, I had a vision of Christ, his sun-bronzed body wrapped around a wooden cross. His limbs contorted into the most tortuous of positions – hard human bones forced, yanked around a wooden stake, a man being twisted on a stick like a snake.

I looked into His eyes and He was crying.

Those are pearls that were His eyes.

I had never seen eyes like those. Eyes that I knew must have surveyed vast kingdoms, eyes which ruled over golden domes and glass citadels, eyes that the angels and seraphims gazed at with unending worship.

I looked at those eyes and saw a love that I had never felt before. In the pond of that sad tear, I saw the reflection of myself. He was there on the cross because of me, for me. This was a love that would sacrifice all the kingdoms of the world for me. In those shining eyes of pain, I saw my Paradise, a treasure that glowed like pure water, the pearl of great price, the pearl of His eye.

After the Tests, my soul felt like it had been charred by

the Red Dragon. It was cold and black, like coal. But now in the silence, my black heart sat like a mineral on the altar and the light from the pearls warmed it. It ignited, and suddenly exploded in the fire of love. I saw myself as Tock Seng must have in his dream. Finally, I was fully myself, Chiah Deng, the lamp, the fire of my family. My soul blazed with the fiery seraphim, singing and rejoicing, consumed by the love of Christ, bursting like a sweet red flame.

17

I swept out of Dagobah Hall in a wave of ecstasy. I felt so calm, so centred, like I had finally attained Jedi Knight mastery of the Force. I felt so Zenned out that I was vaguely tempted to see if I could elevate the Honda Civic on Broad Street with the sheer power of my mind.

I was supposed to meet Steve and my sister at six. I wondered how they would take the news of my conversion. Steve would probably do some piss-taking – like, 'So now you're a Christian, what's your next move? You going to buy one of those hideous giant hats like the grannies wear on *Songs of Praise*?'

But I didn't care. I felt totally tripped out, hopped up. I felt so light, I had to look at my feet as I walked along the pavement to check that I wasn't levitating. Don't worry about Steve, I told myself. You are a transformed individual. You are a cloud of peace; you are a bubble of serenity floating on a sea of happiness; nothing can upset you, you're like the Teflon girl, they can throw anything at you and it won't stick.

Happy, happy, happy.

Wheeeeeee!!!!!!

I am a puff of bliss.

I felt even more virtuous than Mother Teresa, like right

then, as I passed under the Bridge of Sighs, I wished there was a leper there just so I could kneel down to lick clean the soles of his feet.

We had arranged to meet at the Turf Tavern. You walk towards this seven-hundred-year-old tavern via a long, narrow alley, the kind of dark and winding passage that you only go down if you're in the mood for getting raped. But once you've passed the barrels and emerged from damp black, you'll find the beer garden and immediately be overdosed on Ye Olde English charm.

Steve sat by one of the long, brown bench tables, the kind of tables you can imagine Friar Tuck getting merry at with tankard after tankard of ale.

'Greetings and salutations,' I said to Steve. 'How doeth my noble squire on this lovely evening?'

'Prithee, I fare pretty well,' Steve said. 'Your sister is in the bathroom purifying her innards.'

I sat down and gave him a moment to drink in the aura of serenity.

'What? Why are you looking at me like that?' Steve said. 'Are you stoned?'

'Don't you notice it?' I said.

'What?'

'The Glow.' I sat there, hoping Steve would be blinded by the blaze of my inner radiance.

'What? The Glow?' His eyes suddenly widened. 'Oh my God! Who – how – when! – did this happen?'

I stuck out my bottom lip. 'I'm not pregnant.'

'So what's this about the Glow? I thought only pregnant women glowed.'

'And mystics,' I said. 'They glow too, in the fire of love, the *Incendium Amoris*.'

'Oh, I'm sorry, you're obviously talking in Martian. Let me take out my decoder so that it can translate your alien-speak into something that I can comprehend.' Steve took out his Walkman and pressed the 'Play' button.

Ignore Sir Sarkie, I told myself. Remember, you are the Teflon girl.

'I had a mystical experience.' I told Steve what had happened to me at Dagobah Hall. 'It's incredible, like nothing I've felt before. I feel so beatific, I tell you if I farted right now, I would release a fragrant cloud that would smell like a relaxing blend of lavender, neroli and ylang ylang.' I closed my eyes and smiled. 'I am a puff of bliss.'

Steve cleared his throat. 'Uh, yeah, sure.' He nodded. 'You are a puff of bliss.' Steve had the same look the time I plonked down ten quid for 'H_5O', a shampoo that supposedly contained secret chemicals patented by Nobel-Prize-winning scientists. After I used the shampoo, I could see how it had obviously given my hair more body and an almost supernatural shine, but Steve just looked at my head and said, 'Uh, yeah, that looks much better' – but I could see that he really couldn't see anything different.

'I'm sorry, but I just don't get religion,' Steve said. 'I know some people can get really into it, but for me religion is like *Star Trek* or collecting garden gnomes. It's this weird interest that I don't think I'll ever be able to comprehend. But I'm happy for you.' He waved his hand at one of the barmaids, who was mopping up the mess that some rugger bugger had barfed all over the floor. 'Hey there, my lovely serving wench. Send us a pint of your finest Boddingtons to celebrate my friend's mountain-top epiphany.'

'I'm working overtime tonight, but still getting minimum wage,' the waitress said. 'I don't have to take any shite from you, Steve Boulter.'

Steve raised an eyebrow. 'Well, I guess I won't be voting you in as Employee of the Month.'

She threw her puke-stained mop at him. 'Stick this up your arse.'

Steve caught the handle before it hit his head. He leaned

over to me and whispered conspiratorially, 'You know, call me paranoid, but I get a slight feeling that she might still be upset with me for dumping her.'

'Give her a break,' I said. 'You can be such a wanker sometimes. You ought to do something about your "bang them and let them bleed" attitude towards women. There's more to life than being a poster boy for *Loaded*.' I guess that's why I never got together with Steve. It wasn't that I didn't find him attractive – I did, but I also knew him well enough to realize that he couldn't be in a serious romantic relationship for more than three months. Steve was like one of those horny chihuahuas. You know they're cute, you adore them to death, but you know that they're really not marriage material. 'You probably think that monogamy is a kind of wood they use to make furniture with.'

'Fuck, don't go all Billy Graham on me,' Steve said. 'Is this how it's going to be, now that you've been *born again*?' He said those last words in a mock American accent. 'Are you going to try to get people to sign petitions against Disney because they tried to put lesbians on prime-time television?'

'What are you talking about?'

'Remember Bible Bob?' Steve said.

'Bible Bob was a psychotic freakoid,' I said. Bob Jones was an American exchange student we met in our first year at St L'leh. He spent most of his free time at Oxford writing letters to the director of ITV, complaining about the 'lasciviousness' of shows like *Blind Date*. He was a whiz at physics, and after graduation we heard rumours that he was using his expert knowledge to build bombs to destroy abortion clinics. 'Not all Christians are racist, redneck, card-carrying members of the NRA.'

'But still, you've got to make *some* lifestyle changes if you want to be baptized into the C of E.' Steve lit a cigarette. 'You'll have to give up fags and shags for tea and sympathy.' He smirked. 'Your life will have to go from being a lager saga to an Aga saga. You'll have to go to Blackwells to exchange your copy of *Bridget Jones* for *The Rector's Wife.*'

'Shut your gob, that's not true,' I said. 'There's nothing in the Bible against shagging. I'll challenge you to find a verse that says, "Thou shalt not shag thy neighbour".'

'Well, they didn't call it shagging in those days,' Steve said. 'But there are lots of prohibitions in the Bible against fornication, lasciviousness and evil concupiscence. Which is like the King James way of saying "shagging". Now *that* I remember from my tutes with Professor Ad-oy.'

I hadn't considered all this. I had no problem adopting Christianity, but did I have to embrace the Church as well? Would I have to become like those women in *Songs of Praise*? Would I have to move to Middle England and spend my days ironing tea towels, making marmalade and scribbling notes to the milkman? Would I have to *buy a Labrador*? I couldn't even handle the responsibility of owning a house plant, but if I joined the Church, would the ladies expect me to get a dog so that I could walk its legs off on some steep, allergy-inducing hill?

Troubling questions, all these, and I would have pondered on them longer were it not for the loud arrival of my sister.

'Come, come, let me show you what I bought today!' my sister said, plonking down a large shopping bag. 'I tell you, after the Test, I was so depressed. I thought – *ai-yah*, I'm so useless, everything also don't know how to do. So Steve told me to go out and have fun. So I went to Broad Street and joined one of those tour groups. *Ai-yoh*, so *xin ku*, so suffering! Walk, walk, walk – look at old building. Walk, walk, walk – look at old church. Walk, walk, walk – look at another old building. Like this for two hours, I was so tired, so bored, I nearly cried.'

'I'm sorry you had a bad day,' I said.

My sister grinned. 'No! But happy part of story coming! The tour group stopped outside the Edinburgh Woollen Mill. I went inside and found this skirt.' She took out a red tartan skirt. 'It's for children. But I can wear it, since I much smaller than the *ang mo* women. Children's clothes here got no VAT, so very cheap. I was so happy. I can buy so many clothes here, all children's sizes, no sales tax!'

I looked at her face and her joy was genuine, almost celestially ecstatic. Whoever said that money couldn't buy happiness had obviously never met my sister.

'Well, I'm glad you found a bargain because we're going to have to live on a budget from now on,' I told my sister. 'I don't think I'm going to continue with the Tests. I want to go and work for Professor Ad-oy.'

I started telling my sister about what happened to me at Dagobah Hall, but she cut me off before I could finish, snapping, 'Don't be silly, you can't be a Christian.'

'What do you mean?'

'You're Chinese, you can't be a Christian. You have to worship your ancestors, not Jesus. You have to be *xiao xun*.'

'What's that?' Steve said.

My sister drew the pictogram for *xiao* on a coaster. 'The top part of the word means "the old generation". And the bottom part of the word means "child", or "the younger generation".'

'Yeah, the bottom squiggle does look like a baby with its arms stretched out,' Steve said. 'Cool.'

'The word shows that you cannot separate yourself from

213

your ancestors,' my sister said. 'You have to fulfil your duty to them and your parents. If not, bad things will happen to you. To be unfilial is the worst evil a Chinese person can do.'

'She's right, you know. You have an Asian duty to obey your parents.' Steve put on a mock serious look.

'Shut your gob. As if *you* know anything about being Chinese.' I turned to my sister and jerked my thumb at Steve. 'He's the type of idiot *ang mo* who puts milk in his jasmine tea.'

'Hey, I'm not completely ignorant. I'm a citizen of the global village. I've seen *Mulan*. It's all about the lass who took her father's place in the army. That's a classic example of Chinese filial piety. See, I know about Asian values.' Steve smirked again.

'Wind me up as much as you like, I'm not going to be perturbed,' I said. 'You are looking at a new Chiah Deng. I am a pool of tranquillity, I am the quiet shadow of night, I am . . .' I faltered as I tried to think of more images of calm.

'A load of bollocks floating on a sea of shite?' Steve added.

'Could you lay off the irony for just one moment? I'm serious. It's like all my life I've been so focused on what I *should* be doing, I don't even know what I really *want*. For the first time in my life I've found something that makes *me*, not my parents, happy. I want to help Professor Ad-oy work on the *Incendium Amoris*. I don't want to be Huang Tingjian and only be remembered for doing shit work for my family.'

'Who's Huang Tingjian?' Steve said.

'He's one of the Twenty-Four Paragons of Filial Piety,' I said. 'When I was a little sage in Singapore, my grandfather, to lull me to sleep with boredom, would tell me stories of these Twenty-Four Paragons, who were the heroes of Chinese civilization. Huang Tingjian was one of them. He was a general in the army, but spent most of his time emptying his mother's chamberpot. Then there was Cai Shun, who was so devoted to Mummy that if she wanted to call him home, all she had to do was bite her finger and he would feel her pain and run back to their grass hut. And let's not forget Wang Xiang, who nearly died because he spent all winter lying naked on a frozen pond to thaw the ice, so that he could catch fish to feed his Mum. But the best story my grandfather told me comes not from China, but Korea. It's about the man who cured his father of a fatal illness by boiling his only son and feeding the soup to the ailing patriarch.'

'Ach, that's disgusting!' Steve said.

'Asian values are all about sacrificing the life of the child for the parent, and I don't want any part of that any more,' I said. 'I'm sick of being the host for my parents, just standing there and watching them suck the blood out of me while my life passes by.'

'But the Korean story got perfect logic,' my sister said. 'If you kill a child, and still have a father, he can have another child. But if you kill the father, then you cannot have any more children. The old is more important than the young. If you're unfilial, terrible punishments will *polong* on your head. You remember what Nichiren Daishonin say?'

'Yeah, sure, but that's just all myths made up by some thirteenth-century monk,' I replied.

'Who is he? What did he say?' Steve asked.

'Nichiren Daishonin was the founder of the largest Buddhist sect in Japan. He wrote this famous letter listing all the horrific things that happened to people who were unfilial, everything from leprosy to being trapped in a burning boat on a river to Hell. My favourite is the story of Pan-fu, who cursed his mother and was eaten by a giant snake.'

I took out my Mammon CorpS business card and tore it

in half. 'But that's exactly why I don't want to work for Mammon CorpS. I don't want to be devoured by the flying snake.' I tossed the paper shreds into the ashtray. They burned on the glowing embers of a discarded cigarette.

'Blood is thicker than Jesus,' my sister said. 'You cannot escape your skin. If you're not *xiao xun*, you're going to end up like Yu-meng and get struck by lightning.'

'Well, you'd better stay away from me so that when I get zapped you won't get hurt by any stray volts of electricity that might shoot out from my cursed body.' I got up. 'I can't take this any more. I didn't expect you to support me, but I thought that you would at least *try* to understand my decision.' Suddenly the pool of tranquillity welled up into a storm and I left the table before they could see me burst.

I spent the rest of the evening walking the streets of Oxford alone. Everyone else seemed to belong to a group – there were the Union hacks, the Oriel boaties, the Rhodes scholars, the townies from Blackbird Leys, the rugby Blues – everyone roamed the streets in packs, except me.

Even lepers have colonies, but I seemed to have no tribe to call my own. I walked past Dixons. In the window was a row of TVs, all beaming out *Songs of Praise*. Kevin Woodford was interviewing some Laura Ashley model in a creeper-clad rectory. She was showing how she made the church candles from beeswax that she collected from the hive in her garden. Members of the local brass band waved in the background.

I could see my reflection on the glass wall between me and the TVs. I could see both the woman's perfect peach complexion and my own Oriental image. My sister was right. I could never become a Christian, because I could never belong to the Laura Ashley tribe. I could not imagine spending the rest of my life baking Delia Smith cakes to sell at local fêtes, driving my children to school in a muddy

Volvo and getting irrationally upset if the BBC messed around with Radio 4 even one tinsy winsy bit. Hell would be being a Bridget Jones trapped in a Joanna Trollope novel.

That evening, I wrote a letter to Professor Ad-oy explaining why I couldn't be his assistant:

My friend Tock Seng told me once about a temple he visited in Korea.

It was built by King Chongjo, a member of the Koryo Dynasty, who, like all the descendants of the Divine Sea Dragon, had a dragon scale in his armpit.

One day, after listening to the Parental Benevolence Sutra (which explained the debt children owe their parents), he decided to build a temple in memory of his father. The night before they finished building the temple, King Chongjo dreamed of a dragon who soared into the sky and received the Pearl of Truth, the Wish-Fulfilling Gem. That's how the temple came to be called the Dragon's Pearl of Truth Temple.

In my parents' house, there are pictures of lions and cranes – and Red Dragons biting shining globes. They have always taught me that these creatures, like lotus flowers and pomegranates, are symbols of Heaven.

I will be going to Singapore to complete the last part of my Test with Mammon CorpS. Perhaps if I pass the Test, I will find it after all – the pearl of great price, the glowing orb in the mouth of the Red Dragon.

18

'Why you want me to meet you early for?' I said.

My sister arrived at the hawker centre wearing the unofficial Singapore uniform of T-shirt and bermudas. She would have looked like a hawker, only the hawkers differentiated themselves from their customers by having pouch bags strapped to their waists, where they put their change.

'I have to warn you, Ma Ma and Pa Pa think Steve is your boyfriend,' my sister said. 'They're very upset.'

'Why?' I said. 'We're not going out.'

'*Ai-yah*, you know them. Every boy friend you have they think is your boyfriend. They afraid if you have *ang mo* boyfriend, you get married to him, never come back to Singapore.' She sat down and rubbed her hand against the concrete stool. The table and stools were cemented into the ground – a feature of the older hawker centres in Singapore designed, I suppose, to prevent customers from stealing the restaurant furniture, back in the colonial days when Singaporeans might have been poor and *kia-su* enough to want to decorate their flats with patio furniture.

I had planned this dinner to introduce Steve to my parents. Now it looked like a recipe for disaster, but at least the food would be good tonight. Ten hawker stores stood before us. Each tiny green-tiled cubicle was a mini-kitchen, equipped with woks and knives, a fiery altar to the culinary gods. This beat going to a restaurant any day. Each stall displayed all its fresh ingredients in glass cases and the cook prepared the meal right in front of your eyes. White steamed chickens and honey-glazed ducks swayed on hooks in the glass cabinet of the Super A-1 Chicken Rice Shop, red snappers blew bubbles in the tank outside Ah Hua's Seafood Stall, while the Lucky Noodle Shop spread out its wide array of pasta: yellow Hokkein *mee* as thick as Rapunzel's hair, rice vermicelli that was white and stringy like the Ancient Mariner's beard, and Cantonese noodles rolled up like a bowl of golden twine.

My sister perked up. '*Oi*, here they come.'

Our parents waddled towards us, their flip-flops slapping against the concrete pavement.

Ma Ma pinched my cheek. '*Wah*, you're so capable,' she said in Chinese. My parents spoke mainly Mandarin and only understood a smattering of English. 'Your new job got so much money, can take Pa Pa and Ma Ma out for dinner. Now you're going to be rich, I don't need to iron or clean any more. Yesterday I went to MaidSearch Agency. Go and apply for a Filipino. She going to arrive in a few months' time, just when you get your first cheque for your new job. So convenient.'

'And I can stop driving that taxi,' Pa Pa said in Chinese, scratching his stomach through his roach-bitten vest. 'All I need to do at home is read newspaper, relax and shake my leg. So *shiok*.'

Ma Ma slapped his bare bicep. '*Ai-yooooh*!' she screeched. 'You *cannot* spend all the day at home. We spend too much time together, we're sure to fight one.' She turned to me. 'Your Pa Pa forgot the last time we honeymoon in Malaysia. Ha! We spent all our time together. Got on each other's nerves *so* quickly. We ended up fighting over everything – the food, how much to tip the Indian man, how many pillows to sleep with – everything.'

Pa Pa made a face at Ma Ma. 'Ha! You think I want to spend so much time with you? You don't have to stay at home, what. After we get a maid, you can stay out all day and all night. Yah, you go Geok Lim's house to play mahjong and sing karaoke, don't stay at home to busybody me around. Then I can have the karaoke machine all to myself, heh heh.' He rubbed his hands in gleeful anticipation.

'Good idea,' Ma Ma said.

'I'm glad you have it all planned out so beautifully,' I said in Chinese, but my sarcasm was definitely lost on my parents, because they just stared at me with genuine delight. So I said, 'You know, I don't exactly *have* the job yet. And many people who take the Test *don't* pass.'

Ma Ma flapped her hand at me. 'You're so smart, you're sure to get the job. You always got what you tried to get. How many people can get into Oxford?'

'Yah, all my colleagues' children, they all apply for Oxford,' Pa Pa said. 'But only *you* smart enough to get the scholarship. You sure can pass the Test one.'

'You sure can get the job,' Ma Ma said. 'No one in Singapore smarter than you.' She adjusted her black Fifties-style glasses, which looked unexpectedly hip on her, since the Fifties had become the 'It' look at the turn of the millennium. The glasses definitely clashed with the kitsch tackiness of her imitation Smurfs T-shirt, which showed Papa and Baby Smurf playing under a tree, beneath a logo that said – 'The Snurfs'.

'Why is that white devil waving at us?' Pa Pa said.

I turned around. It was Steve. 'Oh, that's Steve. I told him to join us for dinner.'

'Why?' Pa Pa said.

'Is he your boyfriend?' Ma Ma asked worriedly.

'He's a good friend. He's here in Singapore, helping me with the Test.'

'Whew, it's so humid I could chew on the air,' Steve said as he arrived at our table. Steam hissed and spat from the wok near us, engulfing us in a fog. 'It's like eating in a sauna.'

'I wanted to bring you to some place that wasn't so clean and sterile,' I said. 'You know, break the Singapore stereotype.' The more affluent might enjoy having their meals in quiet, candlelit, air-conditioned restaurants, but I liked the riotous untidiness of the hawker centres. Black shoeprints tattooed the wet floor and you always had to wave away the fruit flies to stop them from diving into your claypot of curry. Spatulas clanged against woks and cleavers pounded against wooden chopping boards, cracking bones, slicing flesh. You chucked all protocol down the drain outside, as men rested their bare feet on the stools, placed their elbows on raised knees and used their pinkies to dig their ears. Burping, nose-picking, retrieving bits of meat from your teeth with your thumb then swallowing them – all this was allowed and even encouraged in the raw atmosphere of the hawker centre. The hawker centres might never make it to the Michelin or Zagat guides, but there was nowhere else in the country where you could get a full meal, drink and dessert for less than the price of a large café latte at the downtown Starbucks.

'What's his job?' Pa Pa asked me.

'Steve makes TV programmes,' I said.

'He make how much money, huh?' Ma Ma said.

'Not much,' I said.

'How much is not much?' Pa Pa said. 'Twenty thousand a year? Or less?'

'He makes around that,' I said.

'Hurgh, twenty thousand a year. That's less than me.' Pa Pa looked at Steve, unimpressed.

'How many women has he slept with?' Ma Ma said.

I shook my head in disbelief. 'How can you even ask a question like that?!'

'Why not?' Pa Pa said.

'I can't believe I have to explain this to you,' I said. 'You don't even know him. You have no right to ask such personal questions.'

'Yah, but we don't want to catch Aids from him,' Pa Pa said.

'Has he been tested yet?' Ma Ma asked.

I threw up my hands. 'In the first place, he doesn't have Aids. And even if he did, there's no way you could catch Aids from him. Unless you're planning to have sex with him, or get a blood transfusion. Neither of which is likely to happen while we're having dinner at this hawker centre.'

'You so naïve,' Pa Pa said. 'We're going to eat from the same dishes. What if his saliva gets mixed in the food and we get infected like that?'

'You can't get Aids through saliva,' I said to Pa Pa in Chinese. I resisted the urge to pull at my hair. 'You can only get it through the exchange of semen or blood. I can't believe you don't know this. Were you living in a hut up in the mountains during the Nineties? I really need to rent some sex-education video for you to watch.'

'But what if he has weak gums,' Pa Pa said, 'and they bleed? What if the blood gets mixed in his saliva? Then the saliva gets mixed in the food and we all get infected.'

'Holy shit.' I shook my head. 'Look, Steve is a good boy. It's unlikely that he has Aids.'

'How do you know?' Ma Ma said. 'Has he been tested?'

'What's wrong? Why is everyone getting so agitated?' Steve asked me, not understanding any of the Chinese conversation going on between me and my parents.

'Oh nothing, we're just arguing over what food to order,' I told Steve in English. 'Perfectly friendly bickering about the relative merits of laksa and stewed chicken feet.'

'What's laksa?' Steve asked.

'Noodles in coconut-milk soup base,' I said. 'Which do you prefer?'

'I'm flexible,' Steve said. 'You're the expert.'

'OK. Now just give me a couple of minutes to discuss the dish options with my parents.' I turned back to my parents and said in Chinese, 'Why do you think he has Aids? I've brought lots of other friends along for dinner, and you never think *they* have Aids.'

'They're Chinese,' Pa Pa said. 'They don't sleep with many people like the *ang mo*s do.'

'Yah, whenever I watch those Western movies on TV – they're only two hours long, but the men there always have sex at least three times in those two hours,' my mother said. 'It's a miracle if they *don't* have Aids.'

'But that's just movies,' my sister said in Chinese. 'Fiction. Made-up fantasies.'

'Thank you,' I said. 'Finally, someone in our family who actually has a modicum of common sense.'

'But I always read in the newspaper,' Pa Pa said, 'those Western tourists, they go to Bangkok. Have sex with child prostitutes, and don't use condom. Then they always have to stop over in Singapore on the way back to Europe. Then they pass the Aids on to some naïve Singaporean woman.'

'I've been best friends with Steve for three years and –'

'I thought *I* was your bestest friend!' my sister interrupted.

'I'm sorry, of course you are, my dearest,' I said, patting her hand. 'What I mean is that Steve has been my best friend in England for three years. I know he's really not into under-age hookers.'

'What are you arguing about?' Steve asked me.

'My parents are insisting that we order fried oysters,' I

told him. 'But I said that they always undercook those things, and we'll end up with diarrhoea.'

'Have you been tested?' Pa Pa asked Steve in Chinese. 'Do you have Aids?'

'What does he want to know?' Steve asked me.

'He wants to know if you want the oysters,' I told Steve.

Steve shook his head. 'No, I don't want to risk having to spend two hours in the bog with a dripping arse.'

'Why is your friend shaking his head?' Ma Ma said. 'Does that mean he hasn't been tested?'

'We can't eat dinner with him then.' Pa Pa got up.

'Sit down,' I said. 'Steve said he's been tested. But he tested negative. He's shaking his head to tell you that he doesn't have Aids or any other sexually transmitted disease.'

'Oh.' Pa Pa sat down.

'Why you look so funny?' Ma Ma asked my sister. 'You look like you're going to explode or vomit.'

My sister burst out laughing, a flood of ha ha's accompanied by streams of tears. I'm glad that at least *someone* found my stressful situation amusing.

'What's so funny?' Pa Pa said.

'Oh nothing. I just saw a bird shit on a man's head,' my sister lied. 'So funny, hee hee.' My sister, being the only other bilingual person at the table, was feeding off my pain with unrepressed glee.

'I think we should go and order some food,' I said to my parents. 'What would you like?'

'Anything also can,' Pa Pa said.

I turned to Steve. 'Why don't you come along with me and my sister and see what you'd like to eat?'

We left my parents at the table and walked towards the hawker stalls.

'I'd like to try some Singaporean food,' Steve said.

'There's no such thing as Singaporean food, really. Which is why I find it really weird in England when I see restaurants offering Singaporean noodles, or see a Singapore stir-fry sauce in the supermarket. I mean, you can get Chinese or Malay or Indian food, but there's no dish that you can say is specifically Singaporean. Like there's satay there, which is Malay.' I pointed at a man waving a moon-shaped fan above a charcoal grill. The flames exploded through the sticks of beef, bathing his face in a red glow. 'And there's roti prata, which is Indian.' I pointed to a turbaned Sikh, who cracked an egg into a lump of dough. He pressed the dough shut, then tossed it in the air, twirling it, then dropped it on the black griddle. The prata splat as it hit the hot flat-iron, sizzling to a crispy brown. 'And fried carrot cake, which is Chinese. You can't see it here, but that's my favourite dish.'

'You deep fry a cake in oil?!' Steve said.

'Well, it's not really a cake. And it's not made from carrot either. So I don't know why they call it fried carrot cake. Something must have got lost in translation.' I had never really thought about this before, why they called it carrot cake when it was obviously nothing like an English carrot cake. 'I mean, part of it is made from mashed turnips, and I guess turnips kind of look like carrots.'

'I like most of the stuff you like anyway,' Steve said. 'So get me whatever you're going to have.'

'OK. Why don't you go and order the sugar-cane juice over there,' I pointed to the stall, 'and Chiah Chen and I will go and order the other stuff.'

Steve nodded, so we went on our separate food forays.

My sister and I joined the queue huddled around the carrot-cake store. Office workers fanned themselves with the *New Paper*, while children from the local primary school crawled along the line, looking like baby tortoises in their green school uniforms and giant backpacks.

'Three Chye Tao Kway,' I said to the hawker. 'Table 32.'

She slapped the carrot cake in the wok. It looked like a

225

white, smooth marble slab that quivered like jelly. She cracked an egg over the cake, and the yellow liquid spurted and popped until it wrapped the cake in a crisp golden shell.

'Are you going to get any rojak?' my sister asked.

I looked at the Indian hawker, tossing together the salad made with sweet chunks of pineapple, bitter cubes of fried bean curd, juicy beansprouts and cucumbers, dusted with ground peanuts and welded together with a sticky, candy-like soy sauce.

'Why?'

'Every time I see rojak, I think of you,' my sister said. 'Got a little bit of everything, all mixed up. Very nice.'

We ordered the rojak and went back to our table.

'Hey, the sugar-cane guy is really cool,' Steve said. Five green glasses of sugar-cane juice stood on the table, leaving pools of water at their base. 'I love the machine. He just slides the cane through the roller and it squeezes all the juice out.'

The hawker brought the fried carrot cake to our table.

'Eat, eat. *Qing*. Don't shy,' my sister said to Steve, gesturing towards the carrot cake.

I took one bite of the carrot cake and had an out-of-body experience as my teeth crunched through the yellow crumbly husk, into the soft, creamy cake that teased my tongue with tangy nuggets of sour radishes and shocked it with fiery flakes of red chilli.

'How many women has Steve slept with?' my mother asked me.

'Three,' I said in Chinese, feeling unbelievably annoyed. 'He's been married three times, and he killed all three of them. He pickled their heads in formaldehyde and put them in jars on his shelf.'

'Isn't he afraid that the police will catch him?' Ma Ma said.

'Or is it legal to kill your wife in England?' Pa Pa said.

I couldn't believe it. What kind of monster did they think Steve was capable of being, just because he was an *ang mo gwei*, a white devil? But then I suddenly realized that I could use their ignorance to my advantage. My parents knew nothing about Steve, he was a blank board to them, so I could probably tell them anything I liked about him and they would buy it.

'That was a joke,' I told my parents in Chinese. 'Steve is a virgin. He's a devout Buddhist. He believes in the Four Noble Truths and follows the Eightfold Path. He leads a life of chastity and abstains from alcohol. He meditates three times a day and reads the Tripitaka before he goes to bed.'

A hawker came with the rojak, and another came with a clay-pot filled with chicken curry.

'Cool,' Steve said, as he plunged his fork into a chicken wing.

'If he's Buddhist, why he not vegetarian?' Ma Ma asked me.

'He probably doesn't know that the clay-pot has meat in it,' I said. I snatched the pot away from Steve before he could lift the chicken.

'Hey, that's mine!' he said.

I pushed the rojak towards Steve. 'Here, have this instead.'

'What is it?'

'It's a kind of salad,' I said. 'You'll like it.'

'I can't eat salad for dinner,' Steve said. 'I need meat. That curry looks fantastic, that's why I ordered it. You only want my dish because it looks a zillion times better than your puny black salad. Give my chicken back to me.'

'No, you can't have the chicken,' I said, slapping Steve's hand as he reached for the clay-pot.

'Why he want to eat the chicken?' Pa Pa said. 'What kind of Buddhist is he?'

'If you want the chicken, why don't you just go and order your own?' Steve asked me.

'Just shut up and smile, damn it,' I said.

'What's wrong?'

'Nothing,' I said to Steve. 'You just can't eat any meat tonight.'

'Why not?'

'I'll explain later. Stop asking me so many questions and just do what I tell you. You're stressing me out. Now eat the rojak.'

Steve chewed on the cucumber and bean sprouts obediently.

I smiled at my parents. 'Steve didn't realize the clay-pot had chicken, so he's going to eat the vegetarian rojak instead. And Steve's job in TV is only temporary,' I lied. 'Just something he's going to do for a few months before he goes back to continue his studies at medical school. Steve is going to be a doctor.'

'Oh goody!' Ma Ma said. 'My rheumatism very painful. Ask him how to make my rheumatism less painful.'

I just stared at her, silenced by my ignorance. I knew nothing about rheumatism.

'Well, ask him,' Pa Pa said.

'Steve is going to be a brain surgeon,' my sister said, coming to my rescue. 'He's a brain specialist. He doesn't know anything about rheumatism.'

My parents looked at Steve, deeply impressed.

'Why don't you give them the gifts now?' I suggested.

Steve took out a box of Indonesian bird's nest. 'Uncle, Aunty, here's a gift for you.'

'Wah, Indonesian bird's nest,' Pa Pa said. He turned to Ma Ma. 'If you make it into a soup, maybe it will help your rheumatism.' Pa Pa turned to Steve. 'Indonesian bird's nest very difficult to get. You smuggle it in?'

'Nod your head,' I told Steve.

228

Steve nodded.

'It was very difficult to get,' I told my parents in Chinese. 'What with the political unrest and riots and all that.' I had actually managed to get the bird's nest through some contacts at Mammon CorpS.

'Your friend must be very smart and brave,' Ma Ma said.

'And he's also very good-looking and loving,' my sister told my parents in Chinese. 'He'll make a good husband.'

'Husband?!' Ma Ma balked. 'You don't say such things, give me heart attack. You forgot what happened to Mrs Yap's daughter?'

'What happened to Mrs Yap's daughter?' I asked.

'She go marry this white banker. She think because he's white, can give her so much money. And he has,' Ma Ma said. 'But now she just sit at home, while he has so many affairs with other women.'

'I don't see why you're so against the idea of Chinese people marrying white people,' I said. 'I went out with Tock Seng for so many years, and you really liked him.'

'No we didn't,' Ma Ma said. 'We only pretended to. Oh, when you left him and he disappeared, we were so – whew!'

'Why did you pretend?'

'We saw you so in love with him,' Pa Pa said. 'We sure he going to end up being our son-in-law. So we don't want to say anything bad about him, if not in future will have bad blood in family.'

'But he such a bad influence on you, typical of white devils,' Ma Ma said. 'Go and trick you into making all those bad investments.'

'What bad investments?' I asked.

'Like the chewing-gum thing, you forgot?' Pa Pa said.

'Oh.' When the Singapore government banned the sale of chewing gum in Singapore, Tock Seng persuaded me to invest $500 so we could smuggle in gum from Malaysia. Our scheme failed because, once we got the gum, we couldn't really find anyone to sell it to. Then we realized that, despite all the jokes the Western media made, the Singaporean government was actually right. Nobody really missed chewing gum. Even in England, most of my friends probably didn't buy more than three packets a year. Singapore was gumless, but now it was a land free of the substance that jammed train doors and scarred pavements, a much more pleasant environment to live in.

'Are you talking about Tock Seng?' Steve asked me.

'My parents are just saying how much they didn't like him,' I said, ''cos he was flaky. They expected you to be like him 'cos you're white, but they're glad you're not.'

'Tell your father that I'm not like Tock Seng at all,' Steve said.

'What did your friend say?' Pa Pa asked me.

'He says he's sorry that Mrs Yap's daughter had a bad experience with her British husband, but you shouldn't judge all British men by one white man's bad behaviour.'

'But you never hear any good stories about British men,' Ma Ma said. 'The most famous British man here – Nick Leeson. He go and steal so much money. Now he in prison.'

'Yah, and that Michael Fay also very bad,' Pa Pa said. 'Go and damage the MP's car. They never cane him enough.'

'Michael Fay was American,' I said. 'Steve is British.'

'They're all the same,' Pa Pa said. 'You know why we call the white people demons?'

I sighed. 'Yes.' It was because the Chinese believed that China was the only civilized nation on earth, and everyone outside China was a devil.

'Chinese people always more advanced than the white devils,' Pa Pa said. 'Thousands of years ago, while the white devils were still learning how to climb trees, the Chinese people had already invented gunpowder.'

'God, could you *be* any more racist?!' I said.

'No, no,' Ma Ma said. 'We're very happy you so good friends with Steve.'

'But you should never marry him,' Pa Pa said. 'White children so stupid. Very bad in maths and science.' According to my father, it's a well-known fact that Singaporeans are much better than Westerners at maths and science. And in our market-driven economy, it's very important to excel in those subjects. My father was always horrified at the prospect that some maths-deficient white genes would damage the financial acumen of his grand-children.

'What did your father say?' Steve asked me. 'What's wrong?'

'Nothing important,' I said. 'Just nod your head and smile.'

I smiled at my parents too, but inside I was a total grin-free zone. If the people in the Test were anything like my parents, it was going to be impossible to teach Steve how to win them over.

19

'We're going to put Steve into a typical Chinese scene,' Dr Sidious said. 'In this case, it will be the reunion dinner on the eve of Chinese New Year.'

We were at Mammon CorpS' studio in Singapore. The set looked like the living-room of an *Ah Beng* made good, like the house of someone who had amassed his wealth by frying Hokkein noodles or supplying Sri Lankan workers to construction companies. Someone who, despite his lack of paper qualifications and command of good English, had managed to succeed in Singapore anyway through a combination of street smarts and peasant hardiness. And whose rise in material wealth was not accompanied by a similar improvement in aesthetics. With its Roman columns, Italian marble floor, smiling Buddhas and Koi pond, the room came off feeling like the Renaissance meets Charlie Chan. The home-entertainment system probably cost as much as a Stealth bomber. The owner didn't just get the Sony widescreen TV and the Bang & Olufsen hi-fi system, but also bought two VCRs, a DVD player and a laser disc karaoke machine. An enormous family photo portrait, the size of a cathedral window, consumed most of the wall space on the south side of the room. Facing the entrance of the room was an altar of Kuan Ti, the God of War, placed there because his billowing black beard, tiger skin and rage-like red face would scare away any demons that tried to enter the house.

Draco Sidious turned to Steve. 'When you get on stage, I want you to act like your usual British self. Don't try to fit in. Then Chiah Deng will be able to see when your normal behaviour prevents you from blending in. After you've finished performing the scene, Chiah Deng will be able to decide what Adaptations you'll need to make.'

Dr Sidious turned to Steve and pointed to a door left of the stage. 'Why don't you go to Wardrobe and pick up a costume that you think will be appropriate for the scene?'

When Steve stepped on to the stage, elegant in black tie, a kid ran up to him and said, 'Hurry up, Uncle, we can't start the dinner until everybody sits down.' Steve looked confused. Why was this kid calling him 'Uncle'? Were they supposed to be related?

Teach Steve, I wrote in my notebook, *Chinese thing – you call anyone who's significantly your senior 'Uncle' or 'Aunty', even though they are not from your family.* There's this old joke – you know you're Chinese when all your parents' friends are your uncles and aunts.

There were ten people seated at the dining table, and three empty seats. The kid took his place and Steve was about to sit next to him, but the kid said, 'You can't sit there. It's my brother's chair.'

'Sorry,' Steve said. He touched the back of the remaining chair. 'May I sit here?'

'Yah, OK.'

Steve stared at the steamboat, a contraption that looked like an inverted flying saucer. Plates of raw food surrounded this huge stainless-steel bowl – white fishballs, orange prawn balls, cuttlefish, shrimps and squid. Steve looked at the table as if it belonged to the set of some B-movie

Frankenstein flick. Did they seriously expect him to eat all those slimy pink slivers of uncooked chicken and those bloody jellyish blobs of raw pig's liver? ('Eee-yuh, I don't know how you can even touch that stuff, much less cook it,' Steve once said to me when I bought some raw liver to make pâté. 'It looks like something that someone with tuberculosis would cough out.')

A woman poured some water into the vessel, while a man struck a match against the table. The stick spurted to life and the man pressed the blue flame against the candle at the bottom of the steamboat, lighting the vessel.

Then everyone at the table broke into a flurry of mutual invitations to start eating. ('*Qing, qing*, please, don't be shy, go ahead,' . . . 'No, you *qing*, please go ahead,' . . . 'No, you go first, please, please, *qing*.') The kid next to Steve insisted vehemently that Steve should go and stuff himself silly, so Steve said, 'I thought you said we couldn't start the dinner until everybody was here. Shouldn't we wait for your brother?'

The kid looked at Steve like he was retarded. 'My brother is in Oxford.'

Steve just smiled at the kid, the kind of sympathetic smile that the British reserve for people who are ill-mannered or just obviously insane.

Teach Steve, I wrote, *that in reunion dinners, it is common to save seats for family members who might not be present.*

'Why you so shy? *Qing*, go ahead and eat,' said the man next to Steve.

'What do I do?' Steve asked.

The man jerked his head up in surprise, bobbing it like a turkey. 'Huh? You don't know how to eat steamboat?'

Steve shook his head.

'You just put the food in the water and boil it,' the man said.

Steve went for the fishballs, but instead of picking one up between both his chopsticks, he lifted one chopstick and impaled the ball with that solitary stick. Which, of course, immediately marked him out to be an amateur. I guess it was partly my fault, but as fishballs are notoriously slippery objects, when we were at home I taught Steve to pick them up by spearing them, instead of taking the time to teach him how to use the chopsticks properly.

Steve dipped the stick into the steaming waters, which was a mistake, because he was the first person to do so. *Another Chinese thing Steve must learn – no matter how violently people insist on you going first, you should never be the first person to pick up a piece of food, unless you are the Eldest in the group (i.e., the most senior), or the youngest (i.e., some kid who is too young to know about protocol and thus can be forgiven for any faux pas).*

But anyway, once Steve broke the ice by dumping his food in the steamboat, everyone else went into a frenzy. Slabs of meat splashed into the fog-generating vessel.

Having filled the steamboat to capacity, everybody sat back and watched the clouds rise from the silver bowl.

A middle-aged woman across from Steve threw her head back and sighed dramatically, like she was a lead in one of Sophocles' tragedies. '*Ai-yah*, so *gek sim*. My son have to be away from Singapore for such a long time. Eight years.'

The woman to her right rubbed her jade bracelet and said, 'But I tell you, Er Yi, it's worth it. When he finishes, Ah Loong will be a doctor. From Oxford.'

Everyone at the table, apart from Steve, nodded reverently at the mention of those two holy words – 'doctor' and 'Oxford'.

'Er Yi, you're so *beng ling*,' said a woman wearing three gold necklaces and two gold bracelets. 'So capable, can raise such a *gwai* son like Loong. He's so obedient, such a good boy. What's your secret?'

'I tell you, Da Yi, you have to train them from young,' Er Yi said. 'Every day, after school, I made sure Ah Loong go for tuition, at least *two* hours.' *Explain to Steve the phenomenon of tuition*, I wrote, *the extra remedial lessons that parents send their children to after school. National Singaporean industry – parents can spend nearly a hundred dollars an hour, more than what some people would spend on a shrink.* 'And when he come home, I make sure there's no TV, no comics. I only allow him to read the newspaper, or the *New Scientist* – no story books. And during school holiday, I go with him to Popular bookshop to buy assessment books. We buy all the Ten Year Series, make sure he memorize all the model answers to all the exam questions that came out in the last ten years.'

'Korean ginseng,' said a man with over-permed, puffy hair (a.k.a. 'helmet head').

'Yah,' Er Yi said. 'Every day I got prepare ginseng soup for Loong to drink.'

'Ginseng very cooling,' Helmet Head said. 'Make his brain brighter.'

Tell Steve about heaty versus cooling foods, I wrote. *Too many heaty foods, like fried chicken, cause fever by adding too much Yang to the body, while cooling foods soothe by adding more Yin to the body.*

Steve had that zoned-out look. He obviously had no idea what they were talking about and was getting bored out of his mind. I didn't blame him. I was always lulled into a coma during reunion dinners by all those typically tedious Singaporean debates about the value of Extra Curricular Activities (ECAs) and A-level exams, all so that you could end up with the paper qualification for a banal bureaucratic job.

But my sister would always save me during those zzzzzzzz reunion dinners. We would kill time playing Hangman, drawing the stick figures on the napkins. And we would ·

236

make toys out of the chopstick paper holders. We would roll up the edges of the empty paper tube, put the opening to our lips and then blow. The tube would shoot out violently, and we would keep folding and blowing the tube, until one of us got hit in the eye and started crying and had to go to the ladies' to bathe the eye with water.

Now the food was ready and everyone was getting ready to eat, to *chia cai*. The kid lifted a soggy, flapping flag of mustard green, said 'Kong Kong, eat vegetable,' and lowered it into his grandfather's bowl. Kong Kong smiled and nodded his head, saying, 'Ah Kow, *ni heng dong shi*,' pleased that Ah Kow, the kid, had demonstrated his *dong shi*ness, his 'knowingness', by offering food to his elders before taking any food for himself. *Teach Steve*, I wrote, *that you should always pick up food and put it on the plates of the people around you before you get any food for yourself. And when you want to get something more to drink, you have to top up the cups of the people next to you from the communal teapot before filling your own cup*. Er Yi picked up a snowy flake of fish, stretched her body across the table and flipped it on to a man's plate. 'Ah Gwei, hope this year your business make a lot of money.'

Teach Steve about Chinese food, I wrote. *The items on the menu are there not just because they taste good, but because they are supposed to bring good fortune. Thus you will give* chang nian cai, *'long year vegetable', to the elderly, to wish them a long life, and you will give fish, which sounds the same as the word for 'surplus' in Chinese, to bosses to bless their businesses.*

I was beginning to figure out the naming system for this family. *The women are nicknamed according to their birth order in the family, e.g. 'Er Yi' is Second Aunt and 'Da Yi' is Big Aunt, while the men are named according to their astrological signs, e.g. 'Ah Gwei' is the Rooster, 'Ah Kow' is the Dog and 'Ah Loong' is the Dragon. So should tell Steve*

237

to call himself 'Ah Nieu', because he's born in the Year of the Ox.

Steve goes for the fishball that he put in the steamboat, but the ball keeps eluding his stabs. The chopsticks keep plunging and thrusting until they finally smack the ball and splash the boiling water on to Steve's hand.

'Fuck!' Steve drops the chopsticks and blows his red hand, trying to cool it.

Everyone at the table is silenced, stunned by the expletive that spat from Steve's mouth.

'"Fork,"' Steve said. 'I said, "fork". Could I get one, please? A fork, that is. I just can't handle these chopsticks.'

'We got no forks,' the grandfather said from across the table. 'Ah Kow, pass him the fishball.'

The nine-year-old kid calmly picked up the fishball and put it on Steve's plate.

Steve tugged at his collar, and waved away the steam billowing towards his face. He took off his jacket and said, 'Whew, it's hot.'

'Why you wear until so hot?' a twentysomething Chinese woman said to Steve. All the other men in the room were wearing short-sleeved polo shirts or Hawaiian shirts. 'You just come from a funeral, or what?' She giggled at her own joke.

'I thought this was supposed to be a formal dinner,' Steve said. Steve always wore black tie to formal occasions, and to be fair, he couldn't possibly have known that he was supposed to put on BBQ gear.

'What are you going to wear when you go and *pai nian* tomorrow?' the woman asked.

'I don't know. This is all I have.' Steve pointed to his suit.

'*Ai-yah*, you better definitely don't wear that,' Er Yi said. 'Black and white. So unlucky. You wear that, nobody let you into their house.' *Get Steve to wear auspicious colours*, I wrote, *like red*.

'And you definitely cannot wear the same clothes you wore today,' the young woman said. 'You haven't gone and bought new clothes?'

Steve shook his head.

'*Hi-yah*, what's wrong with you? That's the best thing about Chinese New Year – got excuse to buy new clothes.' The woman took something out of her shopping bag. 'See, I got these Versace jeans.' Designer fashion victims favoured these because of the huge Medusa head that bumped from the back of the jeans, thus screaming 'Designer Brand!' at anyone who happened to stare at their butt. 'I got these at a Katong warehouse sale seven months ago. I haven't worn them yet. Been saving them up for Chinese New Year.'

'Why did you bring them tonight then?' Steve said.

'Oh, I went shopping at Orchard Road before I came here. I saw this exact same brand of Versace jeans at Wisma. So I ask the salesgirl, "How much?" And she said, "Three hundred dollars." Then I showed her these –' she pointed at the jeans on the table, 'and told her I bought it for only seventy dollars. The girl look at me, her eyes big big, and said, "Real or not?" And I said, "Of course it's not fake, it's 100 per cent genuine. See, it says here, 'Made in Italy'."' The woman pointed to the tag on the jeans.

'So you go around shopping for the same item, even after you've bought it?' Steve looked at her like she was barmy.

Suddenly, something beeped 'Twinkle Twinkle Little Star'. The woman took out her fuchsia-pink Motorola mobile. She started screaming into the phone, 'Yah what? Huh? What? Pang Pang called? OK. OK. OK. Yah. OK. Tomorrow mahjong at Tua Pwei's place. OK. You remember to tape the variety show on Channel 8? *Ai-yah*! Why you forget? You useless girl! Humph. Now stupid, don't forget to clean my bedroom tonight. Tomorrow, Chinese New Year, cannot sweep floor, very bad luck.' The woman snapped her phone shut and rolled her eyes. 'Our maid, so useless.'

'You have a maid?' Steve said. *Train Steve to get over his aversion to hiring domestic help*, I wrote. Somehow, Steve's parents had taught him that hiring someone else to do your household chores was a sign of moral deficiency. But most middle-class families in Singapore hired maids, and most of the blue-collar jobs (like construction work) were shunted to labourers from the poorer Asian countries, like Thailand or Indonesia. Another joke: How many Singaporeans does it take to change a lightbulb? None. They'd hire a foreigner to do it.

'Yah, but she's hopeless,' the woman said. 'I keep telling my parents to send her back to the Philippines and hire someone else, but they don't want to lose their deposit. Yah, I was telling you. I like to go round, compare prices when I shop.' The woman explained that every time she visited a new shop and found that she'd bought the same item at a cheaper price at some other place, that made her day.

'OK,' Steve said in a tone he'd use for members of the Flat Earth society. 'Whatever makes you happy.'

Teach Steve, I wrote, *the joy of feeding the* kia-su, *afraid-to-lose-out mentality.* My sister would go into every supermarket she passed by, regardless of whether she needed to buy any groceries or not, to check their price for sea cucumbers, because she derived endless pleasure when she found out that our local wet market still sold them more cheaply ('Because the owner like me, and he always give me a special price,' my sister explained).

'Shopping always makes me happy,' the woman said. 'What makes you happy?'

'What do you mean?' Steve was momentarily taken aback by such a direct personal question from a stranger.

'What you do for fun?'

'I went to watch *Macbeth* at the National Theatre a few

weeks ago. Adrian Noble directed it, with Kenneth Branagh in the lead role and Sharon Stone as Lady Macbeth. Some suspected that they hired Sharon Stone merely to add some Hollywood glitz to the production. But I thought she acquitted herself fairly reasonably.'

The woman shook her head. 'No, I asked what you do for fun. Your hobby.'

'The play *was* fun. Well, maybe not fun as in "ha, ha", but certainly fascinating. I was certainly intrigued by how Branagh decided to play Macbeth the way Dr Bernard McElroy described him in *Shakespeare Criticism*. Branagh's Macbeth is not simply driven by ambition. He is impelled towards evil, yet he also hates evil. And it is this dark–light conflict within himself that torments and spiritually destroys him.'

'Wah, you watch Shakespeare for fun? Very *cheem*,' the woman said. *Cheem*, I noted. *Explain to Steve that it's Singlish for something that is intellectual, profound and difficult to comprehend.* 'I had to study Shakespeare at secondary school. I keep wanting to fall asleep but cannot. At least during science lesson, our science textbook very big – can hide behind the textbook and sleep, the teacher cannot see you. But the Shakespeare book very small, cannot hide your head behind it and sleep. So have to stay awake the *whole* lesson, so boring.'

I really enjoyed the day we went to watch the play – tickets for only eight quid with our student IDs! In the morning, we went to the Tate to see the Cézanne exhibition. We bought a Cézanne-wich from Au Bon Pain for lunch, a sandwich made from ingredients found in Cézanne's paintings. ('Like how stupid is that?' Steve and I both said almost together when we saw the description on the menu.) In the afternoon, we lay by the benches at Gabriel's Wharf, dozing to the slushing lullaby of the Thames. When we woke, we walked to the South Bank Centre, where I bought a secondhand edition of Donne's poetry at the dark market that lay shadowed beneath Waterloo Bridge. After the play we went to a pub and argued about whether the 'unsex me' scene when Sharon Stone ripped open her blouse was a powerful feminist gesture or a gratuitous piece of tit-showing. That day was about as much fun as I'd ever had, but I knew that in order to turn Steve into a Singaporean, I had to *replace Steve's enthusiasm for walking around museums of fine art with a passion for strolling through the air-conditioned corridors of food courts and shopping malls.*

Er Yi chewed on some fish and spat the bones on to the table. She turned to Steve, burped in his face and said, 'You watch Shakespeare for fun? You must be very smart. Which school you go to?'

'I went to Oxford,' Steve said.

'Wah, really?' Da Yi said with her mouth full of eel. 'My son trying to get to Oxford. Maybe you can give him some tips. Which tuition teacher you go to? What assessment books did you use?'

'I didn't go to any teachers or use any books,' Steve said. 'Besides, I would advise you against sending your child to Oxford.'

'Why?'

'Because he'll be treated like a leper. You won't be socially accepted there unless you're white and come from a posh school.'

Da Yi picked up a plastic tube that held her paper towel. She squeezed one end of the tube, so that an air bubble formed at the other end. Then she smashed her free hand against the bubble. The tube exploded. 'But if Ah Kow goes to Oxford, when he come back to Singapore, he'll have a certificate from Oxford.' She removed the towel from its tattered plastic shell. 'He'll have all the 5 Cs. Car, credit card, country club, cash, career. Who care if, for a few years, he got no friends?'

Steve just stared at the tube that had recently boomed in his face.

20

'I hate this place,' Steve said.

We were at Orchard Road, shopping for the clothes that Steve would wear for the Test.

'Why? It's got everything you want in a city,' I said. 'It's hard to imagine this really used to be an *ulu* road.' As suggested by its name, Orchard Road used to be flanked by fruit orchards, pepper and nutmeg plantations. 'Now it's got designer boutiques, five-star hotels, theme restaurants, multi-screen cinemas equipped with the THX sound system.'

'Exactly, it's like an American strip mall running through the middle of a tropical botanical garden,' Steve said. Ferns burst from the tree trunks that lined the road, their branches furry with moss and dripping vines like silky black hair, drooped above the shoppers who wore T-shirts that made them walking ads for Nike, Benetton and the Hard Rock Café.

We sat in the outdoor Borders café, which was next to Burger King next to Starbucks next to Planet Hollywood. The teenagers at the café, still in uniform, slouched a too-cool-for-school attitude by wearing CK sunglasses even though it was night.

'There's nothing special or unique or Singaporean about

the shops,' Steve said. 'They're either Western franchises or international chain stores. It's like Fifth Avenue invaded Shangri-La.' Across the road, the flowers of the Flame of the Forest trees bounced their fiery colours off the shiny windows of the Chanel and DKNY boutiques.

I agreed with Steve, but I couldn't tell him that. I hated the way the coconut trees bowed their bodies painfully towards the asphalt, paying reluctant worship to the BMWs that crawled along the traffic-jammed road. I hated the piped music that leaked out of the stores – bland, middle-of-the-road slush that sounded like it was vetted by the Mormons. But don't get me wrong – I have nothing against Western culture. Americans do American things very well, but the problem is when Singaporeans try to do American things – it just looks tacky, fake, like a cheap imitation, because it's not true to our land, our history, our selves.

'Everything's so sterile,' Steve said. 'This place is like one giant giftshop in a hospital.'

But if I wanted to get the job, I had to persuade Steve to embrace everything that I hated about this city, convince him that the genericanization of Singapore was a good thing.

So I shrugged and said, 'You're missing the point entirely. You see your hotel over there?' I pointed to the Westin Stamford, a white obelisk that dwarfed all the other skyscrapers. 'It's the tallest hotel in the world. A monument to the triumph of a single-party capitalist technocracy. It's designed by I. M. Pei.'

'Wasn't he the geezer who designed that hideous glass pyramid by the Louvre?'

'Yeah. He also designed the Four Seasons hotel in New York. He's an architect raised in China, but who made his reputation as one of the greatest Modernist architects through his work in America. It's no coincidence that he was chosen to design the Westin Stamford. The powers that be obviously wanted someone who could fuse American expertise with Chinese philosophy. You see, Singapore *wants* to be America. Like America, but run by Chinese people. A cyber city built with Western infrastructure, ruled by Eastern values.'

Steve snorted. 'Eastern values. And what might those be? Greed and rampant consumerism? A life centred around shopping and eating?' He jerked his thumb towards a man who had shopping bags flapping from his arms like bangles. He was contorting his upper body, trying to dial the Motorola phone in his right palm with the tip of the dripping ice-cream cone in his left hand.

'Don't knock him,' I said. 'He's to be your model. You've got to look pretty much like him during the Test.'

Steve looked at Mr Motorola. 'But he looks so boring. Can't I dress like him instead?' He pointed to a guy sporting a white sleeveless vest, cargo pants and a Golden Monkey haircut (i.e., black hair tinted blond).

'No, the guy looks too *Ah Beng*,' I said.

'What does that mean?'

'*Ah Beng* is like a term of insult for poorly educated gangsters. They're usually in low-level jobs like waiters, and make extra cash by doing dodgy things like being a bookie or selling pirated DVDs. They like to squat around Orchard Road, waiting for someone to stare at them so that they can go and beat them up.'

I had brought Steve to Orchard Road to show him the full panorama of Singaporean fashion. There were Muslims in their black headscarves, Indian women in their saris, and the *Ah Sohs*, the grandmothers in their Chinese *cheong-sams*. But most people wore a T-shirt or polo shirt with jeans or bermuda shorts. And almost everyone wore glasses.

Steve stood up suddenly. 'Let's go,' he said.

'Why?'

'Nothing. I just don't want to *be* here any more,' he said.

'All right. I'll take you to get clothes for the Test.'

We went to Versus at Takashimaya. It was like every other Versace boutique I'd been to – outrageous leopard-skin sofas and techno trance music. I pulled out a red and yellow polka-dot shirt. 'Hey, it's three hundred and fifty dollars, but it's on sale. Thirty per cent off.'

'I can't wear that,' Steve said. 'It looks like a petri dish filled with infectious diseases. I'll look like I've got chicken pox and leprosy.'

'No, the colours are perfect. Red is the most auspicious colour for Chinese New Year. It shouts "Life! Warmth! Vitality!" And yellow is good because it's a colour that balances everything. It acts as a buffer between the Yin and Yang energy in you.'

'Can't I wear this instead?' Steve pulled out a white shirt.

'Of course not. Do you know what things are white?'

'Snow. Ivory. Milk.'

'Corpses,' I said. 'White is the colour of death. You can only wear it if you're mourning a dead relative.'

I handed Steve a pair of jade-green trousers. 'Green is good. Green is growth. It was the royal colour of the Ming Dynasty.'

When Steve came out of the dressing-room, clothed in what I'd chosen for him, he said, 'I hope nobody I know gets to see me in this.'

'You look fine,' I said. The thing I always liked about Steve was his sense of style. He could be wearing something very simple – like a white T-shirt, blue jeans and black boots – and still look incredibly cool. That's because he scouted obscure shops in Soho and haggled with vendors at Camden to get these basic pieces that fitted him perfectly and were always on the cutting edge of style. I guess I got a big kick out of living with someone who always looked as if he deserved to be on the cover of *The Face*. Now he looked like something that had exploded from a fruit blender, thanks to me. It was like Mammon CorpS was trying to get me to destroy everything I loved in order to keep it. If I didn't adapt my cool friend, I would lose him, but if I did adapt him, he would not be cool any more, and would I still want him to be my friend? I felt like I was being sucked into a vortex. No matter what I did, I would end up losing what I wanted to keep.

We sat in the Speech Lab, where I had to teach Steve how to talk Singaporean.

'What do you know about Singlish?' I asked.

'It sounds like Chinese but it's actually English,' Steve said.

'What do you mean?'

'I remember the first time I heard you talking to your sister on the phone. At first I thought you were talking to her in Chinese. But after I listened more carefully, I figured out what you were saying. I realized that you were pronouncing the English words like they were Chinese ones. Your grammar was all mixed up and sometimes you would use these foreign words. It was still English, but it just sounded like Chinese.'

'You're right. So the first thing you have to adjust is your accent,' I said. 'Basically, you have to smile a lot when you talk.' I took out a mirror and placed it in front of Steve's face. 'Say something – anything.'

'What do you want me to say?'

'Did you see the shape of your mouth when you said that? When English people talk, their mouths are always like an O – very serious, no teeth showing. Look at my mouth. If you grin a lot when you talk, it'll make your words sound a lot more Chinese.'

'OK,' he said. He didn't sound quite right, but with my

248

help, he would get there eventually. I hoped. At the moment, he still sounded English, but with a grin like that when he talked, he looked like Debbie Gibson's twin brother or as if he had spent too much time in some Hare Krishna cult.

'Also, English people talk really quickly. If you want to talk Singaporean, you have to really slow down your speech and lower your pitch. Develop a lazy, slightly stupid drawl. The English say words like "Hello" and "Yes" really quickly, like someone was pinching their ass and they had to squeak out those words as fast as possible. If you want to sound Singaporean, you've got to talk like you've just got out of bed and still feel pretty drowsy. Say "Haaar-low" instead of "Hello", and "Yaaaaah" instead of "Yes".'

'Yaaaah, ohhhh-kaaay,' Steve said, sounding like an Indian guy who was trying to yodel in Swedish.

'Uh, that was excellent for a first attempt.' I handed Steve a set of headphones. 'You'll hear sentences pronounced in the Singaporean way. I want you to mimic them by recording your sentences into that –' I pointed to the mike. 'After that, you can play back what you've said, and see how close you've come to adjusting your accent.'

Steve did what I told him to, and after a few days of practising, he finally got the hang of the accent. Steve was always good at mimicking voices – that's why they called him the Robin Williams of the theatre group when he was a member of the Oxford University Drama Society. He was going to be a lot easier to adapt than my sister.

'Singlish is basically English words spoken via Chinese grammar,' I said. 'But I reckon that it'll take you at least five years to master Chinese grammar. So we don't have enough time during our training period for that. So during the Test, you can just use your normal English grammar, but I'll show you a few Chinese grammar tricks that you can throw in occasionally. So overall, you can kind of fake like you're speaking Singlish.'

'Isn't that a bit risky?'

'No, especially in view of the type of Singaporean you're going to play.'

'Who's that?'

'You're going to play a typical Oxford-educated Singaporean male. Someone who has the ability to switch between Singlish and the Queen's English. One of their main characteristics is their ability to play ironically with both Eastern and Western discourse.'

'So what are some of your tricks?'

'The key technique is compression. Singaporeans seldom speak in complete sentences, and the trick is to know which words to drop. Develop a phobia, especially, for prepositions. So instead of saying, "I'm going to the Sea Palace Restaurant for the steamboat dinner," say, "I go Sea Palace Restaurant for steamboat."'

Then I taught Steve some all-purpose phrases that he could use within any sentence to sound Singaporean. 'Start every sentence with *A*, and end it either with a *lah* or *lor*. And if something happens that upsets you, just say *Ai-yah*, *Wah leow* or its Malay equivalent, *Alamak*. If you want to describe something that feels very intense, say *si peh*, which means "dead father". Finally, if you're questioning someone's motivation about doing anything, you always begin the question with "Why you . . .". If you're asking about someone's willingness or ability to do something, the phrase "Can or not?" will cover it, and the person will say "Can" to affirm his willingness, and "Cannot" to reject your request. Finally, also feel free to use the word "also" as the second word or final word in your sentences as often as possible.' I stopped to take a breath. 'You got all that?'

Steve finished scribbling his notes. '*A, yah lah.*'

I smiled. Then I gave Steve an in-depth low-down on the

education system in Singapore. Singaporeans worship education, so Steve would have to know how to talk about exams, good grades and certificates. In other words, getting the right paper qualifications. From the age of twelve, Singaporeans' kids are subjected to a barrage of life-and-death exams, like the Primary School Leaving Examinations (PSLE), which determine which secondary school you go to. The PSLEs are a really big deal, and most parents would make their children sacrifice their left liver if it could get them into the schools on the top of the Straits Times League Table of Schools – Raffles Institution (RI) or Anglo-Chinese School (ACS) for boys, and Raffles Girls' School (RGS) or Nanyang Girls' School for the girls. When I was at school, my life revolved around taking three to four weekly Continual Assessments (CAs) that trained me to prepare for the exams.

'Guess who invented the first national exam system in the history of mankind? You got it. The Chinese. They came up with the system of using exams to choose the best scholars to serve in the civil service, a system which they created 4,000 years ago. I don't quite know how I feel about this. You know, it's like the English gave us soccer, and the Americans gave us TV. The Chinese, on the other hand, are responsible for coming up with a system where you jam a bunch of twelve-year-olds in a little room. Then you let them sit there for an hour, while they panic themselves into a suicidal state because they can't figure out how to multiply six by twelve.'

'*Alamak*, also that sounds *si peh* appalling *lah*. I also was twelve, greatest worry – try figure out answers to quiz questions on *Blue Peter* TV show – so I can win trip – meet Abba *lor*. All these exams – way to torture children also. *Ai-yah*, *si peh* cruel, human rights violation. Why you Singaporean parents make children go through exam hell, *wah leow*?'

I stared at Steve. What he had just said was gibberish, not Singlish, but I couldn't blame him, he was just following the instructions that I'd given him. It was my fault – I'd never had to figure out how to speak Singlish, never thought about what its rules were, for the words just rolled off my tongue instinctively. How could I pass this gut knowledge on to Steve?

I decided that I would try to solve that problem later, so I went on to fill him in more about the Singaporean obsession with education. 'Well, in answer to your question, Singaporeans are obsessed with exams because they want good grades. They want good grades because those are essential if you want to go to a famous university. There's this joke that goes, "How do you know your parents are Asian? You know your parents are Asian when the only English words they know are Oxford, Harvard and MIT." Also, for Singaporeans, the value of your occupation seems to rise proportionately in relation to the number of years you spend in university. Which is why it's such a big deal if you become a doctor, because you have to study for many, many years, thus demonstrating their superior intellectual capabilities and moral virtue. I don't know why the corporations never clued on to this. If McDonalds wanted to improve the quality of their workforce, all they would have to do is to require their waiters to spend ten years at Hamburger University. Then you'd get millions of hard-working Asians defecting from med school to master the science of creating the perfect burger.'

'Why you Singaporeans have –' Steve glanced at his notes, '*si peh* stupid . . . insane attitude?'

I felt a surge of hope. Steve had actually said a sentence that could pass as Singlish. 'Unfortunately, in order to pass the Test, you must become stupid and insane too. In order to be adapted, you have to annihilate logic and adopt the irrationalities of the group that you're trying to adapt into.'

Then I went on to teach Steve how to talk about food, since most Singaporean social functions revolve around stuffing yourself silly. 'When you want to eat, you say you want to *makan*, which is Malay for "eat". Whenever you eat any food that tastes excellent, you say that it's very *shiok*. *Shiok* can also be used for any incredibly pleasurable experience. Oh yes, and I have to teach you the concept of "heaty" versus "cooling" foods. Various foods can raise or lower the metaphysical energy in your body. If you eat too many foods that are "heaty" – like chocolate, cookies, durians and anything that's fried, your body temperature will rise, and you'll get fever or a sore throat. In order to neutralize too much heatiness in the body, you eat "cooling" stuff, like drinking barley water. By the way, most foreigners hate eating durians, and a good way of getting out of eating this favourite local delicacy is to reject it on health grounds.' I picked up Steve's notebook, so that he would have to form the next sentence without looking at his notes. 'Pretend this is a durian.' I waved the book in his face. 'Come, don't shy, eat durian.'

'Durians are very *shiok*, but *ai-yah*, I have sore throat – doctor told me not to eat heaty food.'

'That was an excellent Singlish response.' I smiled. 'Now you're ready to advance to the more sublime levels of conversation, namely, the ability to swear and insult people. You know you've become a true Singaporean if you know how to complain vehemently about and to your maid.' So I taught Steve how to swear, not only in Chinese, but also in the other two official languages of Singapore, namely Malay and Tamil. '*Jiat sai* is Hokkein for "eat shit". *Si Yan Tao* is Cantonese for "dead man's head". *Ta Ma De Chow Chi Tan* literally means "Your mother's smelly egg" – I don't know why that's a major insult, but it is. I suppose something gets lost in translation. For some reason, many Chinese curses revolve around the state of eggs. Like *hun tan*, which literally means "chicken and duck's egg mixed together", but for some reason is also a swear word. *Tak boleh tahan* is something you say in Malay whenever you can't stand something any more. *Goondu* is what Malays call idiots. Also, since Singapore is a city, there are various slurs that emphasize the rural-like ignorance of the victim. Like, the Chinese phrase *sua ku* literally means "mountain tortoise", i.e., someone who lives in the mountains, knows nothing, and looks totally unhip. Also, an item's primitive incompetence can be highlighted by saying that it's very *ulu*, which is Malay for "village". Another of my favourite slurs is *wayang*, which is Chinese opera. You have these men dressed in robes with huge sleeves, and they spend the whole opera wailing loud songs and flapping their sleeves dramatically. You say someone knows how to *wayang* if they're good at pretending to look busy instead of doing any actual work.'

I took out two handphones and gave one to Steve.

'I'm going to pretend to be a maid, calling you while you're having dinner at a restaurant.' I switched on the phone and dialled Steve's number. 'Hello sir. I finish sweeping the floor already. Can I go Lucky Plaza tomorrow to see my friends? It's my day off.'

'Sure,' Steve said into his phone.

I covered the mouthpiece. 'No, you don't get it. You're supposed to refuse and then insult me according to the best of your abilities. That's what a typical Singaporean would do.'

'I can't do it.' Steve snapped his phone shut. 'I don't know how you Singaporeans can live with yourselves. So, yeah, you have a higher GNP than your neighbouring countries, but there's no excuse for using your superior wages to tempt these poor foreign workers into subjecting themselves to slave labour. Your whole economy is built upon the exploitation of the proletariat, and if there's any justice in the world, the maids should start a revolution to overthrow their capitalist oppressors.'

Steve was obviously a product of a British university, institutions where pockets of Marxism still flourished, despite the fact that most of the world had ditched that economic theory ever since the Soviet Union collapsed. 'Yes, I agree, but if you want to pass the Test, you'll have to burn your little red book and erase your obsession with class struggle and the theory of alienation. Go ahead. Be a Singaporean. Be a capitalist Nietzschean superman who can crush his domestic help at will and send her back to the slums in Manila.'

Steve clenched his jaw. He took a deep breath, then he said, 'OK. *Ta Ma De Chow Chi Tan*, why don't you go *jiat sai*. You think I *goondu*? I know you never sweep my floor properly. I know you *wayang* only. You better change your attitude, if not I *tak boleh tahan*, I'll send you back to your *ulu* country, you *sua ku*.'

'Perfect. I couldn't have ranted any better than you. You're ready to go on to the next stage of the training.'

'Yeah, I'm really proud of myself,' Steve said angrily. Then he got up and left the room.

I smiled, to hide the queasiness that I felt. My stomach hadn't felt this way since my sister's experimental dinner with raw fish three years ago.

'Are you ready for the Test?' Draco Sidious said.

Steve stepped out of Wardrobe. Gone was the fifty quid Ewan McGregor-style haircut that he got from Marcello of Toni & Guy. His hair, dyed black, now sat on his head in uneven clumps, butchered by the razor of some Indian barber. He wore the Versace outfit I'd chosen for him, along with tortoiseshell Armani glasses and a lime-green Nokia phone strapped on his D & G belt. He looked exactly like the kind of boy the Social Development Unit (the dating agency set up by the Singapore Government) would want me to have 2.3 children with, but I thought he looked as sexy as a manual about how to troubleshoot the CMOS set-up on your computer.

'Yah,' Steve said.

'I know you were expecting to act in the Chinese New Year Eve reunion dinner, but there's been a change in plans,' Dr Sidious said. 'We're going to make you act in a different scene.'

I felt ill. 'What different scene?'

'Steve is going for lunch on Chinese New Year Day itself. He's going to Lian's house to *pai nian* and pay his respects to her family..'

'Why do you want to test Steve on a scene which he hasn't trained for?' I said.

'If you remember the principles of Method acting, the crux of the Adaptation process is to train the client to *be* Singaporean, rather than to act Singaporean. If you've adjusted the client successfully, then it wouldn't matter if he's playing croquet on some Oxford quad or eating fried *kway teow* at a hawker centre. In any situation, if he *is* Singaporean, then he will behave like a Singaporean. When you're ready, you can go on stage.'

I looked at Steve.

'I ready,' he said.

21

'*Gong Xi Fai Cai*,' Da Yi said to Steve when he entered the set.

He just looked at her and smiled, obviously not knowing that he had to say *Gong Xi Fai Cai* back and wish her a much money-making New Year.

'Harlow, Aunty, long time no see,' Steve said. OK, so this wasn't the best reply, but at least he remembered to address her as Aunty.

A couple came up from behind Steve. '*Gong Xi Fai Cai*,' the couple said, and gave Da Yi a pair of mandarins.

Steve sensed he had made a mistake by not bringing *gum*, the mandarins that were a homonym for 'wealth'. '*A*, Aunty, I forgot to bring mandarins, *si peh* sorry.' He took out a red sheet. 'But I got bring this for you.' Written in gold was the Chinese word for luck, *fu*, and, according to tradition, Steve stuck the sheet on the door with the word upside-down so that luck would flow into the house.

'Aw, thank you, thank you,' Da Yi said. 'Here, I got something for you also.' She took out a small rectangular red envelope. '*Ang pow*.'

Steve opened the *ang pow* and took out a blue note. '*Wah*, fifty dollars, so much money. Thank you Aunty.'

I winced. Steve really shouldn't have taken out the money

in front of everyone. When I was young, I remember always having to fake a diarrhoea attack in order to go to the bathroom, so that I could surreptitiously check how much money I'd received. After that, I would sneak up to my mother and tell her how much I got, so that if she had given less *ang pow* money to the hostess's children, she could even things out by giving the hostess more mandarins, love-letter wafers or barbecued pork.

'I forgot to bring *ang pow* for you,' Steve said. '*Si peh* sorry again.'

'*Ai-yah*, why you sorry for?' Da Yi said. 'No need. Don't tell me you married already?'

'No,' Steve said.

'So why you want to give me *ang pow* for? Only married people give *ang pow*. When you're not married, you're still a child. A little baby boy.' Da Yi pinched Steve's cheeks. 'Sit, sit, don't shy.' She gestured towards a chicken-wing wooden daybed, a reproduction from the late Qing dynasty.

Steve sat down on the daybed.

'You eaten or not?' Da Yi said.

'I haven't eaten,' Steve said.

'What you want to drink? I got orange, tea, Tiger Beer, Hennessey XO and plain water.'

'Anything also can,' Steve said. 'I don't mind.'

'*Gong Xi Fai Cai*. What's your name?' the male half of the couple said.

'Ah Nieu,' Steve said. 'I born in the Year of the Ox.'

'My name is Tua Pwei Chek,' the man said. 'You can guess why, right?' He rubbed his stomach.

Steve looked blank.

'You don't understand dialect?' the woman said. 'Tua Pwei Chek is Uncle Very Fat.' She rubbed the man's pot belly.

Steve looked slightly startled by the man's derogatory nickname. I smiled, suddenly remembering all the terrible nicknames my relatives had for each other. Supposedly, if you had a really nasty nickname, your life would be more prosperous, because the gods wouldn't envy someone with such a terrible name. I should have told Steve to adopt a more disgusting moniker, in view of the fact that I had two uncles called Chicken Backside and Dog's Bollocks respectively, and a seventy-four-year-old aunt called Pig's Tits.

'I grew up in Singapore and learnt Chinese. But then I went Oxford and study to be doctor,' Steve said. 'I go there for eight years. No got chance to practise my Chinese, a lot of it I forgot already.' I had told Steve to use that reason to get out of any situations where he would have to use his non-existent knowledge of Chinese. Saying that he grew up in Singapore would make him more acceptable to the people on the set.

'Go ahead, eat, don't shy.' Da Yi pointed to the table.

One look at the table and I wished I was up on the set with Steve. It was snack heaven. Most of my Chinese New Year activities centred around devising the optimum ways to consume these pastries. Like the *gong tang* always took special skills, because the peanut flour would crumble like sand once you bit into it, so you had to master the art of stuffing it into your mouth as quickly as possible without choking yourself. Then there were the Love Letters, hollow rolls of buttery wafer biscuits shaped like scrolls, which I would eat by slowly unscrolling them with my teeth. I would eventually turn my attention to the glutinous rice balls, those translucent grey orbs, perfect pearls which released the sweet black sesame paste once you sank your teeth into their chewy, slippery flesh.

Steve bit into a pork floss roll. 'This very good. Like eating brown hair. Sweet hair.'

Then he took a similar-looking roll right next to the pork floss roll. He bit into it and then started coughing violently. 'Hot, hot.' He used his hand to fan his mouth.

'Oh, you ate the sambal prawn roll.' The woman picked up a roll and bit into it. 'Not that hot *lah*. Why you make such a fuss?' Then she picked up a raw green chilli and chewed on it. She handed the plate of chillies to Steve. 'You want?'

Steve shook his head, still hacking like he had just experienced a thermonuclear explosion in his head.

'Why, you don't know how to eat hot things?' the woman said, questioning Steve's Singaporeanness, since a high tolerance towards spices was one of the things Singaporeans prided themselves on.

'No, I like chilli,' Steve said, 'but I got sore throat. Doctor say I cannot eat chilli, it's too heaty.'

A six-year-old girl ran into the room, carrying a plastic imitation-wooden staff. A boy, the same age, ran after her and tried to wrest the staff away from her.

'Give it to me!' the boy said.

'No! Why?'

'Because I'm the Monkey God.'

'You always play the Monkey God,' the girl said. 'This time it's my turn.'

'You can't be Monkey God.'

'Why not?'

'Because you're a girl. In the story, girl can only be *hu li jin*. You can only be the monster.' The boy might be sexist but he was telling the truth. There weren't that many positive female roles in *The Journey to the West*. I remember when I used to play that with Tock Seng, I always ended up being the *hu li jin*, the fox spirit. I would wear a silk nightie and put on some rouge and lipstick. Tock Seng would pretend to be Pigsy, and I would seduce him by planting a kiss on his lips, whereby Pigsy would fall into a deep sleep. Then I would pick up a gingerbread man (who represented Pigsy's master, the Monk Tripitaka) and would be about to eat it, since the monk's flesh would make a demon like me immortal. When I was just about to bite off the gingerbread man's head, Tock Seng would jump up. He would switch his roles from Pigsy to *Su Mu Kong*, the Monkey King-God. Then we would face off each other, making kung fu noises and chopping our hands in the air. I must say that Tock Seng would never have done what the boy did, which was to wrest the staff away from the girl, and then hit her repeatedly on the head with it.

Steve looked at Tua Pwei Chek and his wife. They just sat there calmly, cracking open sunflower seeds with their teeth, sucking out the core and then spitting the shells on to the table, obviously unperturbed by the display of juvenile violence before them.

'You can't be the Monkey God!' the girl said, wrapping her arms around her head to shield herself from the blows. 'You know why? Because you're so fat!' Suddenly, she thrust out her hand and sank it into the boy's pot belly. She twisted his bulging flesh. 'You can only be Pigsy. Fatty! Fatty! Fatty!'

The boy hit her arm with his staff. 'Shut up!' Then he struck her in the face.

The girl clutched her nose. 'You broke it!'

'Serve you right, demon!' the boy said.

Steve probably should have known better and followed the couple's example by ignoring the children. But when he saw blood dripping down the girl's face, he got up and tried to wrest the staff away from the boy.

'No! No!' the boy screamed. 'Mummy, help me! Uncle want to take my toy from me! Uncle bully me!'

'I'll let you have the stick if you stop hitting her with it,' Steve said.

'OK,' the boy said.

Steve was still engaged in the vigorous process of pulling the staff from the boy, so when he unexpectedly let go of the staff, Steve lost his balance and fell on to the table. His elbow hit one of the glasses, sending it crashing to the ground.

'Oh, you broke the glass. You're going to be in trouble.' The boy stuck out his tongue. 'My Mummy sure to scold you one.'

Da Yi rushed into the room. She stared at her bleeding child by the wall and the broken glass on the floor.

'They were fighting,' Steve told Da Yi. 'I had to stop them.'

'*Ai-yah*, how come you don't know? Chinese New Year cannot scold children one. Very bad luck.' Da Yi turned to her daughter. 'Go kitchen and put some ice on your nose.' She looked at the scattered shards. 'Who broke that?'

The boy pointed his finger at Steve. 'Uncle.'

'*Ai-yah*, Chinese New Year break things – *si peh* unlucky.' She patted her heart to convey her anguish. 'Now bad things going to happen all year. All your fault.' She threw Steve a black look. 'After you break the glass, you got say "*sui sui ping*" or not?'

'Um . . .' Steve said.

'*Ai-yah*, why you everything also don't know how to do?' Da Yi said. 'Next time, if you break something on Chinese New Year, must immediately say "*sui sui ping*". You know why?'

'No,' Steve said.

Da Yi turned to her son. 'Ah Gong, tell him why.'

I giggled at the idea of Da Yi nicknaming her son 'Mr Stupid'.

'*Sui sui ping* means "year after year will be safe and peaceful",' Ah Gong said. '*Sui sui* sound the same as the word for broken pieces. So you say *sui sui ping*, then the *sui* thing on the floor will not bad luck any more.'

Da Yi tousled Ah Gong's hair. 'See, my Ah Gong not *gong* at all. So smart.' She turned to Steve. 'Not like you.'

I looked at Draco Sidious, but couldn't figure out how he

felt about the Test. I could see that things weren't going well, though. All the other actors were treating Steve more and more like some ignorant foreigner who needed basic customs explained to him.

'Yah, I thought you said you went to Oxford,' Tua Pwei Chek said. 'How come you everything also don't know? Don't tell me after you go Oxford you forget how to be Chinese?'

'Oh no, I remember Chinese things,' Steve said.

'I bet you don't even remember why we celebrate Chinese New Year,' Tua Pwei Chek said. 'I bet even Ah Gong knows more about Chinese New Year than you.'

'You really want to bet?' Steve said. I had told Steve that the Chinese were addicted to gambling, and if he wanted to integrate, he should use any opportunity to wager some money. 'I bet you two hundred dollars I know something about Chinese New Year that Ah Gong doesn't.'

'I on you,' Tua Pwei Chek said, accepting the bet.

'You know why we wear red on Chinese New Year?' Steve asked Ah Gong.

'Of course,' Ah Gong said. 'Because it's lucky.'

'It's not just that. It's because red will scare off the monster,' Steve said.

'What monster?'

'See, I know more about Chinese New Year than Ah Gong,' Steve said to Tua Pwei Chek.

'Tell him the story,' said Tua Pwei Chek. 'I got to see whether you know the right story or not. If not I won't give you the money.'

Steve lifted Ah Gong and placed him on his lap. 'Once upon a time, got a monster with a lion's head, and sharp sharp teeth. Every New Year's Day it would go to the village and eat people. That's why they called the monster *Nian*.' I smiled, pleased with myself. I had prepped Steve on the more obscure legends surrounding Chinese New Year,

263

so that he could use them to show off his 'specialist' knowledge if an opportunity like this presented itself. 'Everyone in the village all very frightened of *Nian*. They talk to all the wise men, but nobody knew how to scare the monster.' One day, Steve told Ah Gong, the *Nian* arrived as usual. Everybody fled to their huts to escape from the *Nian*, apart from one little boy. 'Like you.' Steve poked Ah Gong's nose gently. 'The boy was outside playing with firecrackers. Not like the firecrackers we have today, but the old type. Exploding bamboos.'

'How you make bamboo explode?' Ah Gong said.

Steve told Ah Gong how the *Nian* was about to eat the boy when the boy lit the bamboo. 'The shoot went "bang!" and burst into flames. The *Nian* got so scared, it ran away. The villagers realize that *Nian* was scared of fire. So every New Year, they put red all over their houses, because red look like fire.'

Steve stretched out his hand towards Tua Pwei Chek. 'Can?'

'Can.' Tua Pwei Chek gave four fifty-dollar notes to Steve. He turned to Da Yi. 'I hungry. Can *makan* already or not?'

'I go kitchen,' Da Yi said. After which, she returned to the room with a huge pot. 'OK, everyone, the *poh piah* is ready.'

'*Qing qing*,' Steve said as everyone gathered around the table.

'You're the guest, you start first,' Da Yi said.

Steve looked at the table. There were plates of prawns, sliced eggs, Chinese sausage, shredded carrots, and a bowl of peanuts mixed with sugar. He lifted the lid of the pot – inside was a brown stew of boiled radishes.

Steve picked up a plate and forked a little of everything on to his plate.

'*A*, what are you doing? You have to put the ingredients in the skin.' Da Yi picked up a thin, round white pancake. 'You never eat *poh piah* before, *meh*?'

Steve scooped the ingredients from his plate on to the pancake. Then he folded the edges of the pancake around the mixture in the middle.

'*Ai-yah*, look at the way you fold the *poh piah*, all wrong! Like that, when you pick up the *poh piah* –' Da Yi lifted up Steve's *poh piah*, and it disintegrated immediately. 'The food fall out all at once.' She turned to her son. 'Ah Gong, show Uncle how to wrap the *poh piah* the right way.'

'Yes, Mummy.' Ah Gong placed the ingredients in the middle of the *poh piah* skin. He folded the sides of the pancake over the ingredients, then tucked in the edges expertly, transforming the pancake into a neat, perfectly self-contained tube.

'That's the way you do it,' Da Yi said.

I grimaced. Steve had just destroyed any respect that he might have gained from telling the *Nian* story.

'Aunty, guess who's here?!' a whiny screech came from the back of the room. In came Lian, in her Versace jeans.

'Harlow, Lian, I so happy you came,' Steve said. 'I got present for you.'

'What? What?' Lian said, clapping her hands.

'I got us two tickets to the Andy Lau concert.'

'Real or not?' Lian said. 'You don't bluff me?'

'No, of course it's real,' Steve said.

'But all my friends try to get the tickets also cannot,' Ah Lian said. 'It sold out.'

'Ah yah, but I booked the tickets with my Gold American Express card,' Steve said. 'If you're member, you get special priority for the tickets.'

Lian looked suitably impressed.

'And before we go to the concert,' Steve said, 'we can have dinner together at the Laguna Country Club.'

'Wah, that country club very expensive to join one,' Lian said. 'I saw in the newspaper they advertise the membership for 117 K.'

'Come, I get some *poh piah* for you.' Steve went to the table and managed to do a fairly decent job of wrapping the *poh piah*.

'Thank you,' said Lian. 'What you do for fun last week?'

'Last week I got no time to do anything fun. I had to go and queue for the property launch for the Good Luck Villa condos. It was so crowded, I almost never got it.'

'But you got it in the end? That condo very good. So near Orchard Road. And got swimming pool, tennis court. Very expensive.'

'Yah, I got it,' Steve said. 'This year I very lucky. I also managed to get a lucky licence-plate number for my new Mercedes. 888.'

'Wah, you must make a lot of money. What job you do?'

'I'm a doctor. Private practice. Skin specialist.'

The way Lian looked at Steve, he must have known that he had scored big time. But then he had followed my instructions perfectly. I had told him that as long as he managed to convince Lian that he could provide her with a lifestyle that had all the Cs – condo, country club, car, career, cash – she would swoon into his arms.

'Wah, doctor,' Lian said. 'You must have studied for many, many years.'

'I study at Oxford for eight years,' Steve said.

'*A*, I got a friend's son who's trying to get into Oxford,' Da Yi said. 'Maybe you can advise him. He can't decide whether to take S paper or not. If he take S paper, maybe it make it easier for him to win scholarship. But S paper a lot of extra work, might affect his A-level results. What do you think he should do?'

'It depends whether he's in Arts or Science stream,' Steve said. 'If he's in Arts, he can get away with doing one S paper. But most scholarship boards expect two S papers.'

I looked at Draco Sidious. He was smiling. By providing insider information on the Singaporean education system, by shining the light towards the road that would lead to the University of Oxford, Steve had gained the adoration of everyone in the room.

22

Draco Sidious clapped his hands. It was hard to know
whether he was applauding or clapping to get the actors'
attention. 'We'll end the performance here,' he said.

'How did I do?' I said.

'I have to consult the other heads about your
performance. Why don't you wait here? I shall be back
soon.'

Steve jumped down from the stage. 'What's wrong?' he
asked me.

'Nothing,' I said.

'So why the Sylvia Plath face? Did I flunk the Test? I
thought that was an award-winning performance. Didn't I
do everything you told me to do?'

'You did. You completely transformed yourself from
lager lout to Chinese *towkay*. They should give you an
Oscar and limo you to Spagos.'

'So why do you look so stitched up?' Steve asked. 'I
haven't seen you look this depressed since your Estée Lauder
perfume disaster.'

A few years ago, I drenched myself in 'Knowing' and
went down to the Turf Tavern, hoping that wearing the
same perfume as Elizabeth Hurley would snag me a Hugh

Grant look-alike. Unfortunately, I spent most of the evening repelling sexual advances from a white-bearded geezer who looked more like Ulysses S. Grant.

'I'm gutted *because* you did so great,' I said.

Steve rolled his eyes and sighed. 'Crikey, there's just no pleasing *some* people.'

'No, don't you get it? Before the Test, you were an artsy bloke who would happily skip a couple of meals to scrape together enough money to see the Georgia O'Keefe exhibition at the Hayward Gallery. But I've succeeded in teaching you how to act like someone whose interest in aesthetics is limited to agonizing over the choice of the perfect colour for his Mercedes. I've trained you to act like a greedy, uncultured git. Three cheers for me,' I said sarcastically. I walked up on to the set and picked up a red *ang pow* envelope. 'Is this what I want to do for the rest of my life? To devote my career to corrupting others?' I opened the envelope. There were eight ten-dollar bills inside. I ripped up a scarlet note.

'What the hell are you doing?' Steve jumped on to the stage and grabbed the notes from me. 'That's real dosh you're tearing up!'

'The CorpS are seducers. They're like snakes who use this apple-red paper . . .' I snatched back the money from Steve, 'to tempt people to pervert themselves. I don't want to become a corrupter like them.'

'So what are you going to do?'

'I don't know. All I know is that I can't work for Mammon.'

Steve shook his head. 'I can't believe you made me go through all this shit for nothing.'

'I'm sorry.'

He glared at me. 'We had a deal. How am I going to get money for my film if you don't work for Mammon?'

'I don't know,' I said.

Steve jumped down and left the room.

I stood there up on the stage, staring at the empty stalls, all alone.

Draco Sidious returned to the set and looked up at my solitary figure.

He smiled. 'Congratulations. All the heads approved your performance. You are now officially a CorpS.'

'I'm sorry, but I can't accept the job,' I said.

Surprisingly, Draco Sidious did not look surprised.

'I'd like to take you on another trip to New York,' he said. 'I'd like to show you something that might make you reconsider your decision.'

'I doubt I'll be interested in what you'll offer,' I said. 'I'm not like your other recruits. All you have to do with those debt-ridden new graduates is promise them tax-free salaries, Maxi Equity ISAs, a low-cost index-tracker pension plan, and Bob's your uncle, you have your man. But I'm not interested in any of those things. I want to spend the rest of my life making people better, not worse. You can put as many digits behind dollar signs as you like, but I'm not joining Mammon Inc.' I was very impressed with my own dramatic monologue. It was noble and virtuous, almost regal in its defiance. I felt like Princess Leia resisting Darth Vader, refusing to betray the Rebel Alliance despite his metallic threats. I felt so majestically martyr-like that I could hear the John Williams soundtrack playing in my head. All I was missing was Carrie Fisher's doughnut hair.

'Very well,' Draco Sidious said. 'But I'd still like to give you the bonus we promised you for passing the Test.'

'The Dali painting?'

'Yes. You deserve it, since you did so well at the Tests.'

'But I don't want to be an Adapter,' I said.

'You can have the painting, even if you don't end up

working for us,' Draco Sidious said. 'It's in New York, though, and you'll have to come with me to collect it.'

The memory of the painting whispered beautiful shadows in the dark corners of my mind. Those melted cheese sculptures lay on a cocoa desert, like milky fruit, a delicious temptation for the eye.

'I'll go to New York to collect the painting,' I said. 'But you do realize that I have no interest in working for the Corporation?'

'Of course.' He smiled.

That night, I lay in bed, wondering what I should do with my life. Should I return to Professor Ad-oy, or was there another path? I looked at my palms.

When we were on the ferry floating towards Liberty Island, Tock Seng had taken my right hand and said, 'Will you let your gypsy friend do a psychic reading?'

'Sure,' I said. 'Prophesy away.'

'There are different types of hands, like the Mercurian Hand, the Venusian Hand, the Solar Hand. You have a Selenian, lunar hand, the most beautiful hand of all. Your upper palm and lower palm perfectly proportioned. Your fingers are long, slender and delicately tapered.' He slid the tip of his thumb around the edges of my hand, and I discovered one of my erogenous zones for the first time. 'People with lunar hands always feel like they've only got half of what they need. They want Yin and Yang, Schubert and the Spice Girls, job security and job satisfaction.' He traced a line on my palm with his forefinger – woah, another erogenous zone. 'Your Destiny line runs up to the Mount of Apollo under your ring (Sun) finger, finishing with a split end. That shows that you want to stand out but you also need to fit in. You want high-heel shoes that say "fuck me" but feel as comfy as slippers. You want to believe in God but party like the devil. You don't want it all because

271

you're *kia-su*, but because those binary opposites are an integral part of yourself. To give any of those things up would be to kill a part of yourself. But now you have to choose. Choose between your friends or your family. Choose between –' he touched my top lip, then my bottom lip.

At that moment, I felt fear and awe, staring at a man who, even after so many years away from me, could summarize my soul in less than two hundred words. None of this was new information to me, so why was I so riveted by his words? But I remembered what Steve once read to me, from *Nineteen Eighty-Four* – 'The best books are those that tell you what you know already.' I read because when someone echoes my soul, I know that my soul is not mine alone.

'I know how you feel because it's how I feel,' Tock Seng said. 'And I have a solution to your problem.'

'What?'

'Me.'

I snorted. 'Yeah, whatever.'

'No, seriously. Did you ever have any other friend in the world who you could play games with based on *Star Wars and* the Shaolin kung-fu movies? Do you know any other person who knows what it's like to be baptized by the Holy Spirit and to burn paper BMWs for his ancestors during the Feast of the Hungry Ghosts?' He showed me his palm. 'Look at the Destiny line on my right hand.'

His line looked exactly like the one on mine.

I couldn't believe it; I felt dizzy, dazed as my mind tried to explain how this could be – maybe he had had plastic surgery on his hand to make it look like mine – but my rationalizations were even more ridiculous and unbelievable than the truth, a reality so surreal and contrived it could only be fiction. But Tock Seng was right – he was the only friend I had whom I didn't have to explain things to, who understood East and West. Could he be all I needed?

I went over to my computer and sent Tock Seng an email:

> *Maybe you're right. Maybe I don't need a tribe, don't*
> *need the company of Mammon. Maybe one Adam is all Eve*
> *needs for her life to be Paradise.*
> *Please contact me.*

But two seconds after I sent the email, I got it bounced back
to me with the message:

> *qmail 31325 invoked by uid 65534. Recipient not recognized*
> *by server – fatal error 2376: unable to find host. Address*
> *does not exist.*

I thought of other ways I might get in touch with him, but
nothing came to mind. I rang his parents but they had no
idea where he was – he hadn't talked to them for years.
After the way I had rejected him at the Statue of Liberty,
God only knows how many years it might be before he got
in touch with me. I might never see him again.

I went out on the balcony and watched the skyscrapers'
cold battle against the heavens. The gentle rain brushed the
steel surfaces, but the buildings, like those monuments in
New York, were blind to any mystery or miracle. The
towers sheared off the rain's tresses and pierced like swords
through the soft swan of the mist.

Times Square was chemical white with electric signs, the
glaring ads for underwear and soda making their maggot
crawl through the dark. The Mammon HQ rotted in its
gangrene floodlights, while far above the mechanical
mountains, untouched by the glow of green dollars, the
distant stars chorused in prelapsarian bliss.

'Where's the painting?' I said. I looked around the
Pinnacle at the Mammon HQ. The walls were blank.

'I wanted to show you something else first,' Draco Sidious said, pointing to a glass wall.

I walked towards the frosted screen.

'We knew that you would reject our job offer. In fact, we designed the Test so that you would do so,' Draco Sidious said.

'But why?'

'Our Tests are an integral part of our training process. In them, we reveal some hard truths about the world. In your sister's Test, we showed you how much contempt and prejudice the West has for the East. We showed you that you could never win the battle for approval.

'We also knew that you would succeed with Steve's Test. And we know how you felt when you triumphed. You felt ill. Because when you adapted Steve, you saw everything you hated about Singaporeans.

'And in that moment, you felt completely alone. Because you knew that you could never be totally Singaporean, since you were so ashamed of their lack of culture and sophistication, so ashamed of their greedy *kia-su*ness. And you knew that you could never belong in England, because they would never accept someone as Chinese as you.

'But do you remember that one moment during the Tests when you didn't feel alone? When you finally felt you had found where you belonged?'

'The Gen Vexers,' I said.

'They were a smart and hip international set. They were the only tribe you've met that you loved and that loved you back. We know how you feel because this is how all our successful recruits felt when they went through the Test. We're offering you an opportunity to be a CorpS, not just because of your excellent academic record, but because through the Test you've shown that you live, breathe, think like a CorpS. We are all looking for a tribe to belong to, and for people like us, the CorpS are

274

the only group that we truly fit into. We are all soul-mates. Will you join us?'

I got involved with Mammon because I was confident that I couldn't be tempted. I knew that the glitter of gold could never corrupt me. But Draco Sidious had known that all along. He knew what I really hungered for – not money, but love. I saw the feast that he offered me. I would no longer be alone, but could spend the rest of my life partying with the Gen Vexers. We would hang out in Italy enjoying foccacia chunky with olives, and suck the bloody wine from the finest grapes in South Africa. Mammon offered me eternal Communion with a tribe who loved me. How could I resist the bait?

But if I bit the bait, Draco Sidious would devour my soul.

'I'm not sure if this is a good deal in the long term,' I said. ' "For what shall it profit a man, if he shall gain the whole world, and lose his own soul?" '

'How else are you going to fill the dark gap?'

'I don't know. Maybe the *Incendium Amoris* will be bright enough.'

Draco Sidious laughed. 'The love of God is a wonderful thing, but it is not sufficient. Even God knew that. He was with Adam in Paradise and realized, "It is not good for man to be alone." Look deep into your darkness. There's a chasm that the divine light can only partly illuminate – you need more and you know it. Remember how you felt at the party? How you felt not alone – like a system that was finally wired into a network that controlled the world? You can feel that oneness all the time. All those Gen Vexers can come and fill your life, hundreds of them, all over the world – you can go anywhere and find company. You need company, and Mammon Inc. is the Company you want to keep.'

The Greeks called their dragons *drakon*, which meant 'sharp-sighted one'. I snapped my head away from those unblinking eyes that exposed my soul. But there was no escape. It was too late. Everywhere I turned, I saw myself, my image reflected in the six TV screens, the gleaming steel tables, the glass walls and the polished floor – it was like being trapped in a room of mirrors. And in those slick surfaces, I saw myself as Eve must have done after the Fall, saw myself without covering, all my weaknesses exposed, realizing for the first time that I had been naked before this giant snake all along.

In the mirror, I could see the amulet that Professor Ad-oy had given me. There was my salvation. That was what would heal me. All I had to do was to look at the bronze snake on the wooden stick, and, like the Israelites in the desert, I would be healed from the fiery bite of the serpent. All I had to do was to believe that two thousand years ago, God in Christ wrapped himself around a wooden pole to save me.

But I couldn't. For to do so would make me as solitary as the man who hung from the cross, cursed and abandoned by all he loved.

Draco Sidious saw the terror of loneliness that would forever enslave me to him: I would rather die in the company of demons than live in heaven and be alone on earth. Christ's crucifixion brought him the kingdom of heaven but I didn't have the strength to go through that, couldn't imagine being without the love of my loved ones for the rest of my earthly life.

I saw in Christ's eyes the pearl of great price, but realized that in order to follow him, I would have to weep those tears as well. I wasn't Christ, but was merely Eve. I didn't have the stamina to bear the cross.

I turned to run, but couldn't move. It was too late, I had fallen. I had made the fatal mistake the moment I stepped into the viper's pit. Draco Sidious's words hooked into me like fangs, sending the venom coursing through my veins. I tried to flee, but I couldn't. The poison destroyed my nervous system, and all I could do was stand there, paralysed.

'What do you want me to do?' I said.

'There's a young man, Maximilian Veers, who is on his way to becoming the top undergraduate scientist at Oxford. He plans to do graduate work on shallow tube wells in Eritrea to help the poor gain access to clean water. We want you to devise a set of Tests to persuade him to work for Mammon CorpS.'

'You want me to corrupt him?' I said. I could see his plans for me, to be a mother of a generation of tainted children. The spreader of original sin.

Draco Sidious simply smiled and snapped his fingers. The glass wall de-ionized into an invisible window that slapped Times Square in my face.

I gasped.

Behold the Great White Way, where busloads of tourists make their pilgrimage to the Crossroads of the World to gawk at the super-sized billboards – the Cup Noodle billowing out real steam, the Coke bottle with the motorized straw. Sharks in suits glanced briefly at the electronic zippers, checking the stock info that sprinted in digital frenzy across the face of the Morgan Stanley Building.

You could see all of New York from the Pinnacle. The gardens and junkyards, mansions and fish markets, art galleries and crack-ridden ghettos, tiny alleys and great lawns, giant malls and mini bodegas, and bright windows filled with Rolexes, spy telescopes, chickens, jewelled Menorahs, belly rings, Swedish designer corkscrews and any other product that you could think of. Everything in the world was on this island, all its glory and grime wrapped in a cloud of fiery pale chemicals.

The Jumbotron, the biggest TV screen in the world, silently flickered reports from mcCNN News at a crowd that scuttled like rats trapped in a giant's madly illuminated living-room.

'See those creatures scurrying into the subway?' Draco Sidious said. 'That's how most people in the world look to us – like subway rats. This is the urban jungle, and everyone is either prey or preyer. You can choose to be with us – at the Pinnacle – or with the rodents down below. Who will you be?'

I looked at the crowd scattered beneath me. Steam billowed out from the grates in the sidewalk, wrapping them in smoky shrouds. 'I want to be a dragon,' I said.

'I thought so.' Draco Sidious put his arm around me. 'You are now one of the new emperors. Enjoy the view of the world, your kingdom.'

I stared out at the glass castles that shimmered in the midday heat. It was like looking down at a field of icicles. They say that Hades has no warmth, and never had I seen a city like this, filled with icy blocks so cold and so hard that not even the summer sun could melt them. The stalagmites of blue and silver wavered in my vision. They seemed unreal, paradoxically unnatural – frozen blocks in hellish heat – skyscrapers shivering like a mirage.

'Don't you just love this view?' he said.

I nodded, smiling bitterly. 'Who can resist the Big Apple?' I said.

The apple in Eve's eye.

Acknowledgements

Many thanks to those who read through early drafts of the novel and offered helpful suggestions: top agents Faith Evans and Emma Sweeney, Jamie Wall, Lucie Sutherland, and Thanhha Lai.

Thanks for the support of those in the Creative Writing Program at New York University, including Melissa Hammerle, Professor Paule Marshall, Lucy Rosenthal, and especially Chuck Wachtel and all my fellow workshoppers in the novel workshop.

Also many thanks to those who offered useful research info for the book, including: Maggie Pringle, Susan Watt, Matthew Branton, Webb Younce, and Marcus Lee.

Maximum respect to Rowland White for being super-efficient editor.

Special thanks to Dr Joe Boulter and Emily Haysom, for patiently rereading drafts of the novel, and also for transatlantic phone therapy.

Thanks to Larry Beinhart, and also all at the Chelsea Coffee Company for providing a writing retreat away from my apartment (a.k.a. The Shoebox).

Finally, thanks to Professor Kirpal Singh, and also to the National Arts Council of Singapore for their support.